His left hand wound itself in her hair. The hair flowed smoothly around his knuckles. She was not the one he wanted, but the hand moved almost against his will.

He increased his grip. He felt everything now—skull, hair, root, the curve of her neck. He hugged her against his groin, his right hand clean and ready on the razor.

His first cut was straight up the spine. The quilted robe split, the pile splintering as it ripped. A moment later blood filled the seam while she screamed against his stomach. He pulled her even closer, his hand deep in her hair . . .

RAZOR'S SONG

JOE MONNINGER

(Originally published in hardcover as
Incident at Potter's Bridge)

AVON BOOKS  NEW YORK

This book was originally published in hardcover under the title *Incident at Potter's Bridge*.

This is a work of fiction. Names, characters, places and incidents either are the product of the author's imagination or are used fictitiously. Any resemblance to actual events, locales, organizations or persons, living or dead, is entirely coincidental and beyond the intent of either the author or publisher.

AVON BOOKS
A division of
The Hearst Corporation
1350 Avenue of the Americas
New York, New York 10019

Copyright © 1991 by Joe Monninger
Published by arrangement with Donald I. Fine, Inc.
Library of Congress Catalog Card Number: 91-55180
ISBN: 0-380-71874-X

First Avon Books Printing: April 1993

AVON TRADEMARK REG. U.S. PAT. OFF. AND IN OTHER COUNTRIES, MARCA REGISTRADA, HECHO EN U.S.A.

Printed in the U.S.A.

RA   10 9 8 7 6 5 4 3 2 1

To
Pete and Deb Shumlin

I have heard that there was once a girl who spent a whole winter in a bear's house . . . and she slept very well through the winter . . . and the bear was a he-bear and he got the girl with child. And the child was a boy, and its one hand was a bear's paw, and the other a human hand, and the one hand he never left uncovered. And once a man wanted him to show it to him, although he said he could not show it because it was dangerous. But the man didn't believe him and insisted . . . And when he had uncovered it for the man, then he couldn't control himself, but tore the man's face to pieces. And then folk saw it was true, what he said about his hand.

—THE LAPP TURI

CHAPTER ONE

GEORGE DENKIN

Portsmouth, New Hampshire, 1979

THE DAY GEORGE DENKIN KILLED HIS MOTHER WAS LIKE
any other day. He had no plan at all except to sit quietly by
and watch his mother do Mrs. Dotty Harris. To "do" meant
to give a facial, a perm, and a manicure to a customer. Dotty Harris was a regular, and Mrs. Gloria Denkin, known to
her customers as Astrid, could "do the do" in a little under
an hour.

On this day, late in September, she only had an hour. She
was closing the shop for the weekend in order to attend a
wedding. The shop was called "Scissors" and it was actually a converted garage off the Denkin home. Astrid's second
husband—not George's father—had done the work on the
shop himself. He had dry-walled the cement frame of the
garage, laid a cheap linoleum floor, built some pine shelv-
ing against the rear wall, and finally jerry-rigged a sink so
that it used the same drainage system as the house proper.
He was not a licensed plumber, nor had he applied for a
building permit, so for the first month after construction he
had instructed Astrid to keep the business under the table.

After two months the second husband, for reasons George never understood, departed.

"Good riddance to bad rubbish," Astrid said.

The beauty shop was hers.

Her client list grew steadily, although the shop remained under the table. She undercut the local beauty shops, charging only fifteen for a trim, ten for a shampoo, five for a brush-out, and a square dollar for a color-me-beautiful assessment. The color-me-beautiful assessment was tied into N-Skin, a multilevel marketing line she sold. Everything in her store was manufactured by N-Skin. She received a commission on the products, charged for them off the top anyway, and was given five percent of the gross for any newcomers she could persuade to become N-Skin sales representatives. One night a week, usually Wednesdays, she gave a N-Skin demonstration party. She baked cookies, sometimes a cake, and spent a half hour giving a slide show on the N-Skin line. Afterward there followed a question and answer period, combined with free samples awarded to the person from the farthest away, the woman with the most children, and so on. She held the show regardless if one woman or thirty showed up. Everyone went away with something.

She often demonstrated the products on George.

She did not worry about causing psychological damage. George was her only child; she had nowhere else to put him. Besides, his skin was flawless. He was a perfect winter, a true brunette, and she could spin the color wheel beneath his face in order to demonstrate the effect correct coloring could have on an individual's appeal.

"Primary colors," she said a thousand times, her breasts holding the boy's head still while she clicked the wheel under his chin. "Not autumn, nothing muted, just reds and blacks."

If the other women said anything, it was only to remark that George was too pretty to be a boy.

On the day he killed his mother, George Denkin was nine-years-old. He was the veteran of countless make-up demonstrations. He was the veteran of endless hours in the beauty shop. His job was to take each new visitor's coat and hang it on the coat rack. He fetched magazines, brought coffee, and, on occasion, held a bloody rag to a woman's toe if Astrid happened to tear some skin during a pedicure. In payment he received odd haircuts, which made him a figure of fun in school. At seven he had his ear pierced. At eight he received razor stripes above his temples. For three consecutive Halloweens his mother convinced him to be a punk. She gooed up his hair in a high spiked ridge, then streaked it purple, orange, and blue. George thought he looked fabulous.

His acquaintances—he had no true friends—thought he looked like a fag.

On this particular Friday, however, George wasn't thinking about being a fag. He sat in one of the visitor's chairs, watching his mom do Mrs. Harris. His mom had permed her own hair earlier, wrapping it in tight curlers and liberally applying the noxious-smelling gunk. She let it set while she worked on Mrs. Harris, who only required a wash, a set, and a comb-out. She was an older woman, perhaps fifty-five, with white-blue hair, pale cheeks, and expensive clothing. George himself did not know the clothing was expensive, but it was a long-standing joke between him and his mother that Mrs. Harris, for all her dough, was the worst tipper on the client list. Mrs. Harris was cheap, but that, his mom said, was the reason she came to Scissors in the first place.

It was a quiet afternoon. Rain came down the panes of the single window in the side of the shop. The baseboard heating was turned on low. The air it pushed out was dusty smelling and old. The radio in the corner was tuned to an oldies station. His mom listened to nothing but oldies and she could sing along with nearly every song that played. She especially liked the Beatles.

But the Beatles weren't on much that day. In fact, George would remember later that the Beatles did not come on at all that afternoon. The DJ seemed to favor the Beach Boys instead. He played a triology of "Surfin' U.S.A." and "My Little Deuce Coupe" and "Little Surfer Girl."

It was during "Little Surfer Girl" that Mrs. Harris began opening her legs for George.

George was not even conscious of the exchange at first.

He sat directly in front of her, his senses dulled by the warmth and hair smells and rain. His mom was behind Mrs. Harris, working to fork out Mrs. Harris's hair. His mom was saying something about a soap opera. Mrs. Harris was chatting in return, mentioning one or two characters George recognized as belonging to "General Hospital." He attended school while the soaps were on, but he often followed the story lines through the ladies' conversations. He knew the characters on "General Hospital."

"So I guess we're supposed to believe they're married, although how they got married I don't know," his mom said. "I tell you, the writers on that show have a lot of nerve."

Mrs. Harris opened her legs wider.

She wore a gray skirt, nicely tailored, which contained a slightly bluish thread. She wore garter belts and stockings. She wore no underwear.

George looked away. He was not even certain he had seen what he had seen, but he looked away anyway. At the same time he felt his penis growing hard. He was unaccustomed to the sensation. He looked away and tried to concentrate on the music.

" . . . little surfer, little one . . ."

Then he looked back and saw Mrs. Harris staring at him. His eyes met hers. He expected her to look away, or at least to clamp her legs closed, but instead she opened her legs slightly wider. His mother came around to shape the hair from the front, so her back was turned and Mrs. Harris continued staring at him, her legs inching wider.

Mrs. Harris nodded her head down, just a fraction of an inch, to indicate her open legs.

The triangle formed by the dress and her legs was dark, but he saw all the way inside.

He looked away again, confused. The sensation was troubling. He felt himself growing more excited. He caught Mrs. Harris's eyes once more and again she nodded.

Then it was over. His mom finished with Mrs. Harris. She spun the barber's chair around and let Mrs. Harris examine the comb-out. Mrs. Harris nodded. As she stood, she caught George's eyes once more.

● ● ●

"Sweep up, will you, honey?" Astrid said when Mrs. Harris was finally out the door. Mrs. Harris had left no tip.

"Sure, Mom."

"I'm going to sit down here and take a load off. You wake me if I fall asleep. I'm going to run the dryer, so if the phone rings, you get it, okay?"

"Okay."

There was nothing unusual in any of this. George often worked around the shop. Astrid said by doing so he earned his allowance, although George never received any weekly sum. He lived off what he could take from his mother's purse, or from the change left over when he ran to get her a soda from Norther's, the local market.

He took up the push broom from behind the door and began to sweep. He herded the snips and cuts of hair in front of him, while his mom made herself comfortable under the dryer. She subscribed to several ladies' magazines, but preferred *People* to anything else. As George swept, he saw her begin reading a story. She turned the pages lazily. The hum of the dryer drowned out the oldies station.

George's erection did not disappear.

He continued sweeping, disturbed by the sensation in his groin. At nine-years-old, he didn't automatically connect Mrs. Harris's open legs to his physical state. His penis was hard, but he wasn't sure exactly why. Twice he put the heel of his hand on the edge of his penis and pressed down. The sensation was excellent. He deliberately began allowing his forearm to graze his penis each time he brought the head of the broom back.

By the time he finished sweeping, his mom was asleep. That was not unusual either. She frequently dropped off at the end of the day, particularly if she had been on her feet through a busy schedule. If she went under the dryer, it was a cinch to happen. This day she seemed more solidly asleep than normal, however. Her head rested against the rear of the drying bell. The magazine dangled on her knees. Her shoulders were slack and her right hand hung, palm outward, on the arm of the chair.

Beneath the *People* magazine, her legs had opened.

That had never happened before. At least, as far as George could remember, he had never noticed it before. He stood in the center of the room, the broom lodged against his penis, the hum of the dryer the dominant sound. He felt peculiar.

He intentionally bent down, pretending to clean something from the bristles of the broom, and casually took a better look at his mother. Unlike Mrs. Harris, Astrid wore underpants. The underpants were merely a white triangle at the end of a dark triangle. He looked for several seconds. He might have looked longer if the broom hadn't chanced to slip away and fall flat on the floor. It gave off a loud crack and George stood up quickly.

His mother did not wake. Carefully he returned the broom to its spot near the door. Then, for no reason he could name, he walked to his mother and turned the drying gauge higher. The dial had settings from one to seven, but the seven, he had been told more than once, was only there for an emergency.

"Like if a girl comes in, her hair all wet, and she needs to get it dried out, then maybe you slip it up to seven. Or if, say, someone comes in late, needs a shampoo fast, and I have to have her out the door in five or ten minutes. You could bake someone under there."

George did not want to bake his mother. He only wanted her to stay asleep. He turned the gauge to seven.

He went to the make-up bar at the rear of the shop and played with the bottles. His mother never minded if he played there, and besides, he liked how he looked in make-up. His eyes looked bigger, more serious, and his cheeks redder. He liked watching women put on lipstick, their faces pouted, their rumps out as they bent to the mirror.

He dabbed on some of his mother's new eye shadow. It was a trial line of sequined eye shadow N-Skin was sending out for test marketing. It made the sockets of his eyes sparkle. He smeared it badly on his right eye, but got the knack on his left. He coated each eye with far too much make-up. His cheeks gathered soft diamonds where the make-up failed to adhere to his eyes.

He covered his top lip with gloss. He had started on his lower lip when he smelled his mother cooking.

He didn't believe his nose at first. She wasn't cooking, he told himself. Her hair was cooking. The dryer was peeling away some of the N-Skin perm sauce.

But the smell made him nervous anyway. He put down the make-up bottles and returned to his seat. He picked up a copy of Spiderman, one of the comics his mom sometimes bought him, and attempted to interest himself in the story.

Spiderman had somehow acquired a black alien super-hero suit. He simply had to think about the uniform to have it magically crawl over him. George knew, from reading future issues, that the suit was actually a living alien. The suit was patiently sucking Spiderman's juices. In this issue, however, Spiderman didn't know about the suit and constantly wondered why he was fatigued. He swung from building to building, his grip loosening on his webs. He had to stop for rest several times.

George read seventeen panels. When he looked up, his mother's legs were spread wider than before. Her mouth was open. Something like smoke seeped from under the bell of the dryer.

You better wake her up, he told himself.

He did not know his mother was already dead.

George stayed in the beauty shop through the entire weekend. No one paid a visit, since Astrid's friends thought she had travelled down to Boston for the wedding she mentioned. He called no one for assistance. He did not go down to Norther's Market in order to ask Mr. Hellman ("just like the most popular brand of mayonnaise," his mother used to tell him) to accompany him back to the shop. He did not answer the phone, although any number of people called.

It took him three hours to gather the courage to lift up the drying bell.

He would have lifted it sooner, but he was only nine and was afraid he had killed his mother by turning up the gauge. In the three hours that passed, he wondered a great deal about fingerprints. He wondered if he would be sent to prison. He wondered if he would have to go live with his father.

In the meantime, his mother's hair began to fall out.

He didn't see it at first. He kept his head down through most of the first three hours. He read a Spiderman, an Iron Man, and an Avengers. He smelled his mother—there was no mistaking that—but the odor only made him nervous.

Wake up, he thought. Wake up, wake up, wake up.

The first shank of hair to fall was a thick clump from his mom's bangs. He happened to look up just as it slid from beneath the dryer's bell. It dropped like a brittle stick. It tumbled across his mother's forehead, then landed across her mouth. It dangled from her lower lip, jutting out far enough to attract other hair. He looked down quickly, afraid to see what else might happen. He tried to push away the thought that his mother's forehead had turned to chocolate.

By that time the beauty shop was all but dark. Rain continued to fall outside. The DJ's on the oldies station had apparently changed shifts, because now the DJ was playing a bunch of Motown songs. George heard "My Girl" and "Stop, In the Name of Love." He heard Ray Charles sing "Georgia." He sat and listened, his eyes still down in his lap.

But the smell increased. It was no longer a particularly unpleasant smell. In certain moments it smelled almost like a turkey basting. In fact, the smell even made him hungry. He hadn't eaten since lunch. It was now close to eight o'clock.

He lifted his eyes a little later. In the dimness, his mother looked alive. Air from the dryer worked its way down her dress and caused the bodice to waffle in the current. The skirt of her dress also fluttered slightly in the hot jet. A shadow from outside—the floodlight was on to show customers where to park—cut her face in half.

"Mom?" he asked.

He stood and took a step. The thing to do, he told himself, was to just act naturally. He took another step and stopped when he saw his mother's hands grip the arms of her chair. No, no, that was wrong. He didn't see her hands move. They were still hanging by her side, the right one with its palm out. What he had seen, he decided, was his mother gathering herself to stand. Her feet appeared to slide over the linoleum, her back straighten. She had just fallen asleep. He was a nine-year-old boy, his mom was asleep, and now she would wake and turn off the dryer and that was that, it was all over.

Except her chest was covered by hair. Her shoulders were covered by hair and her forehead looked like chocolate. Her cheeks had been pulled too high so that she seemed to be squinting at him.

She's eating her hair, he thought.

Because her mouth was surrounded by hair, she looked to be screaming through scraps of hair. He expected to hear sounds, her voice collecting itself to speak to him, except the only noise was a pitch from Feemonti Oldsmobile telling him "TO TAKE THE BEST SHOT, ON OUR LOT, FOR A DEAL THAT'S HOT!"

He moved closer. He circled slightly so he came at her from the side. He reached out a hand and touched the gauge on the dryer. He turned it off, clicking it hard, and the hot jet of air suddenly ceased. It drained out of her dress, letting the skirt go flat first, then the bodice. Finally it released a last trickle of hair. The hair came out of the bell stealthily, like mice fleeing water.

Ten minutes later he lifted the dryer bell.

It had taken him ten minutes to collect himself. For the full ten minutes he had stood in front of his mother, staring at the scream coming through her hair. He had never seen her look that way. She looked crazy. Her mouth was choked by hair and the wrinkles in her skin looked like strings yanking upward from the top of her head. She looked, he thought, almost like a puppet.

When he finally went to lift the dryer bell, he found it was stuck to her head.

He lifted it softly at first, amazed to find it stuck. Even such a slight movement shook his mother, allowing her right hand to finally swing down off the arm of the chair. The radio began playing "Under the Boardwalk." He hardly heard the music because his hands had to work up under the dryer bell to get a grip. And as they did, he felt his mother's leathery scalp, her baked Alaska head, her stickiness.

You killed her, a voice said inside him.

He settled his feet between her legs and leaned across her. He gave the dryer bell a short shove. It shot up suddenly, tilting him off balance, his arms up above his head. He fell forward, crashing into his mother's chest. His chin came to rest on the crook of her shoulder. He pushed away instantly, but not before he caught a glimpse of her alligator scalp.

" . . . on a blanket with my Bab-eeee, is where I'll beeee . . ."

She was a monk. Her hair was gone except for a fine ring of tendrils drooping along the side of her head. The tops of her ears had turned brown. The top of her head had turned into chocolate. Pieces of chocolate dangled from the roof of the dryer bell.

When Patrolman Steve Oldenheimer arrived at Scissors late Monday afternoon, three women were already at the door. They stood flocked together, peeping through the window. As soon as he climbed out, they started in on him.

"Officer, hurry," the first woman said. She was a tall blonde, maybe forty.

"The door's locked," another said, this one a brunette.

"I'll bet he's been in there all weekend," the last one said. She wore a hat.

They hardly watched him approach. That was unusual. In Steve Oldenheimer's experience people at the scene of an accident were always anxious to spill their guts to the police. These women, however, seemed more interested in staring through the windows. He stopped at the button of the small walkway leading to the door.

"Who called this in?" he asked.

"I did," the blonde woman said, then pointed to something inside the beauty shop. "Look at him."

"All right, ladies, step away. Just clear the doorway."

"There's a little boy in there."

"Okay, we'll get it all straightened out."

He thought about his roast beef sandwich, the one he had been eating when he received the call. He also thought about Marla, the new waitress at Goldie's Deli. She wore the most godwonderful little miniskirts and never paid a moment's attention to how she bent over the tables to wipe them down. He had been watching Marla bus a table at the back of Goldie's when the call had come through. And now, from what the ladies said, it was a simple case of a brat locking himself inside a beauty shop.

He went up the walkway.

Bent to look in the window.

Then saw something that made his neck start to tingle.

"What the hell?" he said, straightening and looking at the women.

"See? He looks crazy," the lady in the hat said.

"He's been moving around like that for a half hour. I think he's manic. Isn't that the word? You know, when you can't stop moving?"

This from the brunette.

Patrolman Oldenheimer bent again to look through the window. The kid flashed through the room, trying, it seemed, to stay out of their line of vision. He ran from one side of the room to the other, ducking behind chairs. The kid moved fast. He appeared to be nervous about staying in one spot. As soon as he was hidden behind one chair, he popped up and ran to another.

The kid also wore a wig.

"That's his mother in there. She looks dead," the blonde said. "That's why we called it in. It's so strange."

"The one in the chair?" Patrolman Oldenheimer asked.

"That's Astrid. I had an appointment with her for this afternoon," the brunette said.

Meanwhile the kid continued to jump around the shop. He looked like a bird trapped in a room with mirrors. The kid's wig was long and dark. A Cher wig.

Patrolman Oldenheimer tried the door. It was locked. He gave the door handle a good twist and put his shoulder to the frame. The door didn't budge.

"Son," he called, "open the door now."

" . . . frightened to death, look at him . . ."

"Son, it's all right, open the door."

" . . . he looks so odd with that wig on . . ."

"Son, we're here to help."

Patrolman Oldenheimer didn't wait for the kid. In fact, he could no longer see the kid. He slid his flashlight out of a loop at his side.

"Stand back, ladies. Please."

They fluttered away.

He smashed the window pane nearest the doorknob with the butt of the flashlight.

As soon as the window went he heard a radio playing some Cat Stevens. He also smelled something, he couldn't tell what, released by the broken pane. He slid his flashlight back in the loop at his side.

Carefully he reached his left hand inside and fished around for the door lock. He found the knob easily enough, but had difficulty determining how it unlocked. It seemed to be a button job, a little twisty in the center, but it was hard to work with the glass jabbing up just below his arm.

"Watch the glass," one of the ladies said, as if he didn't have the brains he was born with.

He nodded, his ear close to the upper panes. He fished a little more and almost had the doohickey when he saw . . .

It was the wig he saw. The wig rose at him from the floor inside the door. Patrolman Oldenheimer couldn't help thinking that the kid was a tricky little bastard after all. The kid looked like a graveyard witch, all made up, a freaky wig over his head, his mom dead in a barber's chair behind him. You could make out the kid under the wig, though, just a little kid, a scared little rug rat, so Patrolman Oldenheimer continued to fish at the doohickey. He felt it finally spin, the door start to open. A woman behind him said, "Oh good." But then, an instant later, he saw the kid come up with the barber shears. The kid was suddenly there, jabbing the point of the shears at Patrolman Oldenheimer's wrist.

"Jesus Christ," Patrolman Oldenheimer said, trying to pull his hand free.

He twanged his elbow off a shard of glass and felt it take a little wound. Then he pulled back faster, no longer caring, because the little cretin was playing Woody Woodpecker with the scissors. In his hurry, Oldenheimer smashed his elbow through a second pane of glass and finally pulled back, his arm lined by bloody claw stripes.

"That little fucker," he said.

His hand had been stabbed twice.

He watched the kid go back to his weird routine. The door was locked again.

One of the women, he couldn't tell which one, said: "Are you all right?"

"This just got interesting," Patrolman Oldenheimer answered, trying to plug up the holes in his hand. The holes were deep. Blood came out in a thoughtful way.

Patrolman Oldenheimer pulled off his tie. It was a clip-on jobby, cobalt blue. He wrapped it around his hand, grabbed the loose ends in his palm, then flexed his fingers. Nothing severed, nothing broken. He took a step away from the door.

Then he lifted his right boot and kicked the door to pieces. It took three kicks, which meant it was about as cheap a door as you could find on the market. The plywood splintered, then burst.

Patrolman Oldenheimer took out his flashlight again. It was a four-cell. It weighed about a pound and was made of metal. He glanced again at his left hand. The tie was soggy.

"Stay outside," he told the ladies.

"He's just a boy, Officer," one of them said.

Oldenheimer looked through the gaping door. He didn't see the kid. He kicked the door again to create a distraction, then jumped into the beauty shop. The flashlight was in his right hand. If it had been in his left—he was a lefty—he might have been able to clip the kid on the first shot. Instead, the kid had the drop on him. He came from the left, scissors whacking away. Oldenheimer felt the blades sink into the meaty part of his thigh. He spun, the scissors grinding down in his gristle. In the same motion he clocked the kid with the head of the flashlight, scoring one right on the temple. The kid dropped.

"You little *bastard*." The scissors hung from his right

thigh, clicking a little as he fought to maintain his balance.

The kid did not move. Oldenheimer reached down and pulled the scissors out of his leg. He saw black then white then green. He felt sick to his stomach.

He hobbled over to the kid and put his left boot on the kid's stomach. He hopped into the air, letting his weight come down on the kid's ribs.

"Stop it!" someone shouted behind him.

"Officer, officer . . ."

Oldenheimer let his weight sink back to the floor. It struck him as odd that he almost slipped on his can from his own blood.

CHAPTER TWO

POTTER'S BRIDGE

Colbin College Campus
Coldbridge, New Hampshire, 1991

A MOSQUITO LANDED ON GEORGE DENKIN'S NECK JUST AS he heard the woman walking along the forest path toward him. He had no doubt about who she was. This was her routine and he had followed her every night for the past ten days. One night, just to be certain, he had even followed her into the art center and watched, from a balcony overlooking the potting center, as she molded her clay bowls and cups. That was one of the art center's credos: art was not only to be experienced but the experience should be shared. As a result the potting center spread beneath a circular walkway on which non-art majors at Colbin College could come and watch paintings be painted, sculptures being sculpted, or pots thrown. The atmosphere on the walkway was as quiet and dignified as a library. The architect, an artist herself, had explained at the opening of the building that the old notion wherein artists were secluded from their public was abhorrent to her. She cited Cristo's work in her speech, suggesting the true measure of an artist's achievement was the degree to which he or she involved the public.

George Denkin, in ways the architect had never imagined, was involved in the work of the young potter.

He did not know her name, but her name wasn't important. Even now, standing near Potter's Bridge, a small arc of stone which crossed a creek running through the Colbin College acreage, he did not attempt to give her a name. Instead he listened to her footsteps, checking as well as he could to make sure she was alone. It was her pattern to walk alone—she was, he supposed, the arty, independent type—but something could always change. He understood that. He was cautious, and he was more than prepared to step back into the woods and let her pass if she had picked up an escort as she left the art center.

Another mosquito landed on his wrist. He slapped it gently. The steps were growing louder. From nights spent tracing the path, he knew precisely where she was now walking. She was crossing a small gravel bar that pushed its way into the place where the path curved closest to the creek. After that she would encounter pine needles, then a rooty section where the pines found the soil below too sour. He had tripped once or twice on the roots on his scouting missions. He knew, moreover, that she didn't carry a flashlight. He imagined she might trip, or at least walk tentatively, then straighten herself and begin to hurry over Potter's Bridge.

He put his hand up under his skirt and cupped his penis for a moment. His penis was erect. He twisted it slightly, then let the skirt drop.

He squared his shoulders and shook his head once from side to side, making sure the hair of the wig fell evenly over his blouse. He fought the impulse to glance at himself in the small hand mirror he carried in the pocket of the skirt. There wasn't time; she was coming. He heard her feet slow to accommodate the roots. In four or five seconds she would round the bend, then enter the straight section of path that led up to Potter's Bridge.

George Denkin started to cry.

It was a put on, of course. Nevertheless, it was surprisingly convincing. He slumped down on his knees, put his hands to his face, and began sobbing. He made his shoulders clench and release, clench and release. He took in large breaths.

He heard her coming through the crying. She halted five or ten feet away. He drew in a breath and let it out slowly, careful to raise the pitch. He wasn't sure what kind of woman he appeared to be. Maybe he was a big, dumb woman; maybe he was one of those unfortunate women born to be men. It didn't matter. He simply had to give the impression of a woman to draw another woman nearer.

"Are you all right?" he heard.

But this one was smart. She wasn't stepping any closer.

"I . . . I . . ."

"What is it? Are you hurt?"

"He . . . he . . . he hit me."

"Who? Someone hit you?"

"Ra . . . aped me."

A few steps closer.

"Did he go? Where is he?"

"I . . . I . . ."

George felt the atmosphere change. Caution was giving way to concern. He could sense her moving closer, although he didn't dare let her see through his fingers to his eyes. He stayed slumped down, his face parallel to the ground, his breathing exaggerated.

"Are you okay? No, I mean, of course you're not okay. Are you bleeding? I don't see any blood. You'll be all right, just hold on. We'll get you out of here."

George smelled perfume. He smelled clay and water and something else, something chemical, maybe varnish. Her hand came out and touched his shoulder. He lunged then, still a woman, and hugged her thighs. He pushed his face against the buckle of her belt and sobbed more than ever.

"So . . . awful . . ."

"All right, all right," the potter said.

And while she soothed him he drew a straight razor out of the sleeve of his shirt. He flicked it open, timing his movement to the heave and pant of his crying, then let his free arm wrap more tightly around her knees. A moment followed, a delicious moment, when he could sense her flash of apprehension. Something had changed—she knew that—but she didn't know what it was. He felt her hand still against his head, her legs attempt an awkward step.

"Oh," she said.

He buried his face further in her crotch. He buried it at the same time he slid the razor across the Achilles tendon on her left foot. He pressed down on the blade until he felt the tiny twang of the tendon releasing. A second, more profound twang came as the calf muscle, released from the foot, sprang up and coiled under the skin of her left leg.

"Hey . . . what . . . ?" she still was not sure what was happening.

He sliced the right tendon the same way. This time he pushed slightly with his face against her crotch so that she had no other option but to fall softly backward. She sat, actually.

He did not speak. He stopped his sobbing and pushed her feet away from him. Two pipes of blood drained into the dirt. She had still not recovered sufficiently to speak. She stared at him. Perhaps, he thought, she still wasn't certain what had occurred.

"My feet . . ."

He reached up and cut the small meat between the nostrils of her nose. She began gagging at once.

He crawled on top of her and began smelling her hair. He heard her whimpering underneath him. He tried to ignore her, although she was now struggling for breath beneath his weight, Live hair smelled better than dead hair. He wanted her alive as long as possible. If she understood that, then she might cooperate. He spoke into her ear, his nose still buried deep in her hair.

"Quiet or you're dead."

She went quiet. He resumed smelling her hair. Flex shampoo, he thought. A cream rinse too, although that was more difficult to pin down. As he suspected, she had highlighted her hair. That was a disappointment, but not a large one.

He was on her two minutes before he heard steps coming his way. She heard them too, because she began to make a loud gurgling sound in her throat. He tilted the razor into her mouth and stirred. Then, moving quickly, he grabbed her by the feet and dragged her down underneath Potter's Bridge.

Let the dog go.

That was Lester's first thought when he heard the scream. Let the dog go. The dog was a glossy German shepherd bitch, a genuine beauty named Flick. Glancing down, he saw her eyes looking straight ahead, her ears cocked, her attention fixed on the scream.

Let her go. But he didn't want to have her sprinting across the campus, didn't want to run the risk of someone hurting her, didn't want to be alone. That was the truth, the real skinny, but he didn't like admitting it. He had only been a campus security officer for two months, May and June, and he still wasn't comfortable with the two hundred acres of New Hampshire woods that covered the campus.

But there was another scream.

It was a woman's scream. There was no mistaking it. It was a sort of "No, no, noo," followed by a full-throated one. Lester knew it came from the bridge. If a student had come running into the security office in the center of the campus and said that someone was being raped, Lester would have had one thought: the bridge.

Because the bridge was a freaky place, as some of the brothers would have said in Nam. The brothers would have known about the bridge, would have sensed the evil, swept it for mines once, then stayed clear. They would have known it was a dead end, a dead spot. Would know you do not go near the bridge on a night in the middle of July when the temperature is up and the crickets are all but barking. You do not go near the bridge when the water is so far down that you can walk right under it without getting wet.

Or without making any sound.

But the woman was making sounds. Like she had been pulled down with Billy Goat Gruff and the boys, with the old hairy troll who threatened to gobble people up if they dared cross his bridge. The slight echo of her scream made him finally bend down and slip his lead off Flick.

"Get him," he whispered reluctantly. Very reluctantly, so that his hand trailed down the dog's fur as she left. The dog took off like . . . like what? Like a shot, like a bullet, like a . . . Christ, Lester thought, he should be right behind the dog. That was the drill. The dog was supposed to lead the way, sniff out dope in dorm rooms, intimidate dumb-headed drunks, snarl when appropriate, lay down and endure a pet session with the faculty kids who wanted to pull her ears and yank at her tail.

But he was supposed to be behind her.

And he wasn't, although he listened very sharply indeed to hear what Miss Flick found on that bridge. As soon as the dog was gone he started forward, then stopped because the woods were scary, dark, and deep. He had heard that phrase before. Jam, the crew-cutted, muscle-bound white boy on the force had said it over and over again, taunting him, Lester, with it, making it into a chant—"the wooods areeeee scarreeeyyy, dark, and deeeep." It had been a big joke because Lester was a brother out of Boston, no frucking lumberjack, thanks, a guy accustomed to the Combat Zone, hookers, pimps, sleaze balls, but not snakes and owls and bridges.

He took a few more steps forward. The bridge was only fifty feet away. He heard water trickling and crickets and the gargled huff of Flick's breathing.

"Flick, come here, girl," he called into the darkness. "Come back here, dog."

His voice was lost in the woods. The crickets came back over it, smoothing and smearing themselves as gently as his mama had spread icing on cake. He would have called again, but he was afraid to hear how ridiculously small his voice sounded. Afraid, too, that Flick wasn't going to come jumping over any white rail fence, no Lassie come home deal for Flick. Flick, he was beginning to worry, was now on her way to doggy heaven, though how any-one killed a dog without a sound was beyond him. Killed a German shepherd, which was, any way you figured it, a powerful dog.

Then he heard Flick.

Which made him draw his clunky Smith & Wesson and point it at the bridge. He took a few more steps, placing him only, say, thirty feet away. He could see the outline of the bridge clearly now. It was made of fieldstone and was, when you stopped to consider it, attractive. It looked rustic, Lester had told himself more than once. A little lift, a little arch, and that was that. Right now, however, there was enough heat pressing on the stream running below the bridge to give the arch a coating of mist.

"Flick? Flickeee, come here, sweetheart. Over here."

Fifteen feet away, no more. And still crying, still whining. Lester bent forward again to listen, holding his breath as he did so, the revolver in front of him. The whimpers came again, only this time he couldn't be certain it was Flick. The sounds could have been coming from some nut case trying his best to lure him closer. Some nut case figuring correctly that in the middle of the woods, with the crickets, the splash of the stream, it wasn't frucking easy to know what was what.

"Listen, if you're down there," Lester called, "get out of here. Go, man, I don't want any part of you."

A more solid whine.

He unhooked his walkie-talkie and called in. He tried to think who would be on the desk. Probably Jam. Probably that sick white boy who thought this college campus was Vietnam. But that was okay, because right now Lester would have been pleased as hell to have a crazy white boy to send down under the bridge. The boy was a loopy fucker who couldn't wait to make his first kill in the line of duty.

"This is Lester," he finally said when he got through.

"Go ahead, Lester," the voice came back at him.

It wasn't Jam. It was Eddy, the fat old guy who used to be a fireman until he was laid-off because of local tax reforms. Eddy the fire-code official.

"I'm at the bridge," Lester said. "I heard screams. I think maybe we have a murder—"

"What bridge is that, Lester?" Eddy said in one of those calm police voices.

"The bridge out here in the frucking woods. Potter's Bridge I think it's called. The stone bridge!" he shouted on the walkie-talkie.

"Potter's?" Eddy asked, then a sweep of static took his voice away for a second.

"Potter's Bridge, yes, yes. Get some people out here fast. There was a woman screaming. I've lost contact with her and with my dog."

"Woman screaming?"

Then more static and more popping noises. Lester wanted to scream into the walkie-talkie but he knew that wasn't the way to get their asses moving. Even now, as he strained to hear what they were saying, he knew Eddy was checking the information out with someone else, probably saying stuff like: "Lester's called in, says he hears some screaming." And someone else in the office, maybe Jam, would say, "Tell Lester to stop being such a scaredy-cat. Tell him to get his balls together."

"Lester?" Eddy's voice finally returned.

"Right here, Eddy."

"Jam wants to know how you know it isn't just a prank. You know, some kids playing with you?"

"This is no fucking prank! Get your asses out here!"

Another squawk of static. Then a clear dispatch, all tin-badge police.

"Roger, we're on our way."

Be here, was what Lester wanted to say. Beam your asses out here.

"What do you call the guy who delivers letters to Gloria Steinem?" Jam asked Eddy.

Jam watched Eddy shift the Jeep. Eddy didn't know shit about driving but it was his call, he was the senior hot shot. But still it killed Jam to watch fat Eddy sit there, his nightstick poking up alongside of him like a big fat dick. Eddy needed to lose weight. Eddy needed to lose a small Salvadorian off his waist and gut. Eddy needed to give birth.

"Well?" Jam asked after a few seconds. Eddy never got the punch lines of jokes. Which was okay, no one said Eddy had to be a brain surgeon, but the chump didn't even care enough to ask what the punch line was. He wasn't interested, wasn't curious, wasn't a guy. That was the weird thing about Eddy. The guy wasn't a guy. He sat around in the office reading, sipping coffee, and eating. You could never

get him involved, never get
anything against anyone or a
he got a pruney, holier-than-th
pected him of being sort of half
sometimes gave blow-jobs in re
maybe a guy who liked to lay in th
let football players wearing white t
rub his belly with their toes. Jam ha
that arrested over in Dover the year b

"I don't know, Jam. What, a mailn   ng?"
Eddy finally said.

"No, you don't call Gloria Steinem's le   r carrier a mail
man, do you, Eddy? For Chrissakes, think about it. Do you?
Gloria Steinem?"

"Who's Gloria Steinem?" Eddy asked, jumping the curb
off Pleasant Street and heading down the service road that
went around the cafeteria of Huddleston Hall.

"You don't know who Gloria Steinem is?" asked Jam.

"No. Are you going to tell me? Is this supposed to be a
joke or something?"

"Yes, it's a joke, for God's sake. Gloria Steinem is
one of those lesby feminists. You know . . . a bra burner.
That kind."

"So now start over, what's the question again?"

Jam turned away and looked out the window. He could
not fucking *believe* this guy.

"Screw it," Jam said. "Forget it."

"If you want."

"A person person. That's what a mailman who brings
mail to Gloria Steinem is called. You can't call him—"

"A male or a man. I get it now, Jam."

So was the guy stringing him along, or what? That's what
Jam could never figure with Eddy. The guy was a fireman,
that's what you had to keep in mind. Except he wasn't even
a real ladder rat, just a sort of roly-poly electrician or something. His specialty was fire safety. Jam had heard him go
on and on about how the favorite part of his old job used to
be going to the elementary schools and instructing the kids
on fire safety. Don't play with matches, don't play in the
leaves alongside the curb, don't use a magnifying glass to

ks of wood, because fires could start that
lah, blah. The guy had his own slide show,
with pictures of "do's and don'ts," showing kids
to roll themselves up in a blanket if they caught on
re, check the door before they ran out and got toasted in
an upstairs hallway, crawl out of the house on their hands
and knees.

"Which way here, Jam?" Eddy asked when they came to
a small intersection of footpaths.

"Potter's Bridge is that way," Jam said, pointing left.
"You just follow Lester's glow. He's probably got all his
big white eyes and teeth showing."

"Lester said it could maybe be a murder," Eddy said,
taking the direction Jam had pointed out, not responding
to Jam's usual racist comment.

"A murder? Lester wouldn't know a murder if he fell
over one. Are you kidding? Lester's scared stiff of the
woods, that's all it is. All jigs are. You ever hear of a jig
pioneer, for example?"

"There were black people who went west to settle, Jam."

"Like who? Name one? You got Davey Crockett, Daniel
Boone . . . and what? Tyrone Running Feather? Jerome
Johnson Crazy Horse? Come on."

It wasn't any use to talk to the guy, Jam knew that.
He shook his head and started going over his equipment
instead. He wore a .44 Magnum, way over regs specifi-
cations about power, but who was going to stop him? It
wasn't like Colbin College supplied guns. That was up to
each officer and Jam planned to be one officer who never
found himself under-gunned. Of course, some of the kooks
now carried .9 mm automatics, but he knew that wouldn't
fly with Captain Barney, his boss and chief of the cow-
catchers. He had one at home, an Uzi, which could take
down half the forest if he let it rip.

He also had a knife sheath on his right leg. He only wore
it at night, when Captain Barney wasn't around, because
the knife was way out of uniform. The knife was eighteen inches long, with a Bowie tip and a serrated cutting
edge, the same kind of knife the grunts wore in Nam. Serrated cuts were harder to mend, harder to stitch. They also

had a better chance at incubating infection, which was just fine with Jam. The knife was a rib-saw, a meat grater. He could throw it and make it stick about six times out of ten. A thing of beauty. Reach down to the thigh, make a little flicking motion, and then . . . *boing*! Right in the throat.

"Listen, how do you want to approach this?" Eddy asked.

Jam looked up. They were deep in the woods now. The trees banged against the side of the Jeep. It was hot and buggy. The radio antenna did a dance at the back of the Jeep, twanging forward to where Jam could see it, then shooting back.

"What do you mean, approach this? Drive right up. You think this is some big deal or something? We've got three men. Lester didn't say anything about a battalion out here, did he?"

"No, you heard the report."

"Then screw it. Drive right up on the bridge, maybe put the spotlight on it. I hope the hell something is going on. I'll cut the guy's head off."

"Jam, you're supposed to be a peace officer."

"Wank that, Jack."

It took another five minutes before Jam realized he was lost. No, that *they* were lost. He sat still, trying to get his bearings, but things looked different at night. In winter he could have found his way easily, but now, in the middle of summer, the footpaths were grown over. They were congested with weeds and sumac and all kinds of crap. There might have been . . . he didn't know for sure . . . a path that they were supposed to take off to the left. That seemed right. A path that went up toward Carroll Hall, then over to the science building. Potter's Bridge was off that, just maybe fifty yards further in, spanning the little stream that was really a tributary to the Winnasett.

"Shouldn't we . . . ?" Eddy said after a time.

"Yeah, yeah, I'm just turned around some."

"Lester's counting on us."

Where were they? Where exactly the fuck were they? They didn't answer his radio calls, they didn't come riding through the woods with their siren going, they didn't do shit. For all they cared, he could be dead right now.

Because he was a nigger.

That was the truth. You could bend over five ways to Sunday and never get them to admit it, but the reason they were skylarking along was because he was a black man in a white man's domain. Fact. End of argument.

And that's how Lester was thinking when he saw her for the first time.

She was standing there up in the woods, maybe fifteen yards above the creek.

Lester did not actually take her in at first. Not at all. He was too honed in on the bridge, listening for whines from Flick, waiting to find out what the next appropriate move might be, when he happened to hear a small . . . what? A decompression of soil, a deer stepping across the stream, a human palm slide over the rough bark of a pine tree. Maybe, he didn't know, he had heard a branch crack just like in the movies. Only this wasn't a movie. It was real life, life in 3-D, and she was standing up there looking down at him.

Not moving. She wasn't moving a hemline. All she was doing, in fact, was giving him a frucking major case of the willies.

She looked every inch a witch. She was dressed like a frucking Halloween witch, with a long nose, straight black hair, dark skirt—a hippie-length skirt although she didn't remind Lester of any hippies he knew. There was something earthy and rooted about her. She was as dark as a stump.

She was frucking eerie, that's what she was. She stood there, not moving, her head way too big for her body. She was staring or maybe, just maybe Lester told himself, she was passing some time by putting a curse on him. Not that he believed in curses, but this old dame looked like a piece of New England soil, one of those quaint goddamn rock walls risen up to curse him.

Only . . . it wasn't a woman. That was his next thought. It was . . . something about her posture, her position on the slight incline told him this . . . a man. It was a man dressed like a woman. A man wearing a witch's Halloween costume. A man out of his frucking crazy mind. He knew, sure as hell, this was one mixed up college boy. One mixed up white boy who probably slept in his mother's bed too long, played with his daddy's trumpet, wore his sister's underpants. This was one of those kids who was *out* there, a Ted Bundy type, a guy who pulled a woman's stocking over his head and found that looking through a little nylon mesh with his nose pressed flat, his eyebrows two black lines, was exciting as all hell.

Lester debated about shooting him dead. He even lifted his revolver and aimed it at the kid. It would be a shot, a healthy shot, but he was a fair hand at shooting. But before he decided one way or the other about what to do, the witch started fading back deeper into the woods. She didn't turn, but sort of back-pedalled, feeling with her hands to check for trees, her face, her frucking witch nose, pointed right at him.

Then the siren started. A second later the Jeep pulled up, pulled up from the opposite direction it should have come. Pulled in from the north instead of the south, which meant those peckerheads had gone almost all the way around the campus before finally making tracks for Potter's Bridge. Which meant they had left him out here with the Maidenform girl for a good twenty minutes longer than he should have had to be.

"Assholes," he said, shaking his head at the Jeep.

It would have been bad enough if Jam hadn't jumped out of the Jeep, a machete in his hand, and yelled a jerk-off greeting.

"Yo, Bro," was what Jam called.

Lester shook his head again. He looked up to find the witch. Disappeared. The witch had gone back to his mommy's bed, or down to Zayre's to pick up a pack of opaque pantyhose. But for the hell of it, and to get back at them, Lester pointed up the hill.

"Up there," he said, "the guy got away up there."

Rocky.

Jam wouldn't have admitted it for the world, but whenever he ran up hill, whenever he ran, period, he heard Rocky's theme song someplace deep in his head.

Da da daaaaa, da da daaaaaa . . .

Not loud. Not like it was played when Rocky went up the stairs in Philadelphia. Not like when Rocky danced around on the top step, his hands up, ready to take on the black asshole in the gigantic Uncle Sam hat. No, when Jam ran it was more like . . . like maybe when Rocky was running through the streets of South Philly and the kids ran with him . . . that kind of thing. Just quiet music building slowly, giving him a push to keep going.

He was thankful to have the Rocky theme song at times like these, heading up the hill after some geekster who was supposed to have killed someone. Not that he believed Lester about the guy killing anyone, but he was happy to have someone to chase. Someone to track down and squash, or maybe slip the knife into . . . maybe it would come to that, Jam didn't know, but if it did he would be prepared.

Only right now the hill was pretty slanted. It didn't look like it went up so steeply from the rim of Potter's Bridge. Jam felt himself getting a little winded, which was unusual for a guy who ran probably sixty miles a week. Part of it was the loamy soil, which kept slipping under his feet, and part of it was his adrenalin pumping, and part of it was his black-polished flight boots . . . but that was okay . . . the guy could run but he couldn't hide, because when Jam started hearing Rocky in his head, he could run forfreakingever.

But run where?

There was no point in just running. He stopped on the lip of the hill, the woods gradually leveling out around him. He saw some security lights about fifty yards further on, right where the hill finally flattened out completely. That would be Squatter's Hall, the grad dorm, the museum of bearded assholes. To the south, maybe another eighth of a mile, would be the old science building. Hancock Cafeteria, Gilding Theater, then the Student Union, then Memorial Hall. The geekster could have gone toward any of those buildings, could have found a footpath and just walked off. And the sad hell of it was, you couldn't stop a student and start grilling him about his slimey habits because the ACLU would have your ass over a barrel. You could not say boo. Captain Barney, the student ass-kissing, supreme wimp would stand up for civil rights every time. It didn't matter if you got the guy or not as long as no one trampled on his civil rights.

So there was nowhere to go, no direction to take. Behind him, down on Potter's Bridge, he could make out the flashing lights of the jeep. He heard radio squawks, which meant the two old ladies, Lester and Eddy, were phoning something in. It also meant Chief Barney would be on his way, dressed, no doubt, in baggy corduroys, dressed like a commie college prof, dressed like—

Someone was walking on the path between Memorial and the Gilding Theater.

Walking fast, hustling along. He couldn't see the person too well through the trees. He couldn't see much more than a form walking, moving away from the scene.

Jam picked an angle. It was just like on a football field. You saw the halfback break loose, heading for the end zone, and you picked an angle. You didn't run right behind the guy but picked an angle, doing it instinctively. It didn't matter how fast the guy was. If you picked the angle long enough you caught him. Simple as that.

He picked an angle to the north, an angle that would put him ahead of whoever it was. It wasn't easy to gauge his own speed, going through the woods as he was forced to do, but he was pretty sure he could catch the asshole. He had to hustle around trees in order to keep the angle set up. He tried to be quiet but that wasn't easy, wasn't easy at all with the woods like a box of kindling. Deadfalls, clumps of sumac, stands of birch, and mosquitoes. His head wasn't playing Rocky music anymore. It was playing some sort of African safari music, with the sound of macaws and storks and cheetahs screaming over top.

Luck was with him. He reached the path, just a dirt path, right at a bend so that the asshole walking toward him couldn't know he was coming to a checkpoint. Climbing over the tiny railing that bordered the path, Jam put away his Bowie knife.

He took a position in the middle of the path, feet spread fairly wide, holster open. He leaned forward slightly to put himself on the balls of his feet. Mosquitoes were still all over him, flicking in and out around his eyes, sitting on his arms, doing the back-stroke through his sweat. For a second Jam had an image of himself as Marlon Brando in *Apocalypse Now*, one bald mother, one case of human jungle rot. Rambo or Ninja, whatever you wanted to call him, Jam felt ready.

The only trouble was, it was a woman coming down the path. Just a woman skipping along, probably walking bowlegged from getting it hard and fast for the last couple hours. She was hustling, head down, skirt flapping. The coeds at Colbin were like whores, that was the truth, that was what no one wanted to talk about. Driving around nights, he saw them more than once up in some dorm window getting it every which way to Sunday. Missionary, up against doors, from behind leaning out windows, the guys sawing away at them.

And here was another. She was hurrying home, her eyes on the ground, running along to some dorm where she would pretend to study. Or maybe she would lay in bed and sniff her armpits, recalling Mr. Loverboy's scent, dreaming of the day when they could spend endless hours together.

"Miss, excuse me, have you seen anyone else on this path tonight?" Jam asked. He put his hands on his belt, moved just an inch or two so that he was squarely in the coed's path.

"What?" the girl asked.

Or maybe she said "butt," it could have been butt, it could have been what or butt. Her voice was soft, blubbery, almost as if she had been crying. She still hadn't looked up. She wore a hippie skirt, one of those old-fashioned deals that came down to about mid-calf, the kind women wore with jump boots.

"Excuse me," he said again, "I'm with the school's security office."

And then she looked up.

Which made Jam say holyfuckingshit to himself. Which made him reach for his gun, the hell with his knife, he wanted the .44 out of the holster now.

Because it was not a woman.

No woman looked like that. It was some sort of guy in a woman's outfit, and she was wearing a weird wig. And as he leaned back, slapping ineffectually at his holster, she lifted something out of a fold of her skirt. He knew it was a knife, or a razor, something slashing toward him, but he couldn't do a thing about it because he was looking at the woman's . . . scalp?

It wasn't her scalp. It wasn't her forehead, it was someone else's skin stretched out into a cap and pulled over his head like a Halloween wig. It was the most disgusting thing Jam had ever seen. He was aware he was failing, wasn't handling himself well.

Because she came closer, rising up at him, rushing at him with a razor . . . yes, it was a straight-edged razor, the kind his father used, the kind that came with a strop strap that his dad used on his sonny boy's behind. Jam lifted his arm to protect himself and felt a slice go right down his forearm, and he saw blood shoot up, and then another cut up along his shoulder.

The whole time he was pawing at his gun, but he couldn't keep from staring at the wobbly flesh covering the top of the guy's scalp, couldn't believe that the guy must have actually scalped someone and was now wearing the hair with blood coming down his cheeks.

The blade hit him along the throat. He felt like a pussy for getting caught so easily, and he was still trying to pull his gun but the kid was strong. Very strong. The kid was boring in and Jam felt himself tripping over the guard rail. It was all happening too fast, it wasn't supposed to be like this . . . falling backward, and the kid was on top of him working the razor. All Jam could see was some crazy kid, dressed in a hippie skirt, wearing someone else's hair. Wearing a girl's head of hair and sort of whimpering as she was slicing away, but it wasn't a she, it was a he.

Then the kid was gone. Just like that. Jam heard her going off, him going off, listening to her steps and stared straight up at the sky. He couldn't see much, only trees and a few stars, and somewhere distant a security lamp. The lamp made a nice glow on the tips of the pines. Jam wanted to turn his head, wanted to see where she went, but he couldn't be sure his head was still securely fastened. He couldn't be sure, if he sat up, that his head wouldn't fall right the hell off his neck and roll down the hill toward Potter's Bridge.

CHAPTER THREE

IVY

IT LOOKED LIKE A COLLEGE ARCHIE AND VERONICA MIGHT attend. Jughead would be the water boy, Moose the football star, Mr. Weatherby . . . was that his name? . . . the dean of students.

Only it wasn't imaginary.

That's what thrilled Zelda Fitzgibbon, graduate of Xavier High in Newton, New Jersey, former student council president, staunch member of the New Jersey 4-H Programs, and now incoming freshperson. It was Colbin College, and it was green, and "granite-strewn," as the brochures said, and it had an agricultural lab, and beautiful ivy walls.

It had splendid ivy walls. More than that, it had ivy vines that were slowly beginning to turn in the first week of September. Orange and red and yellow, and then the trees would take on the fever, and within a month, the first week of October at the latest, you would have foliage. You would have state fairs, ox pulls, dog trials, pumpkins, apples, the last of the tomatoes, and a harvest moon. Most of all you would have a harvest moon and a certain night when the

geese went south and the weather was crisp and you felt
an undeniable yearning for cider.

All of which was the reason she had enrolled in Colbin
College. All of which was the reason she pressed her forehead to the window as her father drove her into the circular driveway in front of Sheppard Dorm. She was aware
of acting juvenile, gushy, but she couldn't help it. She
didn't care who saw her, because she had worked too long,
pushed too hard, to care about anyone else's opinion at the
moment. The college was better, much better than she had
remembered.

"Oh look, Zelda!" her mother said from the front seat.

Even though she was looking, even though she was
strained to take in everything, her mother had still latched
on to something to point out. Her mother, Gwendolyn, was
reliving her own college experience at dear old Bard. Zelda
knew that. She was positive about that and it killed her to
watch it. She didn't hate her mother, but she always felt her
mother tried to appropriate what should have been hers and
hers alone. First date, first trip to the beauty parlor, first hair
cut, first manicure, first ballet recital. There wasn't a picture in the entire album of her childhood where Gwendolyn
wasn't somehow muscling in on the scene.

"Yes," Zelda said.

"The sign? Did you see it? How sweet!"

Zelda had seen the sign. She had seen the big ban-
ner made from bedsheets that read: "WELCOME TO
SHEPPARD DORM." It was impossible to miss, naturally,
but it had somehow become Gwendolyn's point of interest.
Gwendolyn was the tour director through Zelda's life.

And Zelda knew her father, Bob, paid the fare. That was,
and always had been, the arrangement. He was the silent
partner, the backer, the money man. He was in insurance,
was good at it, but was not a match for his wife. No one
was quite a match for Gwendolyn, but he was outclassed.
At the moment he was playing chauffeur, sitting behind
the wheel of the family station wagon. He hadn't been to
college. He had gone to work in order to keep his mother in groceries, then had entered the navy, put in his time
and had come out to take on Gwendolyn, a girl from "up

the hill," as they said in Newton. Zelda knew the history well enough, just as she knew her dad now felt he was rising above his station in sending his daughter to a beautiful New England college. On the other hand, Gwendolyn, Service League member, Junior League member, hospital volunteer, showed every sign of returning to a land where she could finally breathe once more, could finally be fully Gwendolyn.

"Do you think I should park right here? They should have someone outside to tell us what to do. You think it's okay if I pull up on the grass?" her dad asked now.

Zelda, looking over his shoulder at the driveway in front of him, couldn't help seeing the bald spot at the very crown of his head.

"There are other families unloading, Bob. Right here, Bob. This is perfect. They expect people to, can't you add it up?"

This from Gwendolyn. She was taking over and of course she was correct. Nevertheless, Zelda saw her dad glance to the right, trying to tell Gwendolyn that this wasn't her moment, so just back off, but he couldn't quite swing it. Zelda watched Gwendolyn dismiss her father by pointing forward, directing his attention to the parking spot. She wanted the car there, right there, and there it would go.

First round, last round, every round to Gwendolyn.

But still Zelda didn't hate her. She couldn't quite bring herself to such a pitch, not now, not on this day. It wasn't an afternoon to hate anyone. Besides, it was all going to be over by tomorrow. By tomorrow she would be a college freshman, freshperson, and Gwendolyn would be back home. Zelda, for better or worse, would be free of her.

So she shrugged as she climbed out. She shrugged as they do in the movies, as they do on TV, shrugged to shake off the first eighteen years of her life. Not all of the eighteen years, not every memory, but enough of it so she could feel she was starting new.

"It's lovely," Gwendolyn said, beginning to climb out. "Bob, why don't you start unloading and Zelda and I will go in and register? Just put the things down here on the grass."

"I'd like to go in by myself," Zelda said.

She hadn't known she was going to say it. It came as a surprise to her, but suddenly it seemed extremely important that she go in alone. She saw her words hit Gwendolyn, who actually rocked slightly backward, leaning for just a moment away from the roof of the car, one foot out and one foot still in the interior. In that instant several things happened at once. Zelda felt immediately that it was absolutely essential she go in alone. She also felt, astonishingly, that this was a moment they all feared in different ways. She saw her mom recoil, struck speechless for just a count. Her dad, bless him, stopped where he stood with his hand on the top of the driver's door. He bent down, gently, very gently, and placed his lips on the back of his hand. With a swell of pain, Zelda realized he was close to crying, that this sad good man had worked all his life for this single moment and now wasn't up to facing it.

There was more, much more, but she couldn't wait to see it or discuss it or be persuaded to some other course of action. She turned around and ran up the stairs, white cement stairs, conscious she was entering what was to be her home for the next four years. It was her domain, her testing ground. From here she would go into biology, work down at the animal labs, become a vet, probably study at the University of Pennsylvania specializing in household pets, not farm animals.

It was here she was going to make a name for herself.

But first Zelda had to take a name tag.

She saw them stuck to a large bulletin board as soon as she pulled open the wide front door. Half of the tags were gone, and for a dreadful moment she couldn't find her own. She couldn't find anything faintly resembling her name, no possible mix-up, no . . .

Then she saw it.

"Hi," the tag said.

Beneath it was her name: "Zelda Fitzgibbon, Room 202."

She pulled off the slick backing and pressed the tag above her left breast. She used the distraction to give her time to look around the lobby. It was old and a little musty. She saw a white patch of tacking on the arm of one easy chair, a lampshade that had been burned black in one spot, an Oriental throw rug that had a badly unravelled edge. But it also had a fireplace, and a high ceiling . . . and boys!

Men, she quickly corrected herself. College men. She wasn't the boy-crazy type, and she certainly wasn't going to take her identity from being the girlfriend of so-and-so big man on campus. But it was a surprise, and a pleasant one, to see boys. She had known, of course, that Sheppard was a coed dorm. She had requested it on the admission form last spring. Xavier had been a Catholic girls' school, which was about as bleak as things could get, so she had jumped at the opportunity to live beside boys, to see boys every day, to be natural with boys. She had figured over the summer—how many times had she figured it?—that if she had been exposed a little more to the company of boys, if she hadn't been so sheltered by Sister Grace, and Sister Pauline, and Sister Bartholomew (and Gwendolyn, don't forget Gwendolyn, she told herself), then maybe Connor wouldn't have happened. Maybe she wouldn't have lost her virginity in the backseat of a Ford LTD to a boy who simply climbed on top of her and took what he wanted.

"Hello, you're . . . ?"

Zelda looked up. She had been patting the name tag and staring around the room, staring at the boys in a glazed sort of way, and had not seen a young woman a little older than herself walk across the room and bend to read her name tag.

"Zelda?" the girl finished. "Zelda Fitzgibbon, Room 202? I thought you were one of mine."

"One of yours?" Zelda said, feeling annoyed with herself that she had zoned out right when she should have been zoned in.

"One of my advisees. I'm your R.A. Resident assistant? My name is Lisa."

Lisa spoke with what Gwendolyn would have called Connecticut lockjaw. She was dressed in jeans and a blue turtleneck. She was tremendously tan and absolutely beautiful. As soon as she finished speaking she ducked her chin just slightly so that it edged under the front peak of the turtleneck.

"How do you do. Pleased to meet you," Zelda managed.

"Pleased to meet you. You're one of the last ones in. Your roommate is here. Martha is her name."

"Is she?"

"All settled. She arrived early this morning, the first one here. Come on, I'll check you through, then take you up to your room."

Get it together, Zelda told herself. For a moment she regretted not allowing Gwendolyn to come inside with her. Gwendolyn would have handled the situation. Gwendolyn would have flourished, in fact. She devoured social situations, while Zelda had always been aware she was more like her dad in that regard.

She followed Lisa to the registration desk. But before they arrived someone squealed. It was a loud scream, a laugh, a cry, all mingled. Zelda was so startled she took a step back, looking around nervously. The squeal came again, this time louder. She turned to the door just as Lisa raised her arms.

"Oh my Goddd," Lisa said.

Zelda saw two girls hurrying across the lobby. They were both dressed in, of course, blue jeans and turtlenecks. They rushed forward with their arms out, their faces tan, their eyes shockingly white against their skin. It was almost a nightmare—three blonde, beautiful women in your dorm, one of them your R.A. Zelda felt dumpy just watching them. Nevertheless, she smiled. It was a ridiculous smile, she was aware, a smile that said, hello, I'm insignificant, but I want to be friends and you three are marvelous and don't mind me right now but someday you'll see that I'm fairly interesting too. And she hated herself for smiling like that, but she couldn't help it, the smile continued to grow until she felt not like the Cheshire cat but like Godzilla preparing to eat the Chrysler Building.

"Where did you two get so tannn... and you lost

weight ... I hate you both!" Lisa said, finally reaching them.

"So have you!" one of the girls said. "How was the Cape? Was it amazing?"

"It was UN-BELIEEVVVABLE."

"Was Chucky there?" the other one asked Lisa.

"Every morning."

The last statement—and all it inferred—brought out another squeal. Watching them, Zelda could think of only one word: mix. That was Gwendolyn's credo, her advice for any social situation. Mix, talk, jump in, don't be a wallflower. Or better still, shrinking violets don't get their share of sunshine.

She took a step forward.

And that was probably not a good move, probably wasn't the thing to do, but Lisa saw it and broke away long enough to wave her over.

"This is Bags and Phillips," Lisa said, "and this is Zela."

"Zelda," Zelda said.

"Zelda, yes, I'm so sorry," Lisa said.

Zelda shook their hands. Lisa put her arm around one of them ... Bags, was it? ... and rocked her head back and forth.

"Zelda, don't listen to a word these two tell you. Not a thing."

And Bags, yes it was Bags, Zelda was pretty sure, leaned forward just enough to whisper.

"I have two things to tell you," she said, smiling her remarkable smile. "Men," she pointed above her, "and men," she pointed below her.

Snoopy.

That was the first thing Zelda saw as she looked over Lisa's shoulder. Lisa had pushed halfway through the door of Room 202, her hand on the knob, her knuckles just tapping the wood.

A Snoopy poster, with Linus and the bird ... what was the bird's name? ... took up most of the wall on the left side of the room. Zelda squinted, trying to read the caption of the cartoon. It said something about "Keep smiling ..."

while Snoopy hung from the front lip of his doghouse. He dangled from his snout, but his mouth, his dog's mouth, was wrinkled in a little grin. The bird and Linus stood down by Snoopy's dish, staring up at Snoopy.

"Martha?" Lisa said.

It was one of those horribly awkward moments. Zelda wasn't sure if Martha felt it, but she knew unquestionably that Lisa did. She knew Lisa had already scoped out the situation and had some sense of Martha. She knew that Lisa had seen Martha hanging up the Snoopy poster, had watched Martha cart in a Snoopy wastebasket, Snoopy sheets, and had cringed. What made it worse was that Zelda saw in the first instant that Martha hadn't a clue. She was proud of her Snoopy paraphernalia. She thought she had made the room habitable and cute and it didn't make a bit of difference that it was all cheap and falsely sentimental. Martha didn't know.

But Lisa knew. As she pulled back, making room for Zelda to step inside, she smiled at Zelda. She smiled as if to say, I'm sorry, this is the luck of the draw, I wanted to warn you about Martha but what could I say? And there was indeed nothing to say. Martha looked like a perfectly nice person, a bit chubby, a bit dowdy, in fact, but not a bad or mean-spirited roommate. Zelda told herself she could have done worse, much worse.

But she couldn't take her eyes off the poster.

"You're Zelda. I'm so happy to meet you. I've just been waiting to help you get settled."

"And you're Martha," Zelda said, shaking hands.

A soft, wet hand, a hand that might rise if placed in an oven.

"I should get back downstairs. I'll stop in later tonight to see how you're doing," Lisa said. She paused at the door, started to say something, then smiled and went out.

Her exit left Zelda standing on the threshold of the room. Again she wished she had brought Gwendolyn in with her, because Gwendolyn would have taken over the situation. Gwendolyn would have mixed, talked, chatted. Zelda was conscious of the silence in the room, and was aware she should say something.

"Well . . ." was all she managed.

"It's a nice room, isn't it?" Martha said, stepping back and quartering slightly to her side of the room. "We look out on the common."

"Do we?" asked Zelda, although she knew that already.

"All the even rooms do."

Zelda stepped to the window and checked the view. She brushed against something and pulled back, afraid she had knocked a knickknack off the ledge. It took her a moment to realize the window was ringed by ivy and she had only touched a leaf. A vine, thick enough to climb on, worked its way directly under the bottom sill. She looked straight down and saw the ivy formed a green mat all the way to the ground. A few of the branches appeared sutured into the wall, chipping the brick to orange. On the top half of the window the ivy had worked into the frame, the leaves glancing inside.

"It's great," Zelda said, looking back and smiling at Martha.

But she didn't look directly at Martha. Instead she looked over Martha's shoulder at the poster. The poster said: "Keep smiling . . ." That was all. There was no punch line.

"I love Snoopy," Martha said, turning and looking at the poster.

"He's neat."

"I wrote to Charles Schulz and he sent me an autographed strip in return. I was only eight. I've loved him ever since," Martha said.

"Neat."

"He's a great man."

"He must be," Zelda said, and looked out the window again.

" . . . but Snoopy all over the place? She has Snoopy sheets. How could anyone . . . ?" Zelda said, trying to find the right words.

"You loved Sting," her father reminded her.

"Sting? Sting was cute and he was a human being."

"Snoopy's cute."

"Dad, nobody can hate Snoopy. It's just that it's so . . .

tacky. I mean, this is college, not summer camp."

"So what should she have on the wall?"

Zelda looked carefully at her father. She was grateful to the waiter who came at that moment to refill their coffees. She hadn't anticipated her father coming to Martha's defense. Usually it was Gwendolyn who threw the monkey wrench in, but Gwendolyn sat calmly to her left, watching the exchange. Zelda knew Gwendolyn understood what she was driving at, but for some reason had decided to keep out of it.

"It just seems childish," she said after the waiter left.

"You agreed she was a nice person, though," her father said. "She stayed around to help you move in. Shouldn't that count for something?"

"Of course it counts for something. I never said that it didn't."

Then she saw it. Suddenly the whole thing made sense. He had defended Martha from the moment he met her, had gone out of his way to include her, had even invited her to dinner this evening because he knew what it was like to be on the outside of social situations. He understood meekness, and awkwardness, and perhaps, yes, even a love for Snoopy. He was telling her right now that there were some people in this world who needed Snoopy to get by, and it was okay, not everyone had to live up to her or other's standards. That was what was in his eyes, that understanding, and it was his last message to her, his final unspoken speech.

"I guess I'm overreacting," Zelda said finally. "She is nice."

"You can get a single next year anyway," Gwendolyn said.

"Probably so."

The waiter brought the check. Her father added the totals, nodding as he did so, then removed seventy dollars from his wallet and placed them on the table. It was over. The last formality was over and in less than a half hour Zelda knew she would be on her own.

"Well," her father said.

"You sure you don't mind about Thanksgiving?" Gwendolyn asked, returning to a subject they had already cov-

ered. "I can arrange for you to go to Aunt Lou's. She'd
love to have you."

"No, I'll be fine here. I'll probably have a lot of work
to do. I'd sort of like the chance to be alone for once in
my life."

"I understand, sweetheart. But we'll be home for
Christmas. It's just that we have some time around Thanksgiving. Your dad has the conference."

"No, Mom, we've been all over this. You go ahead, I
understand. Really."

"I hate to leave you here on your first vacation."

"It's okay. Enjoy it. Florida sounds like fun."

Zelda stood. She knew she was rushing things slightly,
but it was over. There was nothing more to say, nothing
more to do, it was time. She watched her parents glance at
each other. They stood a moment later, first her dad, who
reached over and put a hand on the back of Gwendolyn's
chair. Then Gwendolyn stood, smoothing her dress as she
rose, the skirt of the tablecloth sticking to her for just an
instant.

"I've got something out in the car for you," her father
said when they had regrouped in the lobby.

"The mysterious box," Zelda said, smiling.

"Yes, the mysterious box."

"I'm going to say goodbye here, then. You go out with
your father," Gwendolyn said.

Zelda began to cry. She reached up to her mother and
her mother reached back, and they hugged. Zelda had no
clear idea what she wanted to say. Something about thanks,
thanks for eighteen years, and something about forgiveness,
but there was no point to saying anything at the moment.
She hugged her mother and was startled to feel her mother squeezing her, rocking her, it wasn't just a goodbye hug,
not a little send-off, but something deeper and longer and
more permanent.

"Goodbye, my angel," her mother whispered in her ear
and Zelda, despite herself, whispered back, "Goodbye,
Mommy."

Then they broke and Zelda went outside, not looking
back. It was a little melodramatic not to look back, but it

was okay, she was eighteen, and, really, what more was there to say?

The wind was up. Walking down the driveway of the Alumni Center carrying the box against her chest, Zelda felt cold. Or rather, not really cold but wrung out, worn out, fatigued. She had anticipated this moment so long, this first gulp of freedom, that it shocked her to find she felt nothing but exhaustion. She had nearly allowed her dad to drive her back to the dorm, playing the little girl once again—take me skating, drive me to the bowling alley, can we go to the movies? It took a deliberate effort on her part to refuse the ride. Twice he had offered; she had refused him three times. The last time, refusing him before he had even spoken, she had looked down quickly, concealing her tears, afraid to look at him because he was a good, gentle man.

And then he had given her the box.

She didn't really want to deal with it, didn't want to get caught up in too many emotions, wanted simply to slide away and holler goodbye. But he looked so old bending inside the car, looked so proud when he brought the package out, that she had held out her arms and accepted it. For a moment she thought she might slip away and open it back in her dorm room, open it with Martha and Snoopy and the whole gang, but he had nodded and slipped her purse off her arm to hold it.

"Go ahead, open it," he had said.

She had only the slightest corner off the package when she had started to cry once more. This time, however, she was aware of losing control. It was too much, the whole day had been too emotionally pitched for her as she pulled off the last of the wrapping paper.

"Your size?" he asked.

"Yesss," she said, still not looking up, the tail of her reply getting caught in other emotions.

The package contained muck boots. She had known what they were going to be from the clumpy roll of the boots in the box.

"A vet needs muck boots. You'll be in barns."

She nodded and nodded and nodded. She put the box on the hood of the car and hugged him. He knew, of course. He knew in ways Gwendolyn never would—knew that she would study biology, would become a vet, go to Cornell or Colorado State. He had known it since she was a little girl when they had fixed a robin together, binding its wing, outfitting a shoebox with cotton and twigs, worms from the garden . . .

She had said nothing after receiving the boots. She had hugged him until her arms felt numb, then she slipped her purse off his shoulder and picked up the box in both arms. She had hurried away, not running, purposely not running, feeling she might collapse if she demanded too much of her legs. Halfway down the driveway she heard his loafers scuff on the driveway, then a moment later the solid *whoosh* of the storm door closing on the restaurant. Gone. He was gone and Gwendolyn was gone, and she was on her own at last.

All she felt was cold.

The temperature had dropped. She saw her breath in front of her and felt the metal of her necklace—a golden pear given to her on her sweet sixteen—slippery on the back of her neck. The wind seemed anxious in the trees and she was not surprised to see, when she reached the street, that the gutter was half-filled with leaves.

She stopped at the end of the driveway and tried to take her bearings. She knew she was lost as soon as she looked both ways. She wasn't terribly lost, wasn't going to walk until she perished of starvation or hypothermia, but she was disoriented. She was aware of the irony of the situation—on her own at last and lost within the first five minutes—but she didn't dwell on it. She told herself to calm down, to take things in, which was the advice her father had always given her. Look for landmarks, steeples, streetlights, forsythia bushes, rock walls. She remembered the advice and looked carefully up and down the street once more, but nothing struck her as familiar.

It was dark, that was the problem. The sky was cloudy and there was no moon to speak of and the campus—this hit her with some force—was decidedly rural. This definitely

wasn't Newton, New Jersey. This was New Hampshire. It
occurred to her that Colbin College was laid out on two
hundred acres of woods and farmland and that meant it was
going to be dark at night when the moon wasn't out.

She wiped her eyes and walked to the left, trying to
recall at the same time if they had turned right or left into
the Alumni Center. She guessed right, which meant they
had come from the left, which meant that Sheppard Dorm
was somewhere down over the small hill rising before her.
She walked in the middle of the sidewalk, feeling nervous,
cold, and tired. She clutched the box to her chest, and for
a moment felt like a young girl wandering to school, an
elementary school girl in pigtails and a wide starched skirt,
skipping to class with a pile of books hugged to her chest.
At the same time another recollection forced its way into
her thoughts and she began to remember a Halloween night
when she was ten or eleven, a cold crisp night not unlike
this one, when she had walked down to Cindy Draper's
house and halfway there had been frightened by nothing.

It had been nothing. Everyone later said it was only her
imagination. But that night she had seen a man sitting on a
branch up above the sidewalk. He had been there, his feet
swinging down directly over the sidewalk, his hands held
to either side to steady himself on the oak branch. She had
seen him for several paces, seen him slowly emerge as a
man and not merely a tangle of branches, and he had looked
for all the world like Mr. Hotchkiss, her personal scarecrow
demon. Her first thought was that Mr. Hotchkiss had somehow slithered down from her closet, or perhaps crept out
from under her bed—on Halloween such things were possible—in order to climb this oak tree and sit above her and
whisper, "Come here."

She hadn't imagined the voice. All these years later, she
still couldn't believe she imagined that. Because she could
recall his face, the straw head bending down until it was
almost even with the branch, the smell of his soap, the
black hair on the back of his arm as he lowered one hand,
motioning her forward. There had been one terrible moment
when she realized it was not Mr. Hotchkiss at all, but a real
man wearing a Halloween mask, a deranged man, clinging

from the tree and trying to bring her closer. Their eyes . . .
no, not eyes, their whole souls . . . had met and she had
known in that instant that he wanted her to step closer, to
reach up her hand, to be persuaded to keep silent.

"Come here," he whispered.

He made no promise not to hurt her. He offered her
nothing. When she turned and ran home, screaming that
Mr. Hotchkiss was in a tree near Cindy Draper's house,
she knew no one would believe her. She knew they would
not believe a man had been there, nor would they believe
she had heard his feet strike the ground as soon as she
screamed.

That night was not unlike this night.

Except she was eighteen now, a college freshperson, and
she did not intend to let her imagination carry her away.
This was simply a dark street, a street that would lead her
to the center of town or to some recognizable building. She
turned around once, but not too quickly, not in such a way
that would let her begin to panic, and looked for the lights
of the Alumni Center restaurant. But they were gone, sub-
merged in the pine woods that surrounded it.

She increased her pace. She passed an open field with
white granite boulders. The boulders, for an instant, appeared
to move. They resembled the sides of Holstein cows, pale
and heaving with grass. Their movement came from her
own stride and she commanded herself to stop until they
became only boulders once more.

It was because she was motionless that she heard the
footsteps. For a moment she convinced herself that the
sound was only the echo of her footsteps, but then, in
a quick lament over her own stupidity, she realized she
was no longer walking so how could they be her footsteps
echoing? There was a better explanation, she knew, but she
couldn't think of it at the moment. She couldn't pin anything down, although the trees certainly continued to blow,
and the grass occasionally tugged against its roots until it
appeared ready to peel back like a skin of soil, ready to
open and reveal the maggot world, the land of moles and
worms and corpses, graves gone moldy, spores of conta-
gion floating on the wind . . .

And Mr. Hotchkiss, of course. Mr. Hotchkiss out for his evening stroll.

She saw nothing, but she began to move faster. She cleared the top of the hill and finally saw a few lights below her, which was a relief, except that the footsteps continued to flank her. They moved when she moved, the sound thudding out among the boulder cows. If it was Mr. Hotchkiss, he was a spry old devil. By the sound of his footsteps he was scrambling to keep up, probably covering brushy ground, probably moving crablike with his legs feeling to his side and his eyes remaining on her.

She continued walking, hurrying, the box sometimes jabbing against her chest. She considered dropping the box and heading down the hill in a full-out run, when she saw a pair of headlights approaching. They were coming up the hill toward her, spraying the boulder cows with light. She turned and looked out into the field, squinting to see better, and she stared until she assured herself that there was nothing out there, nothing at all.

She turned back to the road in time to see the car angling toward her curb, the engine going soft, the tires creaking over a pod of pine cones that lay like a brown tongue in the middle of the road. The tires popped the pine cones and the car settled across the road, drifting to her curb. Against the horizon, as dark as it was, Zelda saw round searchlights sticking up like mouse ears from the roof of the car. A police cruiser.

"You lost, miss?" the officer said through the passenger window. Now that the car was near, Zelda saw it wasn't a police car but a campus security vehicle. The officer was a middle-aged black man. He leaned all the way across the seat in order to talk to her. He had his hand on his revolver, his arm bent as if he meant to draw it. He looked nervous, frightened, somehow, as if he had a Mr. Hotchkiss of his own walking around the woods somewhere, as if he had somehow seen the expression of her face and understood the woods could be a dark place.

"I'm new and I'm not sure which way to go," she said.

"Get in, I'll drive you."

She climbed in and closed the door, smelling, for an

instant, a plume of pine scent drift at her from a tiny Christmas tree sachet dangling from the rearview mirror. She looked over at the officer and smiled. He smiled back, but the odd thing was he seemed to be looking across her out at the cow boulders.

"Dark night," he said, turning away and giving the car a nudge of gas.

"I wasn't sure which way we came in. I'm in Sheppard Dorm."

"You were going the right way. You could make it faster taking some paths, but it's a dark night."

He performed a K-turn very slowly. He appeared intent on letting his lights shine out at the cow boulders. He let them linger there, making no pretense of turning the wheel or continuing the maneuver, leaning forward a little in his seat to stare after the high beams.

"You were looking out there when I pulled up, weren't you?" he asked, still letting the car idle in place.

"I was a little spooked."

"Spooky place, this campus after dark. What's your name?"

"Zelda."

"Mine's Lester. I'm going to tell you something, Zelda, you being new and all. You keep your wits about you when you're walking alone. Or better still, you get yourself a boyfriend as soon as you can and you make him walk you everywhere you go at night."

He wasn't saying it to offend her, to put her down. He was just a little old, she figured. She looked at him and smelled the pine scent again. He didn't say anything else. But he kept the lights shining out at the field, his hand restless on the gear shift.

CHAPTER FOUR

OPENING DAY

THE LEAVES WERE TURNING. THE SUGAR MAPLES BEHIND the Colbin College agricultural labs were already red. Up along the Kangamangus Highway the leaf peepers were out in force, stopping their Winnebagoes on bluffs overlooking ponds or valleys, causing, in their excitement to snap photos of this luxuriant turn of nature, traffic jams and accidents, and a swelling in antique prices. The local weather report included in its summary that the leaves would reach their peak the second Saturday in October, if weather conditions remained consistent with weather patterns in the past.

At Colbin College the fall session convened on September 5, the first Thursday after Labor Day.

5:36

This morning Mr. Go Go, a black-and-white tom cat, had killed a snake. He hadn't been hunting for snakes—indeed, he had only killed two before this one in his long and illustrious hunting career—but he had been waiting on the porch of 412 Charlemont Avenue for a chipmunk to emerge from a stack of birch logs when a second and unexpected movement caught his attention. The movement came from a batch of Turk's head irises, and at first even Mr. Go Go could discern no reason for the green wands to be moving. Then, gradually, he saw the snake—or rather he saw the head of the snake, its tongue darting forward to test the air.

It was still dark, with the slightest glimmer of light. Mr. Go Go waited. He sat on the porch railing and stared straight down, his eyes wide, his claws just barely edging out from the soft mitts of his paws. His lips drew back a fraction of an inch, and his tail, a long black tail with a few flecks of gray mixed in, twitched at the very end.

He watched the snake come forward. He could have pounced directly on the snake now, cracking down just behind the garter snake's head, but instinct reminded him that it was, after all, a snake. Snakes could be venomous and there was nothing in Mr. Go Go's intellect to reassure him that this was an extremely mild species of snake.

As a result, he jumped off the railing onto the porch and ran down the steps. He ran with his back flat, his legs crouched. He made no sound. He ran around the newel post of the porch railing, crossed one flagstone, then suddenly stopped. He stopped not more than six inches from the head of the garter snake, although the snake did not appear to realize Mr. Go Go was near.

Mr. Go Go did nothing for a moment. He remained crouched, his tail fidgeting. When he could stand it no longer he reached forward with his right forepaw and smacked the snake a swipe which instantly blinded the reptile in its left eye.

Then he jumped back.

Mr. Go Go left the ground completely, spinning and twirling, retracting his legs so they couldn't be bitten by the thrashing snake. He landed three feet away, a good two feet farther than the snake could possibly strike. He landed facing the snake, his eyes even more intent than before. As soon as he saw the snake wasn't going to defend itself but was attempting to turn and flee instead, he dodged in again and hit the snake twice with his left paw.

This time the snake came closer to scoring its own bite. It turned to strike, following the retreating paw with its open jaws. If the morning had been warmer, if the snake's blood had been heated, it might have at least had the satisfaction of landing a blow in its own defense. Instead it was a bit too sluggish. Mr. Go Go had already moved aside and had hit it three times on its back half, one of the claws hooking into the snake's flesh on the final blow and lifting its entire hindquarters off the ground.

It took five minutes for Mr. Go Go to finish the snake. He played with it for another twenty minutes, frequently falling on his side and lifting the snake above him, ripping down the belly with his rear paws, tossing the snake to one side, then jumping away as if the snake still retained life. He was still playing with it when he heard Gusty, the chocolate Labrador retriever next door, come around the side of the house with his bladder bursting.

Mr. Go Go lifted the snake in his jaws, dragged it for a foot to test its weight, then ran back up the stairs, padded across the wooden boards of the floor and jumped onto the porch railing. He kept the snake in his mouth as he watched Gusty piss. Gusty came by, sniffed once up at Mr. Go Go, then passed on. When Mr. Go Go could no longer hear Gusty's collar, he jumped back down and crossed the porch again. This time, instead of heading down the stairs and out to the yard, he went to the front door and put the snake down on the bushy welcome mat. He knocked it around several times, and once, when the snake slid onto the gray boards of the porch, it even seemed to move. He smacked it a few more times and discovered he could make the tail wiggle just by shaking the snake's head.

6:05

Bonnie Dunfey and Marsha Koln—two local mothers, both with children raised, clean houses, and fifteen extra pounds picked up through the years—crossed the bike path heading up toward Memorial Hall, power-walking as fast as they could. They were both dressed in sweatsuits, Bonnie's yellow, Marsha's red, and both wore Treetorn sneakers. Without speaking, they avoided taking that path. They didn't have to make an issue of it. They hadn't travelled that path since the young woman was pulled down under the bridge and the police officer—a nice boy, they both knew him—had been killed in the bargain.

In fact, Bonnie had been saying for the last month, since the killings in July, that they shouldn't even go on campus. Now, of course, with the students back, the campus didn't seem so frightening. Nevertheless, Bonnie had heard from her husband Frank, who used the same barber shop on Thayer Street as a lot of the school folk and was a man who knew what he knew and you didn't ask him how, thank you very much, that the school president, Doctor Mathews, had hired five new security officers. And why did you hire extra security officers if you didn't expect trouble? Long overdue, was what Marsha said back.

This morning they were moving at a good pace, building steam for the hill up Porcupine Path. Porcupine Path cut over to Gilding Theater, but it gave a wide berth, a very wide berth, to Potter's Bridge. They had gone over Potter's Bridge plenty of times in the past. A queer place, they had said to as many people who would listen, during the weeks following the murders.

"Always damp . . . always sticky," Bonnie usually began.

"A creepy feeling . . . like a swamp, is what it always reminded me of," Marsha would add.

So they were both happy to have a reason to change their path. And Porcupine Path suited them as well, even though the hill, which put them back on Grove Street, was steeper than the one near Potter's Bridge. As a matter of fact, it was a good deal steeper, and as they started up it now they couldn't help slowing down. The incline forced them to lean forward and reduce the swing of their arms.

"Up we go," Bonnie said.

"I hate this hill," Marsha replied.

"So do I. But the hills are where you burn your calories. Three-fifty an hour on flat surface, four-fifty on hills?"

"At least."

"That's a Diet Light Lunch, isn't it? You can have the turkey for three-seventy-five cals, I think."

"You're right."

"So," Bonnie said, pumping her arms as much as she could without entirely losing her breath, "all you'd have to do . . . is walk an hour on this hill . . . and you can eat a shitty lunch."

"Exactly."

Later they would argue about which one saw it first. Marsha said it had to be her, because she tended to bend over farther going up hill, and besides, it was on her side of the path. Bonnie claimed she had just finished speaking—a fact they both agreed on—and as a result she was looking across Marsha and had seen it and called her friend's attention to it.

They both agreed it was a human ear.

"My God," Marsha said.

They stood side by side, their shoulders touching, their hands up to cover their mouths.

"It's an ear," Bonnie said after a moment.

"The earring's still in it," Marsha said.

She felt herself near to fainting. She didn't know where to put her eyes. They were standing in the woods, she realized, and it wasn't very light. It was lonely on the road, and there was no absolute proof that the ear wasn't from a more recent murder than the one last summer. There wasn't any proof that the murderer wasn't still nearby, somewhere in the bushes, watching them this instant.

"Let's leave it," Bonnie said. "We'll send someone back for it. We'll call the police."

She started walking.

Marsha couldn't move. She knew Bonnie was accustomed to calling the shots . . . hadn't this whole exercise thing been her idea to begin with? . . . but she felt in her bones that Bonnie was wrong on this one. You couldn't just walk away. You couldn't turn your back because . . . she wasn't a feminist, not really, but still, you had to stand up for other women. You had to do what you could do to put away the nuts, to face the mug shots, to point the finger at the lineup. Right now the ear was evidence, and if they didn't take it with them, if they left it and a dog ran off with it, weren't they as guilty of indifference and fear as any judge who shrugged his shoulders and asked a rape victim if it wasn't the truth that she had really asked for it?

She bent down and picked up the ear.

It felt disgusting. She kept her eyes off it, but after nearly dropping it she gripped it securely.

"*What* are you doing?" Bonnie asked. She was already five or six steps up the hill.

"It's evidence."

"Just *drop* it. It's disgusting."

"I know it is. Let's go. Let's just call someone fast."

Bonnie looked at her. Marsha made a pouch out of the front of her sweatshirt and placed the ear there. When she knew the ear was completely covered, she began to walk as fast as she could.

6:44

Damian Peule stepped slowly out of his Chevy Vega parked in front of Ms. Fizz's. He was tired from working the night shift at the Coldbridge Grocery Mart. He was tired from filling in for Chuck, the wheezer, who was supposed to be a butcher but who probably was tubercular and coughed all over the meat for a week before he finally called in sick. It was enough to make you toss your cookies watching old Chuckyboy. Even as an employee with a discount on most items, even with a five-finger discount, Damian preferred to buy his meat over at Star Market. No chicken á la Chuck for him.

He walked up the front walk shaking his head at the memory of Chuck. At the memory of the whole damn place, the Coldbridge Grocery Mart. The store was nuts. Kids running up and down the aisles, his coworkers bowling with frozen turkeys and claiming they wouldn't hurt the birds. Bowling with turkeys, for godsakes! The kids ran a few steps, then skidded the turkeys down the aisle, aiming them at a wedge of Del Monte cream corn cans. It was funny, Damian had to admit, but it was no way to run a store. He was just a working guy, not the manager. If he were the manager, if he were . . .

KING OF THE FORESTTT!

He could never think of that expression, king of the forest, without widening it into the song sung by the cowardly lion Bert Lahr.

He heard the first wind chimes now. The sound built with each step until he couldn't hear anything else. There were so many wind chimes on Ms. Fizz's front porch that Damian thought he was in the Orient. Or maybe, he figured, Ms. Fizz thought she was in the Orient, as swacked out as she was half the time. Maybe all that tinkling was just enough to send her into la-la-land riding the heroin horse.

But it was her house after all, and if she wanted to live like the last holdover of Woodstock, that was her business. Live and let live, he thought as he reached forward and rang her doorbell. He rang it hard because it wasn't easy to make yourself heard over the wind chimes. It wasn't easy to make Ms. Fizz answer her own door, because truth to tell, she probably wasn't sure what dimension she was in right about now.

She surprised him, though. She answered on the second ring, her hair actually washed, her eyes halfway open. She looked okay. In fact, she looked good, better than he had seen her look in months. Long blonde hair like that woman actress in the "Mod Squad" . . . Julie, or Janet, or whatever her name was. Clean blue jeans, a fake pearl necklace, flip-flops, and a peasant blouse. The peasant blouse was a bit of a time warp, but so what?

"Hey," she said by way of greeting.

"Hey, you look good," he said, and meant it.

"Thanks, thanks. Come on in . . ."

"Damian," he supplied her with his name, because no matter how cleaned up she was, she was still humming like a four-slice toaster. "I'm Damian."

"Right, right, sure, I know."

She led him through the house into the kitchen. The kitchen was one of those linoleum deals, popular in the fifties. The sink was stuffed with dishes, but otherwise the place looked pretty good. Neat, almost tidy.

"This place looks better than it did last time I was here," Damian said.

"I'm getting a handle on things. Saturn's finally passing."

"Must be it. Things are looking up, huh?"

"Oh, definitely. There were some really bad vibes around. Saturn was playing the devil with everyone. Did you feel it?"

"Sure, no question," Damian said.

"My friend, Baba, says the stars are going to be very forgiving in the next couple months. Very generous. He says we have to prepare ourselves to receive the good fortune. Cleanse ourselves spiritually."

While she talked about cleansing herself spiritually she pulled up a chair to the kitchen sink, preparing to go to work. Damian moved forward. He looked up at the ceiling quickly when she grabbed at his fly. Ms. Fizz was direct about things. There was no conversation, really. Just passing the time of day and gabbing about the stars, then, bingadabing, she was panning for zipper trout.

"So, Baba—that's what everyone calls him, but his real name is Harry—he's Jewish, from down in Brooklyn, but he left rabbinical school because he decided that all religions share the same principles . . ."

He gradually tuned her out. He looked down and saw her hands undoing his zipper, then pushing aside his boxers and letting the King of the Foresssttt step out. Then she did what he liked best, liked more than all her other tricks and specialties. She proceeded to pet his donkey. It was such a sweet thing to do, the only thing about her that didn't seem . . . well, whorish . . . that he always waited for the moment when her hand just brushed the top of his donkey as if to say, hello again, my little man. Corny, maybe, but true.

Then, of course, that phase passed. Ms. Fizz was a pro after all, even if she did look like the blonde girl out of the "Mod Squad." She put her lips on the edge of his penis and hummed. She didn't pretend to hum, but really did hum, her lips buzzing to "Yankee Doodle Dandy," or whatever it was she hummed. Then she smiled up at him.

"*Mmm*," she said.

But the odd thing was, the only thought that came to his mind was working the night shift at the Coldbridge Grocery Mart. All he could think of were the kids bowling their turkeys, and the deadpan voice of Lou Canaseco, the store manager, reading the specials . . . "shoppers, today's special is" . . . static here . . . "four pound bag of Alpo dried dog food" . . . more static . . . "and six, twelve ounce cans of Diet Pepsi for only three dollars and twelve cents" . . . and the shoppers moving like zombies, like people pushing around their own wheelchairs, their own hospital gurneys, waiting to drop forward and be buried right in the metal carts.

"Doesn't that feel good?"

"Oh, it feels great."

"But you're not real . . ."

"I know, I will be in a second."

He had to consciously prevent himself from thinking of the grocery store. He concentrated on Ms. Fizz doing her work. Even though he wasn't entirely into it this morning, wasn't really a taut little springboard down there, it still felt like heaven. He leaned into her a little and felt her hands press against his thighs. Then she pushed away a bit and reached to the sink. She lifted her mouth off his penis and looked up again at him.

"I'm just going to . . ."

"I know, I know."

She took a drink of lukewarm water and sloshed it around in her mouth. Then she moved her lips over the head of his penis and suddenly he was in warm, warm water, and he felt his little man begin to stand up for himself. In fact, it took no time at all to be up at attention, her tongue and lips keeping the water moving.

"Oh, that's nice," he said, and grabbed the back of her head to haul himself deeper, but she politely removed his hand and gave him an extra slosh of water for releasing his grip. She spit the water out in the sink, then took another drink.

"Give me the fizz," he said.

She looked up at him and gargled. It was sort of her trademark, he knew, all this water business. When she gargled she closed her eyes and pretended to like what she was doing, but it was just a way to earn fifty bucks, just Ms. Fizz getting to the next syringe.

She grabbed for the tablet of Alka Seltzer and dropped it right in her mouth. He heard a little *kaplunk* as the tablet hit the water, then she gargled some more, and before long the whole thing was foaming up and coating her lips. She had her eyes closed, her head back, a foaming fountain, and he felt himself getting ready to shoot. It was all sort of perverse, he knew that, but it worked, she was good, and he grabbed her head and pulled it forward so that she didn't have any option but to take his penis in her mouth. All around it was foaming, tingling, and he didn't know if he really felt anything special or whether it was just knowing a woman was gargling an Alka Seltzer to make him feel good that set him off. But he did get off, Ms. Fizz peeking to see if he was done yet. For a second he wondered what she felt, what with all the fizzing going on, the warm water splashing around.

She spit the water and Alka Seltzer into the sink. He had to hold himself up for a second to keep his legs from wobbling. He saw the half-dissolved tablet down by the drain and listened to Ms. Fizz still trying to get her breath. He patted her on the back and felt sympathetic for an instant. What a way to earn a living. But then he realized that the whole thing had taken, what, ten minutes? She was up fifty in ten minutes, which was probably enough for her to get a little horse, a few cigarettes, another wind chime.

"How was that?" she asked a minute later.

"You're the best."

"That's fifty. You should know I'm putting my price up to seventy-five. From now on, I mean."

"That's a little steep."

"Well," she said.

Damian pulled up his zipper while she tidied up the sink area. She used a bottle of mouthwash and rinsed and spit, then rinsed again. He pulled out his wallet and counted out fifty bucks. She took the money as soon as she saw it and put it in a drawer to the right of the sink. Everything about her seemed a little more efficient, and Damian wondered if she wasn't under new management. Maybe this Baba was the new boy. Maybe he'd go national and you'd be able to find a Ms. Fizz in every town.

"Okay, then, I'm going to take off," Damian said.

"Okay."

"See you again some time."

"Sure."

He followed her to the front door. As soon as she opened it he heard the wind chimes clanging. It was early morning, but late at night for a guy working the night shift. The sun was waiting outside, waiting to melt him just like a vampire.

He shivered and smiled at the thought.

7:15

A fanatical Catholic. It reminded him of Brother Dick, the old madman principal of Trinity High, circa 1971. It reminded him of that old S.O.B., the walking Dick, Brother Love, the guy who wanted to suspend him, Len Barney, in the spring of his senior year, for kissing a girl! Brother Dick who talked about the Apostolic Church, the mission of Catholic education, who said from the lectern more times than Barney could count, "We have one way to go . . . the Catholic way!" He didn't even have the sense to call himself Brother Richard.

Captain Len Barney hadn't thought about him in years until this morning. But that's what Colbin College's chief of security thought about as he watched the seven o'clock national news. He couldn't concentrate all that well on the story because he was down on his hands and knees, playing Hulk Hogan with his five-year-old, Seth. But it seemed to him like the guy in handcuffs being trundled off in the back of the TV cruiser was wearing one of the biggest crucifixes since Brother Dick's.

"*Shhh*," he said to his son, who was, at that moment, trying to throw a flying forearm into his father's forehead. Trying with such zeal, such joy, that Barney actually turned away from the television, shocked at the intensity of the five-year-old's expression.

"*Whooaaa* there," he said.

"Hulk . . . Hogan," the kid grunted, whaling away with his forearm. Although it didn't hurt, it was very annoying just then.

So of course Barney turned the play session into a reprimand, a lesson, which was exactly what he wanted to avoid. He didn't see enough of his son to allow play opportunities to slip by, but neither could he allow the kid to give him a forearm smash. So he glared, conscious he was doing so, and felt the room go still, the TV grow louder, and he heard himself say in a tight voice:

"Stop that."

The boy's lower lip began to tremble.

"Now come on, Seth . . . I didn't mean to . . ."

But it was too late. Off to the kitchen in near tears. Off to mom, to the primary caretaker, to the breast, the maternal hug. And who could blame him?

"Aw, Seth, daddy just wanted to hear the news report," Chief Barney called after his retreating son, knowing at the same time that it wasn't quite the truth. The truth was he didn't want to be bothered right now, not the minute he woke up. He was down on his knees so quickly because, well, because he thought it was what fathers did with kids. Little boys, at least. Wrestle around, pull a coin out of the kid's ear now and then, take him to a baseball game and buy him hot dogs until he couldn't eat anymore. That's what his father had done with him, bonding the old-fashioned American way.

He stayed for a few minutes more on his knees, watching the tube. The story about the Catholic was gone, taken up by a hard-news report. A man with a poorly planted toupee stood in front of a municipal dump, seagulls flying over his head. The guy wore a raincoat and nearly shouted into the microphone, trying to be heard over the squawking gulls, the wind sawing into the microphone, the rattle of a backhoe.

Before Barney could find out exactly what was going on with the dump, the kitchen door swung open and Matty came out with Seth in hand. Seth's face was marked by tears and his lip was pushed out, and it was clear he had gone in and brought back the biggest gun he could find. Mom would fix it. Mom would show him. Barney didn't like to see such cunning in the kid's eyes, but it was there.

What Barney couldn't read, never could read, was Matty's expression. Whose side, after all, was she on? He had been married to her for twelve years, the last five with Seth floating around her like a satellite, and he still couldn't predict how she would jump on any given issue.

"Sorry, sorry, sorry," Barney said.

"He's just a little boy," Matty said.

"I know. Come here, Seth. Daddy's sorry. I didn't mean for you to stop completely. I wanted to keep playing but you were getting a little crazy."

Captain Barney stayed on his knees and held out his hands.

But Seth didn't move.

"We can play some more. Who should I be? Brutus Beefcake? I know you're Hulk Hogan . . ."

It was lame. He could say this about his son, the kid wasn't easily conned. Puckered mouth, hand on the seam of his mom's jeans, back of his wrist pressed against his eyes. Above him, Matty smiled encouragement.

It might have worked. It might have all toned down if Captain Barney's pager hadn't beeped at that exact moment. Family interruptus. He placed one hand on the kill button and pressed, but it was too late. He saw Matty's smile die. He saw Seth's face cloud over.

"Hey, will you call that one in for me, Lieutenant?" Captain Barney asked Seth.

He saw immediately it was a good move. A great move, in fact. Seth looked up at his mom, his mom looked at Captain Barney, and for a second they were all there. Joy to the world. Dad was being a good guy, and sonny was gainfully involved, and Mom was proud of her two pumpkins.

Seth ran off, grabbed Captain Barney's hat from the piano stool and plunked it on his head. He looked at his dad and his dad looked back.

"Go ahead. I'm coming."

The kid ran off into the kitchen. Captain Barney stood.

"I'm sorry," he said to Matty.

"He just looks up to you so much."

"I know."

"He's a little boy and he loves his father. That's not a sin, you know."

"I know."

Captain Barney kissed his wife. He kissed her hard and bent her over a little backward. She pushed at his arm for a second, then she gave in and he ran his hand quickly over her breasts.

"Brutus Beefcake," Captain Barney said when he broke off the kiss.

"No, that was Hulk Hogan."

"You think so?"

"Definitely."

"I guess it was, wasn't it?"

He left her to turn off the TV and went into the kitchen. Something was bubbling on the stove and he turned it down, then crossed to the backdoor where Seth was up on a chair, punching in the phone number of the campus security office. Seth looked like a midget cop.

"Yes," Seth said to someone on the other end of the line. "Yes?"

"Say hello," Barney whispered.

"Hello?"

Captain Barney sensed the person on the other end wasn't exactly getting it. That would be Eddy, this time of the morning. Eddy or Lester, but probably Eddy. He wanted to take the phone from Seth—he was captain of the security force, after all—but he saw that cloudy look on Seth's face again. Seth was telling him not to take it away yet, not to ruin the game, but it wasn't a game and Barney didn't want it to go on too long. But he couldn't wreck the kid's day twice in ten minutes, so he stood beside his son, nodding at nothing, his hand itchy at his side.

"Okay, I better take over now, Lieutenant," he said after another few seconds.

"Over," Seth said. "Over."

"Okay now . . ."

"Over."

Barney held out his hand. Seth looked up at him, his police hat clicking backward, his smile disappearing. But he handed over the phone. Barney bent down and gave the kid a kiss, kissed him on the neck and shoulder to make loud sucking sounds, then hoisted him off the chair and placed him back on the kitchen floor.

"Captain Barney," Barney said.

"Barney? I didn't know if that was you. Were you chewing something?"

It was Eddy.

"Right here, Eddy. What's up?"

"You better get in here. Someone found an ear."

"What do you mean, found an ear?"

"Just that," Eddy said. "A woman's ear, I guess. We think it's part of that woman being killed at Potter's Bridge. The city cops are on their way. President Mathews is coming over."

"I'll be there."

"A woman's ear," Eddy said again.

"Be right down."

Barney hung up. He lifted his hat off Seth and put it on his own head. He smiled, made a gun from his index finger, and pretended to shoot. Seth shot back, raising his hands to a machine gun and drilling his father dead with spit bullets.

7:59

Zelda Fitzgibbon heard a rat down at her feet somewhere. It was a bold creature. It rattled a paper loud enough to bring her just to the edge of consciousness, where she hung, suspended.

She didn't mind rats. She had kept two white ones for her biology teacher, Mr. Paterson, one summer. He said his wife hated the things, wouldn't have them in the house, and was there anyone who might like to . . . She had raised her hand instantly, beating Johnny Fosleman to the punch, knowing, just as the sun would rise, that she was Mr. Paterson's favorite and he was pleased to see her raise her hand. The rats came home, Sylvester and Tweety-Bird, and they stayed the summer in the garage out back, then returned to school and died two weeks later. Died, she had hypothesized, of lead poisoning. Someone in Mr. Paterson's new biology class had lined the rat pen with pencil shavings, and the rats had keeled over just like that.

But this one was a persistent rat.

She opened her eyes slightly and raised her hand to fend off the sunlight. She was flat on her back, and for a moment felt dislocated. It wasn't her room at home, she was certain about that, but it wasn't familiar either. Somehow there was a sense of urgency about waking up, she had things to do, but her eyes wouldn't spring open. She squinted again at the sun and this time saw Martha, her silhouette square in the middle of the window.

Martha, Our Lady of the Pop Tarts.

"Morning, sleepy head," Martha said in that singsong voice that Zelda thought was simply not in the catalog for anyone under forty-three. It wasn't the way girls talked, not any she knew, and Zelda let her hand slip back until her eyes were buried in the crook of her elbow.

"What time is it?" Zelda asked.

"Almost eight."

"What are you eating?"

"Pop tarts. Strawberry."

This was the second twist. In addition to having a corner on the Snoopy market, Martha also possessed more junk food than anyone Zelda had ever encountered. Pop Tarts, Fudge Pin Wheels, Malomars, Almond Joys, Snow Caps, microwave popcorn. It was like living in a Stop & Shop.

"Is that what you eat for breakfast?" Zelda asked.

"All my life. I know, I know, I should eat something more nourishing, but Richie eats them too."

"Does he?"

"Yes!"

Giggle. Richie formed the third corner of the triangle that formed, and informed, the loveliness that was Martha. Snoopy, junk food, and Richie. Richie, the engineering student at Lehigh. Richie, the hometown boyfriend from Goffstown, New Hampshire. Richie, whose picture took a prominent place on Martha's desk, dwarfed only by Snoopy hanging from his doghouse. They reminded Zelda of a pair of hamsters, happily chewing their way into a diabetic state.

Zelda climbed out of bed, grabbed her robe from the back of the door and wrapped it around her. Up the hallway she heard someone switch on Mick Jagger. Martha, if she noticed the sound, didn't say anything. She dug into the waxed paper again and came up with a second Pop Tart.

Zelda picked up her plastic shower bucket and opened the door. The music was a little louder outside. It sounded all right, not really too raucous. If you let it, she decided, it would actually get you going. She allowed it to chase her down the hall, her blood responding, her eyes opening more fully. She passed two girls—hair up in towels, their legs shiny from just being shaved—and said good morning. They said good morning back.

She walked into the bathroom and was hit by steam and the hiss of deodorant. Back in the showers she heard someone singing a show tune, something out of *Cats*. Lisa, her R.A., stood in front of a long mirror that stretched over the row of sinks. She wore white underpants and a white bra, and she was blonde, remarkably blonde. She was bending forward, pooching her lips, waving on mascara with a small wand. She looked so adult, so stylish, that Zelda was reluctant to brush her teeth at the same row of sinks.

"Good morning, Zelda. You have a ten o'clock?" Lisa asked.

"I do," Zelda said, taking out her toothbrush and loading it with toothpaste.

"Nervous?"

"A little."

"Nothing to be nervous about, I promise. Just like high school, really."

"I've got biology."

"You are serious," Lisa said, stopping for a second to examine herself closer in the mirror.

Zelda stuck her toothbrush in her mouth and brushed. She worked her gums, then back along her cheeks so her mouth was good and frothy, clean as a whistle, when a young man came around the wall from the showers, wearing only a towel. The amazing thing was, he didn't seem to find himself out of place in a girls' bathroom. Not at all. He moved to the sink beside Lisa and actually reached out a hand and rested it on the saddle of her back. He rested it where her back was scooped and hollow from bending forward to the mirror. His hair was washed and his smile was bright and he seemed in the most robust health of any human being Zelda had ever seen.

"Zelda, this is Chucky. Chucky, Zelda," Lisa said, not even halting for a minute the application of her make-up.

Chucky said good morning. Zelda, the toothbrush pushing her jaw out to a round lump, nodded. She nodded and pinched the top of her robe closed. Pinched it so prudishly closed that even Sister Bartholomew would have been proud. It was instinctive, a natural reaction, but Lisa caught it and smiled.

"Guys are always in here," she said.

"I didn't know."

Lisa smiled. Chucky smiled. Zelda looked in the mirror and saw her own lips were white, and as perfectly frothy, as the mouth of a rabid dog.

9:11

Captain Barney couldn't get the coffee machine to work. He had plugged it in, filled the top with grounds, poured in water, then switched it on. The machine gurgled, growled even, but did nothing else.

"It sounds clogged," one of the women said behind him.

It was Bonnie, he thought. It was Bonnie or Marsha, the woman in the yellow sweatsuit, anyway, who seemed to be ready to jump up and come around to help. He turned around and smiled, tried to give them a helpless male smile, then turned back to the coffee machine and shook it. He shook it pretty hard and water slopped out a little bit, but something clicked down inside and the water started dripping through the filter.

"We had one like that and when I cleaned it out I found a pencil in it," Marsha said.

Barney watched the coffee water drip through for a few more seconds, then went back to his desk chair. The coffee machine continued to wheeze. The women had been in his office for close to forty-five minutes. They had gone over their testimony, explained where they had found the ear, had repeated the story once when Detective Giamoona from the Coldbridge police had arrived to take away the ear, and were now waiting to tell it again to President Mathews. In the meantime there was nothing to do but wait and watch the coffee, and work on public relations. "Make them comfortable. Contain them," President Mathews had told Barney on the phone.

So Barney contained them. He had given Marsha a sweatshirt out of the lost-and-found to replace the one she had wrapped around the severed ear. He had offered to send out for breakfast, something from the cafeteria, or McDonald's if they liked, but they said they were on diets. When he mentioned coffee, however, they had teetered. They looked cold, even though it was warming up nicely outside, so he had insisted, telling them he made the best coffee in the office. That was a whopper, though not a mean-spirited one, intended to get them off the track. Because, God knew, they were on the track. They were like two bloodhounds, or maybe like two mismatched Miss Marples, lady detectives ready to hear about the whole case. But he couldn't tell them much. He couldn't tell them—though they asked— that the ear had probably belonged to Miss Toni Glennon, a grad student majoring in journalism. Couldn't mention that Toni Glennon's corpse had been discovered under Potter's Bridge lacking not only an ear, but the entire scalp. Couldn't say the body had been mutilated and the assailant, whoever that might be, had gone off with a human fright wig, cut hastily but cleanly with a razor or scalpel, and had managed to kill one of his officers, Jam Steifken, in the bargain. He couldn't say, furthermore, that he didn't have a clue as to the attacker's identity, nor could he speak his secret suspicion that the attacker was a fellow student of Miss Glennon's, a classmate, a year-book candidate with the future inscription: "Most likely to be the next Ted Bundy."

So the ladies sat waiting to hear what he couldn't say. He sat there listening to coffee and containing the situation. And President Mathews, wherever he was, certainly sat somewhere, probably discussing core curriculum decisions, or tenure obligations, or the new gym for the Fighting Mules, but not helping much to contain what probably couldn't be contained anyway.

The coffee stopped, sighed, then started to drip once more.

"Almost done," Marsha said. "You can tell when they pause like that."

"I have paper cups but I can get you some porcelain ones if you don't mind using someone else's."

"No, paper is fine," Bonnie said.

"I was wondering," Marsha said, "if you don't think . . . now, I know you can't tell me, or us, I know it's privileged information—"

"Really, Marsha," Bonnie interrupted, "he's told us more than once he can't disclose the details of the investigation. How would they ever catch anyone if they let the public know everything? The murderer could just read what's in the papers and stay one jump ahead of them."

"I was just going to ask for his opinion. His conjecture," Marsha said.

"Oh, you've been watching too much television. Conjecture on part of the witness, Your Honor. I saw the same show you did."

Barney turned to watch the coffee.

"What I was going to say," Marsha said, "was that it makes no sense to think the ear was just sitting by the road all this time. I mean, how could it? Someone would have seen it. We take that road ourselves every morning now. I bet it was back in the woods somewhere and a dog carried it out. Either that, or the murderer was moving the body parts."

"That's gruesome," Bonnie said.

Fortunately, President Mathews arrived right then in a three-piece suit and a cloud of Aramis. He came in, frowned, bent his face around to tell them he understood what kind of a morning they must have had, how upset he was in behalf of the college community, how busy he was, and how he was doing absolutely everything to speed the case. The interesting thing was, he seemed to be carrying it off. Barney, standing and coming around the desk to make the introductions, was startled to see President Mathews sort of flirting with them. Not flirting exactly, no one could accuse him of being insensitive to the situation, yet he was about their age, and he was a man of some physical charms, a tweedy professorial type, and he was covering each of their hands as he shook them, giving each a grieved look that said he understood. Although Barney didn't think they bought it completely, they seemed flattered nevertheless to have the president's full attention.

"Would you like coffee, President Mathews?" Barney asked.

"Coffee? That would be great," the president answered, taking up a seat on the corner of Barney's desk. "Ladies, what a traumatic morning this must have been for you."

Barney poured coffee and carried it over to the ladies. They each took a cup. President Mathews continued to look at them. He waited until they were settled with their coffees. He took his own cup and placed it by his right thigh. Barney went back around his desk and sat down.

"Now," Mathews began and spread his hand to include Barney, "our captain has informed me of the circumstances of your discovery. I won't ask you to repeat it—you've done more than your share. I hope he had also told you the importance of keeping this information confidential. In any case of this kind, from what I understand—I'm an old professor, so this is as new to me as it is to you—certain details are withheld from public knowledge so that the investigation team can know with certainty when they've captured the correct individual when the time comes. Has he made that clear?"

The ladies nodded.

"We don't know what we're dealing with yet. The police don't know. You've met Detective Giamoona?"

"Yes," Marsha said.

"Good, good. In a case of this nature, the Coldbridge police will handle the investigation. Our college security team will contribute where it can, but that isn't really its function. Our security team is here to regulate parking, keep the students under control, that sort of thing."

"Do you think it's a student? The killer, I mean?" asked Marsha.

"I doubt it. Detective Giamoona doubts it as well. I spoke with him on the phone just now. He's been in touch with the state hospital in Concord. Since the deinstitutionalization process began, a number of patients who might have otherwise been kept in the hospital . . ."

Barney didn't know why at first, but he saw Mathews halt. He saw him suddenly cease talking, and it was a remarkable thing to see, a pleasant thing to see really, because he was stopped by Marsha leaning forward on her chair. Under any other circumstances she wouldn't have been a match for Mathews, not even close, but she sat forward with such urgency that even Mathews paused. For his own part, Barney leaned forward himself, bending slightly to see around the president. What Barney saw was a look of profound distaste on Marsha's face for what she was hearing. She didn't believe Mathews. It was that simple. She had, it seemed, been snowed before, and Barney realized that Mathews had underestimated the woman.

"I'm sorry to interrupt, but I'd like to hear you admit that you don't know," Marsha said.

"I admit we're not sure," Mathews said, covering fast, but she interrupted him again.

"I didn't stay around here to listen to you, President Mathews. I'm sorry, but I didn't. I stayed around to ask you what you intend to tell the girls on this campus. That's all."

"We've already hired five extra security guards. Captain Barney can tell you—"

"But it's dark on campus," Marsha said, her voice rising. "This campus stretches for miles. There are woods, and the girls are going to keep on walking around if they aren't told."

"It was in the papers. I'm sure you heard about it yourself."

"That a girl was chopped up? That there is a psychopath loose on this campus? These girls are in danger, Mr. Mathews! I want to know how you intend to tell them that. Tell them there is something bad going on around this campus. Because if you don't, I will."

11:12

Halfway through lunch period, Tony Corposaro—twelve-years-old and just on the edge of puberty—swung his book bag as hard as he could and watched as it smashed into the side of Wayne Steele's head. It didn't seem possible that he had actually swung the book bag. It didn't seem possible that he had actually landed the shot, because Wayne Steele was at least thirty pounds heavier than he was, and twice as mean.

But he was tired of being ridiculed by Wayne, tired of the whole group of bullies who followed him around the hallways of Coldbridge Junior High calling him "computer head" and "nerd" and "pen-pocket." He was tired of being mocked just because he cared something about school, wanted to go on to college, and took an interest in his classes.

Notwithstanding, as soon as he swung the bag, before he even knew what he was doing, he regretted it. He was in the right, Wayne deserved anything he got, but the timing was all wrong. The playground was crowded, kids were everywhere eating their sandwiches, and now he couldn't run away.

He swung his bag again, only this time he didn't have surprise on his side. Wayne, still bent over from the first blow, brought his hand up in time to snag the bag and rip it away. Tony couldn't believe the violence in Wayne's short movement. He heard Wayne's leather jacket creak, heard some sound come from deep in Wayne's chest, and saw a pack of Camels fly out of Wayne's shirt pocket. All he could think of was the look cartoon characters got on their faces when they suddenly ran off a cliff and were suspended in air, that "*oops . . .*" He knew the look wasn't far from what was on his own face. You don't hit Wayne Steele with a book bag and expect to live to tell about it.

Around him, Tony heard the whole playground go quiet. Some of the kids were already on their way inside, but the quiet pulled them back. The kids, mostly the boys, started running in his direction, forming a circle.

"You stupid mother," Wayne said, touching his ear a little to see if it was bleeding. "You dumbass pen-pocket, I'm going to kill you."

"Just stay away from me."

"Or?"

"Or nothing."

Wayne stepped to one side and kicked Tony's book bag. He kicked it twice before it broke open, a geometry book skidding across the macadam, the pages waving. A pack of pencils broke and scattered. His protractor, a plastic half-moon, shot up in the air, following the arc of Wayne's foot, then caught the wind and fluttered like a leaf into the crowd.

"You're a little puke," Wayne said, and started forward.

A girl, bless her, said in apparent disgust, "Oh, Wayne." But all Tony Corpasaro could fix on was the look on Wayne's face. The kid was nuts. The kid was worse than nuts, he was a pyro. A Bic-bug, his dad called kids like him, and his dad should know because his dad was a fireman. Tony also knew his dad was right, knew Wayne liked to start fires in Paul's Woods back behind the school, had come close, several times, to burning the whole place down. Wayne was on a list down at the firehouse, and on the computer at the cop shop, and it didn't matter how many times anyone went and talked to his mom, the kid was going to burn something up someday, because he was a fat creep and a bully and—

"What did you say?" Wayne said.

"I didn't say anything."

"Yes you did, four eyes."

All the talk, Tony realized, was just a way for Wayne to warm himself up. He was stepping closer, his leather jacket shiny, his hands out at his sides. Tony thought this was probably the moment when the four-eyed kids in TV land suddenly folded their glasses, raised their fists like the Marquis of Queensberry, and proceeded to give the bully the drubbing of his life. Only it didn't work that way at all, so that when Wayne swung, a lazy roundhouse that crashed into Tony's ear, he was hardly surprised.

The blow made Tony spin, made him actually turn his back to Wayne. Tony felt something else hit his shoulder, a fist or a slap, he couldn't tell. Then Wayne hit him again, punched him in the back so that Tony's lungs emptied, he coughed and felt himself close to crying.

"Leave him alone," someone said, the same girl, Tony thought. But Tony knew Wayne wasn't going to quit now.

Without knowing he was going to do it, Tony began to run.

He wasn't a great runner but he was shifty and was always hard to catch when they played Spud or Block-tag or Sardines. So he ran now, a coward, he knew, but what was he supposed to do? The crowd separated in front of him, the kids jumping sideways. Right behind, he heard Wayne pumping after him.

Tony headed for the entrance to the cafeteria. He ran on the macadam, dodging around the slower students who still hadn't scattered. He shifted directions once and heard Wayne skid on his shit-kickers. Tony wore Michael Jordans and that was an advantage, a solid advantage, although he didn't know what to do with it.

He ran across the basketball court, dodging across mid-court. He cut down to the basket where he stuck out his hand and hooked the steel pole. He swung himself around, going off at about a ninety-degree angle from his previous direction and again heard Wayne slip.

And that was when Tony came up with a plan. It wasn't a surefire plan, but it was the only one he had. He ran as hard as he could, hard enough to get a slight lead on Wayne, then turned around, back-pedalling. Wayne was almost on him, almost tackled him, so Tony planted hard and shifted

directions. Wayne went past a little bit, a stupid looking
bull, then dug his heels in and stopped.

"You're chicken," Wayne said.

But he was breathing hard.

"And you're an asshole," Tony said.

Which would, of course, make them enemies for life.
Tony knew that. Yet he also felt remarkably calm. Wayne
was everybody's enemy for life. Wayne wanted to burn
down the planet. So what Tony said next was a stroke of
inspiration, the perfect thing to goad Wayne. He waited
until there were a few people around so that his words
would be preserved for all time, then he dodged away once
more and said two words.

"Sufferin' succotash."

"You jerk," Wayne said.

"Sufferin' succotash," Tony replied.

Daffy Duck. He was the Daffy Duck, and Wayne was
a slow-witted watchdog, and when you thought of it that
way Wayne didn't seem quite so frightening. Tony knew
he could outrun Wayne.

"Sufferin' succotash," he said again, deliberately spraying
his words.

Wayne charged, his arms out wide to grab something,
anything, but Tony dodged expertly.

"*Woo-hoo*," Tony cackled like Daffy Duck.

And now a few kids had caught on, they were laughing.
Wayne stopped and looked around.

"The guy's chicken," said Wayne.

"Sayyy," Tony said, spraying again.

"Hey, sufferin' succotash," someone else in the crowd
said.

"Tony's Daffy Duck," another guy said.

Tony jumped in the air. Not high, he didn't want to leave
his feet for too long, but when he was up in the air he locked
his knees together and kicked his feet out. It was the way
Daffy always moved before he took off like a demon.

"Sayyy," he said again.

"Kiss your ass goodbye," Wayne said.

A few guys—Jimmy Zitch, Flippy Light, Tommy
Polumanus—started "succotashing" Wayne. They didn't

want him charging them, Tony knew, but the whole
fight was spreading out over the crowd, and it no longer
seemed quite so personal. Even Wayne seemed to know
it, because he smiled, a forced smile, and pretended to
give up.

And he almost got Tony that way. Tony almost got carried away, jumping up and down, flicking his feet, playing
to the crowd. As he ducked away he felt Wayne grab the
back of his jacket, and felt that sensation of pulling away
just in time. Wayne even lost his footing, or their feet
touched, something, because the next thing Tony knew
Wayne had crashed to the ground. A second later he was
holding up his hand, examining his palm, pretending, Tony
suspected, to be hurt worse than he was.

"Sayyy cut it out," Tony said, making the words slurry
in his cheek.

"Hey, Daffy," one of the kids yelled.

Finally the bell rang. Tony trotted back to his book bag
and scraped it together. He looked up now and then to see
how Wayne was getting along. Each time Wayne bothered
to look away from his palm, he flashed Daffy Duck his middle finger.

A real psycho, Tony thought, scared and proud all at the
same time.

12:06

In Jaddley Cafeteria, George Denkin pushed his tray along
the metal pipes in front of the steam table. He had already
selected a pint of milk, a plate of cottage cheese, a cup of
yogurt, and three peaches. It was too much dairy. He would
have preferred some wheat germ, or perhaps some simple
nuts, but he understood that was expecting too much. College students expected swill and got it.

Nevertheless he took his time. He had exactly forty-five
minutes left on his lunch break from the admission's office,
and he didn't propose to gobble his food. Next to the milk
on his tray, he had three manila folders stacked neatly and
covered with a napkin to protect them from splatters. The
folders comprised his lunchtime reading.

He was aware that he moved too slowly to satisfy the students behind him, but he didn't care. He refused to be rushed. He caught the eye of an attendant behind the counter and bent forward to make his voice heard.

"Could you tell me, do you have any granola left over from the morning?"

"Gra, what?" she asked, stopping for a moment her explosive mixing of spaghetti sauce.

"Granola. From this morning."

"Been all put away."

"I understand, but would it be possible . . . could you see if maybe you could find some?"

"Morning's morning. I'm not going to shovel out that stuff just for one student. There's plenty of food."

"But no grains."

"No grains? What the hell you think this is? You talk to the dietician, you want grains. They's got a suggestion box over there."

George Denkin stared at the woman. She stared back, then shook her head and returned to beating the sauce. George Denkin pushed his tray a little farther along the metal runners.

"Can we get a move on?" someone—a male—said behind him. "I got class."

"Tell him," the attendant said without looking up. "Thinks we're going to all go worrying over his colon. This ruffage thing'll be the death of me."

Someone—not the same male as before—snorted and laughed. George Denkin resisted the impulse to turn around. They didn't see *him*, of course. They saw just another student, a part-time worker in the admission's office, so they couldn't be blamed. He put his hand on the admission folders and made sure the napkin completely covered them.

He pushed his tray along, examining the offerings. Hot dogs, burgers, limp fries. The salads were a joke—all iceberg lettuce and greenhouse tomatoes collapsing under the weight of a thick Russian dressing.

"My, my," he said to himself.

He stopped one last time in front of the desserts. They were set out on a stainless-steel countertop like so many globs of sugar. He picked up a wiggling plate of jello, smelled it to see how fresh it might be, then checked to see if the attendant was watching him. She was busy with the boy behind him, ladling out spaghetti and her awful sauce. He thought briefly of dropping a gob of spit in the whipped cream that topped the jello, then shook his head as if he had found the jello inadequate and slipped the plate back among the desserts.

Keep yourself focused on the target, he instructed himself.

12:22

George Denkin cut his last peach in quarters, then used the slices to complete a floral design he had arranged on top of his yogurt. Six petals, a small dot of peach flesh in the center. He kept his last peach for a snack later in the afternoon. He swirled his spoon in a spare glass of water he kept for that purpose, then wiped it meticulously on a napkin at his side. He inspected it to make certain it was immaculate.

The yogurt tasted cool and sour. It was the one food source he could depend on in this dreadful cafeteria. He scooped up a thin slice of peach with his second taste, and was rewarded by the tart seriousness of the fruit.

He settled the spoon across the edge of the yogurt bowl and pulled his notepad closer.

Greens and grains, he wrote. At least four ounces of each.

He resumed eating. He had approximately fifteen minutes left, then had to return to the admissions office. Mrs. B., his supervisor, was a clock watcher. Naturally she wasn't fair when it came to enforcing her rules about tardiness. She played favorites. She was particularly sympathetic to the young women who worked in the office, pretending not to notice when a covey of them came in late from lunch carrying shoe boxes and crinkly shopping bags. On the other hand, she watched his hours scrupulously.

He tilted the bowl and worked his spoon away from him to finish the last swabs of yogurt. He saved one last wedge of peach to top it all off. Then, with his silverware lined up again and covered by a napkin, he pulled the manila folders closer.

They were admissions folders. Against policy, he had taken them from the admissions office. He stacked them neatly in front of him, pushing the tray to one side. He checked the area immediately around him to make sure no one from his office had followed him. Two girls sipped tea at the next table. A young man, a football player from his appearance, greedily ate his third hot dog. They weren't interested in him.

The first file was not at all promising. It was the admissions application of a transfer student. Elementary education major. Combined S.A.T.s of 950, G.P.A. 2.7. She was a C+ student and was currently doing her student teaching at the Kennedy School in Manchester, New Hampshire. She had been admitted under a minority program. American Indian. He had selected her folder on the basis of the picture stapled on the upper right hand corner of the application, but he saw now he had been mistaken. She was not good enough.

Neither was the girl pictured in the second folder. She was blonde, quite beautiful, and apparently vacuous. Her S.A.T. scores barely topped 800. In fact, she had been admitted under academic probation. She was obliged to fulfill a math and a composition competency requirement. Her application essay was a complete muddle.

He closed her folder and went on to the third.

He had saved this one for last because, at a glance, it was by far the most intriguing. He opened the folder and read carefully. S.A.T.'s just shy of 1,200. Essentially straight A's in high school. Member of the New Jersey 4-H program. Her father in insurance, the mother a graduate of Bard. In her application essay, she stated she hoped to be a veterinarian.

He studied the picture for several minutes. Was there something familiar about it? He had not seen the face of the girl he had followed, when the security car came along. Never mind. He saw the face now and it took all his attention. He was no longer aware of the people around him. He stared at the woman's face. A thin, handsome face, perhaps just shy of being beautiful. But lovely, very lovely, with excellent hair. The hair, he imagined, would be dark and fine textured, the kind that fell into place at even the suggestion of a comb. Yes, he thought, she would do.

He leaned to one side and dug in the front pocket of his trousers. He came out with a small egg of Silly Putty. He opened the egg and took out the putty, rolling it into a seamless ball. Then, massaging gingerly, he flattened it into a square roughly the shape of a three-by-five card.

He took the square and pressed it on the girl's photo. He started at the bottom, then rolled it toward the top of her head. When he finished, the girl stared out at him from the depths of the putty.

He looked around once more. The girls drinking tea were gone. The football player was up at the steam table, fetching something else to eat. George bent forward and unzipped his pants. His penis, erect for the last several minutes, popped out. Moving smoothly so he would draw no one's attention, he took the putty and pressed it face down on the head of his penis.

The girl's face remained on his flesh after he lifted the putty. The impression was slightly off center, so it appeared she was looking not directly up at him, but at the wall beside him. Nevertheless, Zelda Fitzgibbon was an excellent fit.

1:24

Zelda felt ridiculous. First of all, for standing in the shadow of the barn with a pair of muck boots under her arm. Not that the muck boots weren't right. Mr. Kim wore a pair himself, but his, she noticed, were patched like an old innertube with bright orange and red spots. They had been used, used hard, while her own pair squeaked their newness from under her arm whenever she moved.

She also felt ridiculous because Mr. Kim had never heard of her. She had written him three letters over the summer, all unanswered, telling him of her interest in veterinary medicine, her desire to help around the barn (without pay, she was positive she had written), and now he stood with a currycomb in hand, shaking his head.

"Zelda Fitzgibbon . . . I wrote you," she said again.

When he didn't answer she thought maybe he didn't speak English, in which case her letters, and her ridiculous position by the barn door right now, were lost on him. If he couldn't speak English, if he was a relocated Cambodian, for example, work in a barn would have made sense. No words, just animals.

"I thought . . ." She started once more, not sure where she was going, but he cut her off in perfect English.

"Are you horse crazy?" he asked.

"Horse crazy?"

"Horse crazy. Horse crazy, you know what I'm talking about. Are you one of these girls who can't get enough of horses?"

"I like horses."

"You don't have a wall of jumping ribbons? Nothing like that?"

"No."

"You ever been in a horse show? You ride?"

"No."

"You don't have any horse britches? The ones with little pouches on the sides?"

"Mr. Kim . . ."

"Yes or no?" he asked, taking a step toward her.

"No," she said.

"And you don't want any pay?"

"No."

He looked at her. For an instant Zelda wondered if he was coming on to her. He looked her up and down, but he didn't seem to stop at any particular part of her body. He didn't leer.

"Clean out the stalls. Sweep out the barn," he said.

He went back to the horse he was currying. The horse was beautifully groomed. It stood calmly in the center of the doorway, its nose down to sniff at the floorboards.

She sat on a stack of feed bags and changed into her muck boots. She also watched Mr. Kim. She had not spent a great deal of time in barns but she knew enough to understand that Mr. Kim was obsessive about his duties. The barn smelled only faintly of manure. The rest of the smell was a combination of hay and straw and damp boards. Glancing up, she saw sunlight coming through three windows cut high in the wall.

She didn't know where the pitchfork was, didn't know her way around the barn at all. Mr. Kim, she was certain, waited to see what she would do next. He curried the horse with extravagant sweeps over its brown skin. What she wanted to do, of course, was ask some questions. Where is the pitchfork, what should I do with the hay? But she sensed, no she knew, that was the wrong thing to do. It was a little test, and Mr. Kim was going to be very attentive to how she handled it.

She stamped her feet in the boots, forcing her toes up to the front, then walked down the center of the barn. There were five or six stalls, she couldn't count them as she walked, but she noticed a family of pigs in one, a mule in another. The mule, she noted from the name plate on the stall, was named Jaspar; the pigs, which had no names, made a commotion as she passed.

She found a pitchfork at the rear of the barn, arranged neatly near some other tools. It was heavy. She carried it at waist level back through the barn until she came to Jaspar's stall. The mule seemed to nod when he saw her but made no move to step away from the gate.

Again she wanted to ask Mr. Kim a few questions—does Jaspar bite, kick, press you into the side of the stall—but he wasn't watching her. Or, rather, he pretended not to watch her, because she noted he had switched sides on the horse. Now, merely by lifting his head, Mr. Kim could watch her over the horse's back.

She unlatched the gate. Jaspar backed a few steps. She squeezed the gate shut behind her, then raised a hand to touch Jaspar's muzzle. It was a heavy thing, slightly wet from drinking and surprisingly bristly with whiskers.

"Good Jaspar," she said.

She began, cautiously, to scrape the straw and woodchips from around his legs. The bedding wasn't dirty, but she understood that wasn't the point. The point was whether she could work around animals. It wasn't complicated.

She scraped the bedding into a pile. It grew rapidly, grew until Jaspar moved over and put his nose in it. He pushed it apart, spreading it and chewing it so that she was forced to lean against him and ease him to the other side of the stall.

When she had most of it raked into a pile she skewered a forkful onto the prongs. Holding the pitchfork in one hand, she unlatched the gate, stepped through, then closed it. Careful not to tilt the fork and soil the clean center aisle, she walked toward Mr. Kim, who said nothing to her as she passed.

She carried the hay into the barnyard, looking for a compost pile. The yard, however, was clean; the dirt was raked. She went to the right side of the barn and looked along the exterior wall. Nothing. She walked to the left and saw, with gratitude, three or four piles of straw mixed with manure.

She carried the hay to the first pile and threw it on top. The fork came out of her hands and jabbed into the hay. She grabbed it back, looked quickly to see if Mr. Kim were watching, then went back to the barn door.

Jaspar stood outside the stall, tethered to a metal ring dangling from a center beam. Mr. Kim was back beside the horse. He didn't stare at her, but he didn't look away either.

"I see," she said.

He said nothing.

And for a second, just a second, she almost said more. She almost said he was being a jerk, playing the sensai out of *The Karate Kid*, but she simply walked past him and returned to the stall. When she stepped inside she saw a small trap door opened at the rear. It opened directly onto the sideyard, the same spot where she had carried the soiled hay a moment before.

"I see," she said loudly enough for him to hear.

But she wasn't sure that she saw at all.

2:27

Psychology professor Farley Simon returned to his office from the cafeteria with a styrofoam cup of Orange Mandarin tea and a bran muffin. He closed the door after him, carefully cleared his desk of papers, files, and text books. He wasn't particularly prepared for his 3:10 Introduction to Psychology lecture but he didn't particularly care either. He had notes on Durkeim's seminal work, *Suicide*, and the topic, he knew from experience, was always a crowd pleaser. The lecture hall would be littered with freshmen and sophomores, half of them bent on self-destruction, and the information on suicide would feed their greedy hearts.

The lecture would work. Taking the lid off his tea, he closed his eyes and rummaged through his long list of anecdotes. Yes, there was one about a woman who committed suicide by letting an iron rest on her chest until it melted down into her spine, for whom, Farley could say, suicide was a pressing issue; there was Portia from *Julius Caesar*, who swallowed burning coals; there was a boy, Danny was his name, who had climbed a pine tree, handcuffed his arm to a branch and then tossed away the key. Oddities, that was the ticket with a large lecture hall. Although the anecdotes were on shaky theoretical ground at best, they never failed to satisfy.

He took a sip of tea and broke the bran muffin into thirds. He was watching his diet. He had lately felt the rumbling of a gallstone, and from everything he had read the pain he was going to experience if he didn't curb his diet was nothing to take lightly. He had vowed to himself that he would give his bowels sand. Oatmeal for breakfast, bran muffins for snacks, no fried foods, clear soup for dinner, and so on. It was bland living, but there was something gratifying in such mealy consistency. He felt somewhat creative for the first time in years. His mind, as if swaddled in fat for the past half-decade, had suddenly shaken itself free from professional lethargy, had actually embraced the new regimen and made him feel . . . he wasn't getting carried away, it was occurring . . . that he might still have some scholarly articles left in him. Something on college and its manner of perpetuating adolescence was nibbling at his thoughts the past week. It was potentially an abstract, nothing more, but it seemed to bear thinking about.

He finished his muffin as someone knocked. He looked at the crack beneath the door, expecting, as usual, to find a pair of sneakers lurking there. Another student, probably a grad student, wanting to discuss theories. Wanting to discuss—although the students were never this precise or candid—life and discord and their own mind-splitting impatience. It surprised him to see a well-shined pair of black wing-tips instead.

He brushed the desk clean of crumbs, picked up his tea, and turned his swivel chair to face the person as he entered.

"Come in," he said.

It was a security officer. The man seemed a senior security officer, although Farley prided himself on being ignorant of symbols of rank. Nevertheless, the man looked competent, and that, Farley assumed, would be sufficient among the Keystone Kops of campus security to make him, at the very least, a lieutenant.

"Yes?" Farley said.

"I'm Captain Len Barney," the man said.

"Captain?"

"Of the security force here on campus."

"Don't tell me. My meter has run out again."

It was a dumb joke but it served Farley's purpose. It gave him a moment to study the man. Captain Barney did not seem on official business. For a moment Farley feared the man might think that he, a professor of psychology, would be operating a small clinic out of his office. Divorce, obesity conferences, smoke-enders, and of course student counseling. Divorce seemed a likely guess, because the man looked troubled.

Given the entire picture, Farley nevertheless found himself surprisingly intrigued. It was the diet, no doubt, but he admitted to himself that he was willing to listen. He could redirect the man, send him elsewhere if it came to it, but for the first time in years Farley felt something approximating intellectual curiosity.

He didn't speak. He remembered that much from his training in clinical psychology. Let the patient disgorge, then examine the material.

"May I sit down?" the officer asked.

"Of course."

Troubled, Farley concluded. The man sat on the edge of his chair as if still deciding if he had come to the right place. Farley took a sip of tea. In looking down at his cup he discovered a large crumb from the muffin perched on a fold in his necktie. He whisked it away.

"I wonder if I might ask you a few questions in confidence?" the officer asked.

"Certainly, but I must tell you I'm not a clinical psychologist."

"No, I need a regular psychologist to help with some theories."

"I only have a few minutes. I have a class, you see."

"I want to ask you about the murders on campus last summer. You've heard about them?"

Farley, despite himself, leaned forward. "I've read the newspaper reports. I've followed it fairly closely. You take what news you can get in New Hampshire."

"Then you know a young woman was killed beneath Potter's Bridge. One of my officers was killed too."

"I read that, yes."

"The body was mutilated."

"The man or the woman's?" asked Farley. The news about mutilation hadn't come out to the press, he realized. It made things significantly more interesting.

"The woman's."

"How exactly?"

"With a razor or a scalpel. Probably a razor."

"Are you feeling guilty?"

"Guilty?" The officer seemed thrown off by the question.

That the officer should feel guilty made perfect sense. Survivor guilt. Guilt of the person in authority over his inability to protect his subordinates. It would be something the officer was happy to suppress. Farley sipped his tea once more. It was lukewarm and tasted like Hi-C.

"Oh, I see what you're saying," the officer said a moment later. "No, I'm interested in knowing what type of person might actually dismember a body. Is there a category of some sort? A type of . . . dementia?"

The man was college educated. Farley sat back and reconsidered. The man was definitely more shrewd than he had first given him credit for.

Farley asked how the body was dismembered. The officer told him in a flat monotone, probably the tone of official reports: Scalp gone, ears sliced away, other slash wounds. Farley watched him closely while listening to the story. If the man felt guilt, he showed no signs of it. He looked tired, yes, but he seemed to have perspective on the murders.

"Well, Captain, the killer you're describing is a psychopath, although now he would be identified under the umbrella of antisocial personalities," Farley said when the officer finished.

"What does that mean?"

"Well, it's just a diagnostic tool. As our colleagues in other departments will gladly inform you, we are not engaged in an exact science in the psychology department. We can't put stickums on this or that part of the brain. We can only approximate. I suppose that's the word. A psychopath, or an antisocial personality, is a nut, Captain. A nut, potentially a violent one. He doesn't know the difference between right and wrong, or if he does, he can't delay gratification. He is impulsive. Sometimes he is addicted to alcohol, or drugs, and sometimes he is a sexual deviant."

"What would he want with the dismembered pieces?"

"Who knows? To eat them, to wear them. Sometimes they are necrophiliacs—they make love to the dead, or they keep the dead around them. There was a serial killer in Indiana or someplace who kept bodies propped up in his closet. He moved them around the room, had dinner with them. You tell me."

"I don't know."

"But you think this killer could be disturbed in this way? You say your officer, the one who survived, thought the murderer was dressed in a woman's clothes? A transvestite?"

The Captain nodded.

"Well, the murderer probably identifies himself as a woman," Farley said. "The other half of the personality—the one that goes through the day, parks the car, buys groceries, that sort of thing—may despise the female part. It's doubtful one side of the personality knows the other . . . or rather, it's possible the sane portion of the personality wakes up to find itself confronted with the gore and residue of the murders, but doesn't quite comprehend where the bodies came from. We don't know that much about the true psychopath, as he used to be called. I wish I could help you more, Captain, but it's getting close to class time."

And that was a half-assed lecture. And Farley Simon didn't care. He saw Captain Barney nod. Farley crushed the styrofoam cup and grabbed his briefcase. It was 3:09 and time for class.

"Any suggestion about how we might catch him?" Captain Barney asked, standing.

"Catch him?" Farley said. "Oh, he'll be caught. He'll want to be caught. Some part of him, anyway. But until then it will no doubt be difficult."

"Yes, that's the problem."

"Look for some place where he can play dress up," Farley said, standing and brushing his front once more. He was thinking as he spoke, coming up with a possibility. "Look for some place where he can keep the bodies, or the body parts. If he's a psychopath on the order of what I've described, he'll need a place where he can become female and where no one will contradict him. Until then, any female he meets will remind him that he is not truly female. He's dangerous, Captain. Extremely dangerous."

And *that* was not a half-assed judgment.

5:00

The five o'clock whistle went off in a twelve-second blast. The whistle was located in New Market, on top of the old firehouse. The sound, in winter, was sometimes reported as far away as Dover or Rochester. On this day, in early September, it barely reached Coldbridge, located only 14.7 miles away up Highway 34.

Captain Barney was tidying up his desk when he heard the whistle. A moment later he heard the door to the security office tentatively open. The door was fitted with a buzzer so that the office personnel, Mrs. Shell, the parking lady, or Mrs. Cawdor, the lost-and-found lady, would know they were needed. But the ladies only worked until four, so they weren't there to insist that the person close the door. As a result the buzzer went on buzzing, increasing in volume, gaining strength and annoying brilliance until it became the only sound in the building. As it built, Barney was aware that it might be deliberate, it might be a kid coming in to play a trick, but whatever it was, it was intentional and a very good cover for anything going on.

He stepped around the desk and found himself reaching for a nightstick. He didn't carry a revolver himself, never saw the need on campus, but when he picked up the nightstick he also let his eyes pass over the shotgun case at the rear of his office. He didn't look seriously, but he looked, which meant he had the heebie-jeebies.

"Hey," he said, more to make a sound than anything else. It helped to have a little noise besides the buzzing, because although Captain Barney wasn't positive, he thought he was alone in the building.

"Hey," he said again.

The door did not close. The buzzer kept on. Barney took a breath, then stepped out into the hallway. He saw someone at the door, but he couldn't make him out.

Moving faster, Barney went down the hallway toward the reception desk. He raised his nightstick, cocked it by his side, because, after all, the guy killed with razors.

He put both hands on the nightstick and got ready. As he approached the reception desk the door suddenly yawned wider. Someone stepped through, dragging something, and Barney felt his stomach go cold. When the man turned there was an instant, just an instant, of fright on both sides, so that Barney knew he had scared Lester Draabo, for God's sake, as badly as he had been scared.

Lester recovered first.

"Hi, Captain," he said.

"Jesus, Lester. Close the door."

"I will, just a second."

Lester stood in the doorway looking out. He was waiting for something. Barney couldn't see what it was, but he lowered his nightstick.

"Come here, boy," Lester said.

Lester pushed the door open wider, making the buzzer short for a second, then continue. A moment later a small German shepherd puppy came through the door. It wasn't exactly a puppy, it was an adolescent dog with long legs, a soft face, and deep brown eyes.

"Captain, this is Goliath."

"Goliath?"

"Goliath the dog," Lester said, speaking faster. "I bought him with my own money. I'm going to have him trained myself. There's a guy over in Portsmouth who runs a security class."

"Close the door, Lester."

"Okay, okay."

The buzzer finally went off. The dog had obviously been frightened by the buzzing. It shied sideways when the door shut, then, gaining confidence, came forward and smelled Barney's shoes.

Barney stood for a second letting things calm down, then squatted in front of the dog. It was probably the wrong thing to do. He didn't want to encourage Lester. The office had no money for another dog, none to train it. Everything had been used, and more, to hire five additional men. President Mathews had borrowed from an emergency fund to find salary money for the new men, and besides, an untrained dog would just be a nuisance.

But the dog put its snout on Barney's thigh, huffed once, then sat down to be petted.

"Lester . . ."

"My own money, Captain. Flick was a real asset. You said it yourself," Lester said, talking even faster than before. Barney had a notion this was a rehearsed speech. "Flick was good public relations. Everyone feels better around a well-trained dog."

"I know, Lester, but—"

"My money, Captain. This guy in Portsmouth, he said Flick probably didn't attack right away. He said Flick probably didn't figure out the difference well enough. You know, between criminals and just, well, you know, normal people."

It would have been easier to say something to Lester if he himself hadn't been carrying a nightstick in his own office. Lester's eyes had locked on the nightstick and he had understood. Lester had been through it, he had seen the man wearing a dress, and he had been there later when they had picked up Jam in a body bag. Lester would have understood Professor Simon's explanation.

"You're a good dog, aren't you, Goliath?" Lester said. "Give the captain your paw. . . . paw, Goliath."

Goliath gave Barney his paw.

6:12

Tony Corposaro, alias Daffy Duck, stood fifteen feet up in the notch of a beech tree. He could hardly see Jimmy Ryder at the bottom of the tree because it was rapidly becoming too dark. He could hear him, though. Jimmy Ryder was dragging branches to hand up. Tony guessed from the sound of dragging and cracking that Ryder had pine branches mainly. That was okay. The pine branches could be fitted just right so that in maybe another hour they would have a flat platform, four-by-six, for their deer stand.

Not, of course, that they expected to shoot any deer. Neither one of them owned a rifle. In fact, Tony couldn't think of any kid his age who owned a rifle except for Glenn Mathis, and that was just an air rifle. Mathis liked to stuff pieces of mud down the barrel and shoot it straight up in the air. You couldn't kill a deer with hunks of mud, but Tony envied Mathis the gun anyway.

"What do you have?" he asked Ryder. He leaned over the first portion of the floor. It was surprisingly solid. He didn't even need nails, just old twine he had taken off a cache of wooden crates he had found behind the state liquor store. He had roped the sticks together as well as he could, keeping in mind a picture he had seen of Kon-Tiki, the raft this

Scandinavian guy had floated across the ocean. That's what
he was building in the tree. A Kon-Tiki deer blind.

"Bugs are killing me," Ryder said.

"What do you got?"

"About five six-footers. What do you need?"

Tony saw Ryder below him now, dusky in the little sun
left to them. Ryder wore jeans and a hooded sweatshirt
and he had the hood up to protect his ears against the
mosquitoes. Tony could picture Ryder's nearly bald head
underneath the sweatshirt. The poor kid's dad believed in
military haircuts, so that Ryder always looked like a cue
ball. Ryder's dad, Tony knew, did something over at the
military base at Pease. Only the military base was closing down and Tony's own dad said Mr. Ryder was going
to have to make a living somewhere else besides the military bread-line.

"I need a couple three-footers," Tony told him. It was
the third time he had said the same thing.

"I can break these."

"No, pass them on up. We can break them up here."

He leaned down over the flooring, checking it as he
shifted his weight. The floor was solid. Tony grabbed one
branch, lifted it, put it behind him, then reached down for
another. It was like what the Scandinavian guy had done
to sharks. He had seen the pictures or he wouldn't have
believed it. All the bearded guys sitting out in the middle
of the ocean waiting for sharks to swim by, then grabbing
them and yanking them aboard. It was crazy but brave.
They did it to check some theory, but Tony didn't understand the theory exactly. It wasn't about sharks. It was
about navigation, but they grabbed the sharks anyway to
have something to eat. Sharks and flying fish, that was all
those guys ever ate.

As he reached down for the fourth branch Ryder suddenly stopped.

"Oh puke, do you smell it?" Ryder said.

"Yeah."

"It's wicked bad."

They had been smelling it most of the afternoon. Tony
could smell it even more from up in the tree. It came to

them whenever the wind blew from the north, which meant it was coming from the direction of Cooly's Stream or the graveyard. This late in the year, it was probably Cooly's Stream, which wasn't much of a stream at all but was more like a damp fungus you discovered in your basement after a hard rain. In the spring you could find snapping turtles and panfish in some of the deeper pools, but by this time of year most of the stream was just mud and slime and stink.

"Something's dead, Tony," Ryder said, stopping to pinch his sweatshirt across his nostrils. "It smells like a cat or something probably got stuck down in the mud. Something like that."

"It could be the graveyard," Tony said.

"Naw, that's just a colonial graveyard. Everyone in that thing is older than George Washington."

"It's bad."

"It's wicked bad."

The wind changed. Tony could still detect the dead smell but it wasn't nearly as strong.

He grabbed the last two branches from Ryder, then told him to climb up. It was getting too dark to do much more, but he wanted to try to finish off the floor anyway. You could still see close up. When you looked into the woods, though, all you could see was the dark outlines of trees.

It was right around then that the jay started calling.

It called three or four times, screaming like crazy on the last call. A jay going off was always a sign something was moving in the woods, at least if you believed Mr. Harmon—Mr. Hard On, the whole pack called him—of Cub Scout Troop 73. Hearing it, Tony squinted to see deeper in the woods but the undergrowth was too thick. It was probably a deer. Probably a deer, or a racoon, or maybe just some crows moving in on the jay. More likely, the jay was scolding something away from whatever it was that was dead, because jays were great for chiseling in and taking their share.

But it was scolding awfully hard.

That wasn't really unusual. Nevertheless, there was something he didn't like about the jay calling that way. It was like a jungle movie he had seen when a zombie was sneaking up on the white hunter guy, and the white hunter was stumbling around in the woods, real scared. Then the hunter heard a macaw, or some jungle bird suddenly start to scream, and the next thing you knew the zombie was right behind him, blended in with the trees so that only the audience could see him, but the white hunter kept backing and backing and backing—

The jay started calling again.

At the same time Ryder finally stuck his bony head up above the level of the deer-blind floor. Ryder's sideburns and temples were scratched with sweat. He had two plugs of Tootsie Rolls stuck on his incisors, so that when he got Tony's attention he snarled. It was supposed to be some chocolate vampire thing. It looked, instead, like Ryder had two enormous cavities in his teeth.

"Jeezum, this is decent," Ryder said, looking around at the flooring.

"*Shhh.*"

"It's just a jay."

"I know."

Ryder finished climbing up, sat against the trunk of the tree, legs stretched in front of him. He pulled out the rest of his Tootsie Roll, which was curved from being in his pocket, and ate it in two or three bites. Tony tried to hear around the commotion Ryder was making, but all he could tell for sure was that the jay was moving through the trees. He heard it coming closer.

"*Shhh,*" Tony said, even though Ryder wasn't making noise any longer.

"It's probably a deer coming to drink. We're right over a game path."

"*Shhh.*"

Tony leaned across the flooring and pushed Ryder down. Ryder didn't resist. Maybe, Tony thought, Ryder was still figuring it was a deer, and a deer was worth seeing from your own blind the very first day you built it. The only thing was, Tony had a sense it wasn't a deer coming along the path.

Then, before he knew what was happening, Ryder poked him in the side and pointed. Tony couldn't see what he pointed at, but he was pleased that Ryder was finally quiet and paying attention. Shaking his arm for emphasis, Ryder pointed again. This time Tony followed the line of Ryder's pointing until he saw a man walking the path, a young guy, probably a student from Colbin, hurrying up from Cooly's Stream. He was coming along the game path, the bushes snagging and slapping as he came. It was odd to see someone down that way, especially coming back from Cooly's, because there was nothing worth seeing down there except moss and lichen and some decent spider webs. But before Tony could get his mind around it, he felt Ryder go up on one elbow.

"Sufferin' succotash," Ryder said, then lay back down on his side, laughing, his breath smelling of chocolate, his bald head so thick with bone that Tony didn't see how he kept it square on his neck. Tony reached over and dug his nails in Ryder's forearm, squeezed for all he was worth, because he somehow knew this wasn't the time.

The steps stopped below them.

They stopped twenty feet before the tree, right on the game path. The jay called again. The breeze shifted so that the odor that had been tagging them all day rode in right through the branches. Tony reached out his hand and would have set his nails in Ryder's forearm again, telling him in this way to shut up about the smell, only this time Ryder nodded and put his finger to his lips.

Tony leaned slightly to his right, careful not to let the flooring rattle, and looked over the edge.

The guy was there. He was looking around, his eyes at chest level, scanning the game path forward and back. He was listening—that was clear. He was listening because he had heard something peculiar in the woods, had heard Ryder's "sufferin' succotash" and wasn't sure where it had come from. He was looking hard. You could see this guy wasn't scared. Even though he was in the woods, and it was getting dark, and he had heard something strange, he wasn't frightened. He was . . . he looked pissed off, actually. He looked all tight and angry.

Ryder went up on one elbow.

Tony shifted his own weight fast and slapped his chest on Ryder's back and reached one hand up to cover Ryder's mouth. Ryder, the stupid a-hole, was laughing. He was going to call "sufferin' succotash" over the edge, because he still hadn't figured the whole thing out. Tony heard the flooring slide, the wooden poles creaking against one another. Tony was certain that if he had looked, the guy down on the path would have been even more interested than before.

"Be quiet," Tony whispered into Ryder's ear.

All Ryder would do was laugh. Tony, his chest flat against Ryder's back, could feel his friend's ribs shaking and could smell small pants of chocolate coming. He also smelled the odor again, this time stronger, this time the smell of something rotting, a deer with its ribs open to the hawkweed and tansy and asters, grass pushing up through the nostrils and between the leathery ears, a beetle perhaps burrowing under an antler so that it could work its own type of decay from the safety of the soil.

And with the smell the jay started screaming again. It fluttered to a larch not more than ten feet away from Tony, alternated its attention among Tony and Ryder and the man below. It stepped sideways along the branch, shaking it, then suddenly took wing, following the deer path farther south.

Tony heard the man walking off. At the same time, beneath him, Ryder pushed up hard and shrugged, so that Tony felt himself almost go off the edge.

"Stay off me! Jeezum, Tony," Ryder said.

"He's going to come back."

"So what if he does? He's just some jerk from the college."

Tony threw himself at Ryder with such force he was shocked by it himself. He grabbed Ryder around the throat, hooking his elbow exactly under Ryder's chin, and squeezed. He squeezed steadily, not in a herky-jerky method, so that Ryder would understand he could call it off by just being quiet. And with the squeezing Tony swam up his friend's back, pulled himself along by holding onto Ryder's neck, and finally got his lips next to Ryder's ear.

"The guy's coming back. Remember what they told us in school about the murders? I'll bet anything that's the guy."

"You're . . . dreaming," Ryder said, his wind cut off and forcing him to speak in two distinct words.

"He'll kill us. I know it."

But he didn't know it. He knew it but he didn't know it. Yet something in his voice worked, because Ryder finally nodded his head, and Tony let up on the pressure. He let up on the pressure expecting Ryder to start shouting or laughing or doing something nuts, but Ryder seemed finally to understand. He didn't move at all. He didn't do a thing. A mosquito landed on Tony's neck and he was sure Ryder could hear it too, but neither of them slapped at it because below them, directly below them, they heard a single crack of a man stepping on a branch he couldn't see in a woods full of darkness.

9:36

Captain Barney sat in the common room of Sheppard Dorm's second floor and listened to a talk about condoms. He was the only man in the room. The woman giving the talk was Samantha Fielding, the campus gynecologist. She was a plainspoken woman. She was about fifty, with white hair and an intelligence that came through even this rather pro forma speech. Talking to her before the session, Barney had learned she delivered this speech at the beginning of each term to every girl in every residence hall. Thirty-three talks a year. Thirty-three "Sex Talks" as the girls called them. Senior or freshman, graduate or sophomore, it didn't matter how many times you had already heard it, you had to hear it again. Preventative medicine, Dr. Fielding had called it.

And of course the girls were too mature, and too sophisticated to actually think they needed the talk—and there were lobbying groups on campus demanding to know why the same talk wasn't being given to men—but for the most part, Barney saw, the girls listened. They listened because they felt they were getting the straight scoop. Samantha

Fielding delivered her speech in a clinical fashion, a fashion that would not entertain embarrassment. So they could ask about condoms, or diaphragms, or the pill, and hear straight talk in response. They could also hear about AIDS, and herpes, and tubal pregnancy. Love stew, Dr. Fielding called it. The whole messy world of human sexual relations.

Barney sat in the farthest corner of the room, near the door. He wore his uniform, complete with hat, so that he would seem like a crossing-guard come to give a bunch of third graders a talk about ... pedestrian safety. Sexless. He tried to keep a look of ... what on his face? Not boredom. Boredom was not an appropriate message to send, and besides, he wasn't bored. Not condescension either, because some of the matters Dr. Fielding discussed were new to him. No, he tried to keep a look of pointed interest on his face. It was the same look, he realized, he had used to get him through Rutgers.

He was concentrating so hard on managing the proper facial expression that at first he almost didn't realize Dr. Fielding was calling on him. He heard her voice from far away.

"Captain Barney, if you want to give your talk before we go on to questions, then perhaps you can leave and allow us to talk together as women."

"Certainly," Barney said, rising.

"I think it would be more comfortable."

"I understand."

Barney had to turn sideways and squeeze past two rows of young women on his way up to the front of the room. Halfway there he realized he could have stayed where he was and accomplished the same thing. But he was already on his way, so he kept sidling up, saying excuse me, pardon, aware the entire way that he was a male in a room full of some fifty women.

When he reached the front of the room he removed a typed one-page statement from his front pocket. It had been typed up by President Mathews' office and sent over by student-courier. Barney knew its contents and he also knew it was out of tone with Dr. Fielding's speech. It wasn't frank; it wasn't candid. It was a cryptic message, complete with euphemisms about "potentially dangerous situations" and "serious consequences." Double-speak.

"As most of you know, or should know," be began, not consulting the paper, "a young woman was killed on this campus over the summer. Murdered, I should say. She was murdered under Potter's Bridge, and her body was mutilated."

The room was very hot and very still. Barney had to consciously refrain from looking at the paper in his hand.

"I am here to inform you that we do not know very much about the killer. It might be someone from the outside . . . a non-student . . . and then again, it might be someone from here, on campus. Staff, faculty . . . you understand me? You should also know that the murderer apparently dresses as a woman . . . at least one eyewitness recounted it that way. It's possible the man is confused in his sexual identity . . ."

"Do you have any leads?" a young girl asked. Barney wasn't even sure who had spoken. He responded to the voice.

"We have an investigation under way, but no . . . right now, we're in the dark. The Coldbridge police and the campus security force are working together on the investigation. I won't kid you, though. This campus is comprised of some two hundred acres of woodlands. That makes it very difficult. We have three thousand residents in and around the community who are affiliated with the college. Naturally, it's possible the person isn't connected with the college in any way."

Barney glanced down at the paper. He knew what the paper said but he wasn't going to use it.

"What this means to you, particularly as young women, is that you should be very alert. You should keep to well-lighted paths and avoid walking through the woods at night. Walk in pairs. We have established an escort service. You may call an officer for an escort if you're coming home late or have to be out for a class, or a recital, or a play. Our officers will try to do as much as they can, but they can't be everywhere. Report what you see if anything seems out of the ordinary. Report any strangers on campus. Get to know the people in your dorms, the men . . ."

Here there was a laugh. A tension laugh.

" . . . so that you can recognize and report anything, or anyone, who doesn't seem right. This is a serious matter. The murderer killed one of my officers in addition to the young woman. Killed him with a razor blade."

Barney stopped. He knew President Mathews wouldn't like the last line if he heard it reported later. But the young women took a collective breath, which also meant the young women were taking his talk seriously.

"Any questions?" Captain Barney asked.

There weren't any.

Captain Barney turned to Dr. Fielding and nodded. She nodded back. It was time for him to leave. He started back toward the row of girls, then stopped.

"I want to say one last thing," he said, surprised himself that he was going on. "Some of you, at some point, may be in a position to ignore what I've said here tonight. Maybe you will have had a few beers . . . or maybe you'll figure it's only a short walk through the woods, and what's the point of calling a security officer or waiting around for someone to escort you? If you think of my talk at all at that moment, you may decide it was just one more adult being overly cautious. I'm asking you now not to dismiss what I'm saying. The danger is real."

Barney headed for the door.

Dr. Fielding, behind him, said, "Thank you, Captain Barney."

Barney kept going. He walked down the hallway. By Dr. Fielding's count, there were only thirty-two more talks to present.

10:57

" . . . so Richie . . . his dad has a cabin in Maine, I hate it, but Richie loves it, and if you're going with a guy, if you're as serious about a guy as I am about Richie . . . I mean, we're almost married, really . . . Anyway, Richie says that he has to have a flannel shirt if he is going up to Maine, so I went out to this really nice place on Chestnut Street, and I bought him this red shirt with a sort of glen plaid pattern . . . he looks great in red, because he's dark . . . he's best in primary colors . . ."

Zelda reached forward and took a handful of Doritos from the bag on Martha's lap. Sometime during the night Zelda had decided she was going to put on a cool twenty pounds by rooming with Martha. It was inevitable. Martha herself was like a force of nature, a large, gooey wave of indulgence and junk food.

But Martha was also, to Zelda's surprise, an extraordinarily funny storyteller. She was self-deprecating and sarcastic. She also possessed an exact understanding of what she, Martha Baird, offered to the world. She knew she was pudgy; she knew she was not particularly pretty. She also knew—and this was the largest surprise in the whole evening—that the Snoopy posters were childish and sentimental. She had even made a joke about Snoopy's balls—how, if Snoopy were a male dog, after all, he must have a pair of dangling testes under his furry, swollen stomach. She went on to talk about Snoopy with a boner, Snoopy humping Lucy's leg, Snoopy squatting like a canine Buddha to do his business. The whole rap on Snoopy, and most of the stories, were actually pretty off-color. In different company, or even on a different night, they might have been too scatological to be funny. But listening to Martha as she sat in a furry bathrobe gobbling Doritos and talking about Snoopy and sex and her boyfriend Richie, well, Zelda was enchanted. Martha, with her outlook on the world, was a revelation.

"So did Richie wear the shirt?" Zelda asked, sitting back farther on her bed.

"Well, he did. He thought he was a lumberjack, but Richie . . . you know I love him, but he's a nerd. We're both nerds, really. Richie has this tackle box and it's set up by color. He has the red lures on one side, and they gradually get lighter until the yellow ones take up the middle, then blue . . . well, he's anal compulsive. Anyway, we went out on the dock at night and we were going to make love and he took off his pants and all he had on was this shirt. And the tail on it was really long, so that everytime he moved, his thingy jumped out, then ducked back in, like an actor ducking out of a curtain to take a bow. And I started laughing, and he kept saying, what, what is it? But he was moving around and his thingy was out—"

Someone knocked.

"Who is it?" Zelda asked.

She stood and grabbed another handful of Doritos. She heard someone out in the hallway running. Someone else laughed.

"Who is it?" Zelda asked again.

This time someone yelled back.

"Open up, quick."

Zelda opened the door and found five or six girls waiting there.

"Your room's next," one of them said.

"Next for what?" Martha asked from the bed.

"Scope night."

At the same time, Zelda heard someone tapping on the window behind her. That was impossible, they were a floor up, but the tapping was definitely coming from somewhere. She wasn't sure what she was supposed to do, but she didn't have time to figure it out anyway. One of the girls started squealing at the sound, pointing to the window. Zelda turned in time to see something hitting against the window, tapping for attention.

"It's a periscope," one of the girls said. The girl had dark hair and was vaguely familiar to Zelda. A hallmate.

"What do they want?" Martha asked.

"It's scope night. They want to look at you, and you get to look at them. At the guys above you."

"Can they see in?" Zelda asked, still not sure what was happening.

"Only if you leave your blinds open."

The dark-haired girl crossed the room and pulled open the blinds. Martha sat up. The other girls—there were four of them—came into the room. Zelda saw the glass eye of the periscope tapping at the window. As soon as the blind was open she heard someone, a male, whooping from the room above her.

"They're going from window to window, scoping us out."

A second girl, this one with brown hair, came into the room carrying a long periscope. It was the kind of periscope people used at football games, only longer. She went to the window and opened it wide.

"Make yourselves at home," Martha said.

"It's a tradition. Every floor has a scope night," the new girl said.

The girl carrying the periscope stuck it out the window and put her eye to it.

So there were two periscopes, one going up, one looking in. The girl holding the periscope started waving everyone closer with her free hand.

"Okay, you two have to stand up and let them see you. If you want to," the first girl, the one with dark hair, said.

"Do what?" Zelda asked.

"Just stand up and let them look at you," the girl with the periscope said. "They're pointing. They'll go after they see you."

Zelda looked at Martha. Martha shrugged and climbed off her bed, brushing Dorito crumbs off her bathrobe. Zelda, despite herself, brushed her own sweater.

"What do we do?" Martha asked.

"Just stand there. Some people pose. You know, vamp a little."

"I don't vamp too well," Martha said.

Zelda stood next to Martha. She felt ridiculous but she also felt strangely excited. The whole hall was awake. People were running up and down, and it would have been small on her part not to go along. She put her arm around Martha. Martha put her arm around Zelda and they stood stiffly, facing the window.

"Are they done scoping us?" Martha asked. "Do we get to scope them now?"

"In a second."

It was like having your picture taken, Zelda thought. She stared at the window, her smile—she was smiling, she told herself—fake and insincere. In some way it would have been easier to vamp. At least then she would have been able to move. As it was, she had to stand with her arm around Martha, looking, it occured to her, like the famous primitive portrait of the Midwest farmer and his wife, pitch-fork in hand.

"Okay, they've got you. Your turn," the girl at the window said.

Then, before anyone could move to the window, the girl squinted into the periscope and said, "Oh my God, they're stripping."

"Strippers!" someone at the door called.

Zelda heard people running. Girls from up and down the hall were coming. The doorway suddenly became crowded. The room was close and hot.

Zelda followed Martha to the window. The whole thing was odd. She didn't really want to look. But then she saw Martha taking the periscope from the girl's hand, bending out the window to adjust the line of vision.

"They're in their undies!" Martha said.

"Boxer men," the girl who owned the periscope said.

"They're in their boxers," Martha repeated.

Zelda stepped next to Martha. Martha pulled her eye away and handed the periscope to Zelda. Zelda bent to look into it but at first she could see nothing. Bricks, a venetian blind, a glimpse of light. Then, holding it steady, she finally saw into the room above her.

Two guys. One well built, the other skinny. The skinny one was flexing, turning right and left, occasionally hoisting the legs of his boxers into a sarong bottom. The well-built one was handsome but had a strange expression on his face. He didn't move, really, but stood staring straight ahead.

"It's Shawn Casey," the girl beside Zelda said. "The good-looking one. He's amazing but weird as hell."

"Who's the other one?" Zelda asked.

"That's Tripper. I didn't know he was so scrawny."

"Casey is a definite ten," a girl at the doorway said.

Zelda handed the periscope back to the girl who owned it. The girl at the doorway wrote something on a clipboard. She was ranking them. Casey was a ten, she announced. Tripper was a five.

A few more girls came in and took turns at the periscope. Zelda stepped back until she eventually had to climb on her bed to stay out of the way. By the time the fifth or sixth girl had looked, Lisa stuck her head in.

"All right," she said. "They called down. On to the next room."

And that was it. The girl with the periscope lowered it, shut the window, and pulled the blind.

"Do we get rated?" Martha asked her before the girl left.

"You get rated, but they don't show us the rating."

"Do you show them ours?"

"No way."

"Then give that scrawny little jerk a four. I never saw uglier legs on anything that walked," Martha said.

Except for Mr. Hotchkiss, Zelda thought.

11:16

Mrs. Grace Corposaro—Daffy Duck's mom—finished her rosary by kissing the crucifix. She dropped the beads in the front pocket of her smock, then blew out the votive candle that stood in front of the small statue of the Virgin Mary. Behind her, she heard her husband, Benny, stir in bed. He said something—jeez, or come on—then rolled away from her so his eyes wouldn't be exposed to the bathroom light.

"A second, a second," Mrs. Corposaro said.

Mrs. Corposaro undressed in the bathroom. She combed her hair. When she finished she slipped into a flannel nightgown. She took a moment just before turning out the light to look at her face closely.

It was an Italian face. Dark eyes, dark skin, a nose not entirely straight. Not straight at all, as a matter of fact, though it was nothing new for her to see this. Her nostrils were wide. In fact, her right nostril had always been slightly larger, so that she was often conscious of it stealing air from the left. To smell anything clearly, she had no doubt about how to hold it. She held spaghetti sauce, perfume somewhere near her right cheek. Her large nostril always found the scent and identified it.

She looked at herself once more, then turned off the light.

Her husband snored gently. She left him and walked down the hallway. She was guided by a Santa Claus night-light left over from Anthony's childhood. The light was at least ten-years-old, bought for him on his second Christmas. It had remained on, miraculously, every night since. The bulb had not been changed. It burned from behind Santa's face as resolute as blood or liquor.

When she reached her son Tony's room she opened the door carefully. The window was up and at first all she sensed was cold air. Taking a step inside the door, she saw Tony. He ran in his sleep, his legs gently paddling under the covers. The blankets cut across him lengthwise so that his back was exposed to the air.

She went to the bed and covered him. She didn't move with great caution because Tony, unlike his dad, was a sound sleeper. As a baby he had slept in grocery carts and car seats, in strollers and playpens. It was his constitution and, she liked to believe, his clear conscience.

When she finished by the bed, she stepped back and watched him. He still ran under the covers, his knees like cat paws kneading the blanket. He ran with long gentle strides, running a distance rather than a sprint. His head, now and then, turned ever so slightly on the pillow. It turned almost as if he were looking back over his shoulder.

She was tempted to kiss him but she left without doing so. It was late. She closed his door. She turned to go back down the hallway. Her husband's snores came like a trail to her. She wrapped her nightgown closer and saw . . . it was strange. At least it wasn't anything she had ever noticed before. She glanced down at the plastic night-light and was surprised to see Santa Claus looking at her. The angle had changed. It had to be the angle because she had never seen him twisted to watch her. He was supposed to stare straight out, stare dumbly ahead, only now he had somehow turned himself to watch her.

No, not twisted himself. Someone had probably brushed past it and tapped it out of line with his ankle. Probably Tony. There were mud clods next to the wall where Tony had stamped his way to his room after she had sent him there for coming in past curfew. He came in, she guessed, from Cooly's Stream, where he was *not* supposed to play. All of the children in the seventh grade had been told not to play in the woods alone. Bad things went on in those woods. And Grace Corposaro, for one, did not think the bad things were over. So Tony was grounded, and wasn't happy about it, but all he said, over and over, was "sufferin' succotash."

Still, she was fairly certain the Santa head hadn't been turned when she had come past it a moment ago. It had turned, almost as if it followed her. Its face was ruddy and its mouth was too wide. Its shadow fell across the floor in a strange pattern. Light came intensely through its eyes, came like small powerful beams. The eyes appeared to be looking up, waiting, which was obviously impossible. All of it was.

For a moment she thought about going back in Tony's room and waking him. The Santa head, she felt, was a sign. She didn't question her feeling. She was accustomed to signs, believed in them as solidly as she believed in the Virgin, and this one, she was certain, was telling her something.

She held out her right hand and formed the sign against the evil eye. She held her index finger and her pinkie in the shape of horns and pointed them directly at the Santa Claus head. If it was an omen, she would try to understand it. If it meant mischief, if there was a curse anywhere in her life, she would send it back to whomever had cast it in the first place.

She stayed against the opposite wall as she passed. She lifted her feet so that the light would not touch her. The head didn't swivel to follow her, but she kept the guard against the evil eye pointing at it. When she was past it, she backed down the hallway, letting her husband's snores guide her into her room.

11:30

George Denkin knocked on Ms. Fizz's door at exactly eleven-thirty. He was precise about appointments. Like his late mother. He listened to the wind tickle the wind chimes. Not such a pleasant sound, really. It made the air feel fragile.

When no one answered the door after his second knock he took a step back and checked the street number. Forty-three East Federal. Two-story white-painted clapboard house. Wind chimes on the porch. That was the number on the card given to him by a man he had met at Cathcart's, the topless place on Route 17. Baba had been the man's name. He was a self-styled holy man, although George saw through him. The man was a pimp, nothing more.

But the card—the woman's services—intrigued him. Baba had phoned to arrange things. The memory of the phone call encouraged George to knock again. This time, however faintly, he believed he heard someone stirring inside. A moment later a light flicked on in the hallway. A female voice called something unintelligble.

More lights. George took a step back, preferring not to let her fully glimpse him when she opened the door. His head knocked against a wind chime. It chattered rapidly, then gave way to a steady cadence. Its ringing passed off the porch into the darkness, then curled back and infected the other chimes.

"Just a minute," the female's voice said, suddenly closer to the door.

Finally she was there. She pulled open the door. She was, George noted, more attractive than the man at Cathcart's had indicated. She appeared extremely drowsy, her face somewhat full with sleep, but she was indisputably pretty. Her hair was long and straight.

"Yes?" she said.

"Baba sent me."

"Oh, well, it's late, isn't it?"

"He called, didn't he?"

"Yes, but I told him to tell you not to come by. I said it was too late. Did he tell you to come anyway?"

"He said we had an appointment at eleven-thirty."

"Really? That's too bad. I mean, it really is kind of late. I was sleeping."

"Would it take long?"

"Well, no, it depends."

She held the door against her chest. She looked confused. She seemed not completely there, but her hair was excellent. It came down past her shoulders, corn-silk blonde. He felt his penis growing solid.

"I have money," George said. "Perhaps I could add a little to make it worth your while."

"That's nice. That's good, but, well, I was pretty mellowed out for the night. I was reading this book on elf spirits, you know? I'm not sure I'm in the mood."

"How much do your services usually cost?"

"Around seventy-five. That's what I'm charging nowadays. It used to be fifty, but with inflation and everything. Baba takes some off the top. Where did you see him, anyway?"

"At Cathcart's."

"The strip place? You know, I told him to stay away from there. A lot of bikers go there and two of those guys hate his guts. Cathcart's has bad vibes, don't you think?"

"Maybe so."

"Well," she said, opening the door wider, "come in then. You might as well come in. The place is a mess."

George stepped inside and closed the door behind him. She was already walking in front of him down a long hallway. She wore a quilted bathrobe. He watched her hair. It swung from side to side against her back.

He followed her. He wore jeans, a flannel shirt, and a large hunting jacket. The hunting jacket had seven pockets. It also had a large pouch in the back where you could keep a dead bird without worrying the blood would soak through. He had other uses for the bird pouch, but he did not want to think about that right now.

"Let me just clean up here," the woman said. "I left the dinner dishes to soak, but you'll feel better if they're cleaned."

"That's fine."

"I wasn't expecting anyone. Well, you know that by now. So what was Baba doing out there? At Cathcart's, I mean?"

"Watching the show."

"Those women are such cows, though," she said, flicking her finger under the water stream to see if it was hot enough. "I don't understand why guys get so excited about seeing some fat ladies take off their clothes."

George said nothing.

"Whatever floats your boat, I suppose. I'm finally waking up. What did you say your name was?"

"George."

"George, huh?" she said, her hands moving around in the sink. "Mine's Mary. Real Catholic name, isn't it? I was raised Catholic but it didn't take. I still believe in the spirituality of the Catholic Church, if you know what I mean. The Father, the Son, and the Holy Ghost, that's something when you think about it. Three in one. It's like that old Certs breath-mint commercial, you know? Two, two, two mints in one?"

"I see."

"There," she said, shaking her hands, "all done. That didn't take long, did it? Well then, if you want to come over here."

"By the sink?"

"Didn't Baba tell you? That's my specialty."

"He mentioned it."

George stepped closer. Mary pulled a chair away from the kitchen table and dragged it to the sink. She sat. George looked away when she unzipped his fly. He caught his reflection in the window over the sink. He turned his head and looked in the other direction.

Her hand went inside his pants and pulled him free.

His right hand went inside his coat pocket and clasped the straight razor.

"Now just relax and enjoy," she said.

His left hand wound itself in her hair. The hair flowed smoothly around his knuckles. She was not the one he wanted—he wanted Zelda, the girl in the dorm—but she was here. This wasn't intended, he didn't need this one, it was dangerous. Baba, the man at the bar, might remember something about him. He had left a track to this woman's door, and he was smarter than that, much smarter, but he felt his hand grabbing deeper in her hair. The hand moved almost against his will.

"Easy there, George," she said. "Ouch, that hurts."

He increased his grip. He felt everything now—skull, hair root, the curve of her neck. He jerked her head to one side and pushed her cheek against his penis. He hugged her against his groin, his hand clean and ready on the razor.

"George, that hurts. *Ouch*, stop it. Stop that."

She tried to stand. He leaned against her. He held her head steady. She hit his thigh, then reached up, trying to get at his testicles. He squeezed her closer, squeezed her until there was nothing between her cheek and his penis.

He brought the razor out.

His first cut was straight up the spine. The quilted robe split, the pile splintering as it ripped. A moment later blood filled the seam while Mary screamed against his stomach. He pulled her even closer, his hand deep in her hair. The next time she screamed he jerked her head back, placed the razor against her mouth, then shoved it backward until it clicked against bone.

Midnight.

Opening day at Colbin College was over.

In his bed, President Mathews sipped brandy and turned the heating pad up higher on his aching lower back. He couldn't get much relief. Propped against three good-sized pillows, he read *How to Swim with Sharks and Not Get Eaten*. It was a very silly book but he kept reading anyway.

Two miles across town Captain Len Barney made love to his wife Matty. She had come to bed wearing the WHO T-shirt she had bought at a concert in Boston. No underwear, no jewels, no earrings, just the WHO. Now, quietly, so as not to disturb Seth, they moved together under a single sheet. It was one of the good times, one of the times when their flesh felt young and they were not too fatigued and life seemed open and yielding, as it had in the beginning.

Marsha Koln—that was her last name, although Len Barney had long since forgotten everything about the woman except the way she had found the ear, then pinned down President Mathews—was finishing a sampler in her sewing room. The sampler said "God give me the courage to change . . ." Marsha loved Jack Kennedy and had made, at various times, four samplers with the same inscription. This particular one was earmarked for the wall of her mother's semi-private room in the Elton Nursing Home.

Farley Simon, psychology professor and now nurse to a potential gallstone, slowly pushed away from his electric typewriter. He reached forward and pulled his paper from under the platen. At the top it said: "College and Its Effect on Prolonging Adolescence." Followed by a colon and: "Why Kids Refuse to Grow Up." It pleased him immensely to see his own thoughts typed cleanly on a piece of paper. He reached behind him and turned up WEVO, the local branch of National Public Radio. They were playing Chopin, the sonatas.

Zelda Fitzgibbon, in Room 202 of Sheppard Dorm, slept with a copy of E. B. White's *One Man's Meat* on her chest. The book had been assigned for Composition 101. The teacher, a young graduate assistant named Hugh Campbell, was an E. B. White fan. He believed E. B. White to be the greatest stylist America had ever produced. He believed *The Trumpeter Swan, Charlotte's Web*, and *Stuart Little* to be the greatest trilogy of children's books ever written. Naturally he assigned E. B. White's collection of essays in his class. Zelda liked them, but still had fallen asleep.

And while Zelda slept Lester Draabo was driving down Dunbarton Road at fifteen miles per hour. He reached over to the passenger side and checked to make sure the doorlocks were down.

It was the third time he had checked in the last half hour.

As he pulled back behind the steering wheel, he brushed his hand across Goliath's back. Goliath turned and gave his wrist a quick lick. A damn good car dog. No car sickness, not much barking, no jumping forward and back on the seats. He was too young to be of much use, but that would come. Right now, right this second even, Goliath was learning the business. And whatever he learned on this job would be reinforced over in Portsmouth under the tutelage of Suds Peterson. Suds Peterson knew dogs. Suds Peterson talked dog and went to sleep dog. Suds Peterson would make sure that Goliath didn't share the same fate as Flick.

He drove carefully down Dunbarton, then took a left onto Tower Road. Woods out here. Woods and old farm fields and white stones that breathed sometimes if you just caught sight of them out of the corner of your eye. Then maybe, if you let your imagination run, you sometimes saw figures and forms walking near the trees. It always took a good three-count to disassemble the figure and turn it back into a shadow. Because that's all it usually was . . . a shadow, a flame of birch shadow or maybe an oak tree, its leaves cordovan-brown, cutting man-sized forms out of tall grass.

"See anything, boy?" Lester asked his dog. "You see anything?"

Goliath perked up his ears, looked about, then bumped his snout twice against Lester's shoulder. Lester reached a hand back and rubbed under Goliath's chin.

CHAPTER FIVE

CHIMES FOR MS. FIZZ

LESTER WAVED HIS HAND ACROSS HIS WAIST, RIGHT TO left.

Goliath sat.

He raised his hand in an Indian salute—How, Paleface Motherfucker.

Goliath went down on his belly.

Lester made a little stop sign with his hand, flashing his open palm at Goliath's eyes, then said, "Stay." He walked ten feet away and turned.

Goliath stayed.

"I want you to do that twenty times after our session. Get him sitting, get him down, then make him stay. He's a smart whip, that Goliath. He's coming along."

This from Suds Peterson. Lester nodded. There were five other dogs in the group. A golden retriever, a chocolate lab, a rottweiler, a Rhodesian Ridgeback, and Goliath. The retriever and lab were working on simple obedience. The Rottweiler, Ridgeback, and Goliath were working security.

"Circle them," Suds said.

Lester released Goliath. He said, "Free." Goliath jumped up, came over, sat, then waited while Lester hooked up the leash.

"Goliath, heel," Lester said, then started around the outside perimeter of Suds Peterson's barn. He kept Goliath on his left, the leash dangling from his right hand. Goliath walked exactly even with him.

"People, you got to do your homework," Suds lectured as they circled. "Do fifty down-stays, fifty sits, fifty recalls. The dogs learn by *reinforcement*. Repetition. Dogs need constant repetition. Okay, put them down."

Hand across his waist, sit. Hand up in an Indian salute, down.

"That's it for you two," Suds said to the owners of the lab and golden retriever. "Take them home and keep working on the down-stay. Your lab is quivering, Jocelyn. It wants to get up, that means you're not doing your homework."

"Sorry," Jocelyn said.

"Your money. You want to waste it, it's your business," Suds said, and shrugged.

Lester stood by his dog. He watched the lab and the retriever go out. A few minutes later he heard two cars start. Goliath was in a down-stay. Goliath did not quiver, because Lester Draabo did his homework. Fifty sits, fifty downs, fifty stays. Every morning, every night. No praise until the dog was sitting. No treats unless the dog locked into a down-stay. Goliath was frucking tight.

Suds went to the back wall of the barn and began putting on the padded suit that hung there. Lester watched him. The owners of the two other dogs stood beside their animals and said nothing. Suds discouraged friendliness among the three men. Friendliness, name calling, created an air of camaraderie. The last thing, Suds had advised, that anyone wanted in a guard dog was a sense of camaraderie. The last thing anyone wanted was a friendly face-licking crotch-sniffing spineless K-9. What you wanted in a guard was go-to-the-throat loyalty.

Lester agreed. He ignored the other owners and their dogs. He watched Suds Peterson waddle out to the center of his barn in the padded suit. Suds had a catcher's mask on, but the mask was flipped up onto the top of his head. He looked like the Michelin tire man.

"Okay," Suds said, "I want all three of you to lock your dogs down. I'm going to take them one at a time. Remember, you are in control of your dog at all times. Even when the dog is deliberately out of control, when it is in an attack phase, you are carefully monitoring your dog. Is that clear? Okay," Suds said, flipping down his mask, "give me Benji."

The Benji name was a joke, Lester understood. It was a joke because in the movie Benji was a cute little ass-hole lap dog. Look in the camera, cock his head, beg for table scraps. The Benji in class was a hundred-twenty-pound Rottweiler with a muzzle as square as a stump and a chest as deep as a lobster pot.

"How do you want him?" Benji's owner asked Suds.

"I'm going to walk in the barn door like a perpetrator. I want you to sick him on me, then I want you to call him off and put him into a guard phase."

Lester felt his back get tight. He felt his skin turn slightly clammy. The barn was hot and smelled like dog. Lester glanced at the owner of the Rottweiler and saw the man was nervous. He wasn't nervous, Lester guessed, out of worry about how Benji would behave. He was worried because it was a strange feeling to sick a dog on another man, a strange feeling to unleash all that energy, all those teeth even on Suds the waddling Michelin man.

Suds went out, pulling on a pair of thick gloves as he went. Benji's owner unhooked the catch from the dog's choker. He doubled the leash around the dog's collar so that he could drop one end of the leash when he gave the attack command. This was called a "slip-release"—let one end go, the other zing out from under the collar and *voila*, the dog was launched. They all knew the drill.

A few moments later Lester heard the barn door start to open, heard it creak on its hinges and saw the sound register in Goliath's ears. He put his hand down—stay—and Goliath settled. But the Rottweiler inched forward, leaving their lineup, while the owner bent slightly at the knees. The owner even lifted his hand, pretended he had his gun out.

He looked like a guy playing cowboys and Indians, only he was serious and intent.

Let the dog go, Lester remembered. Suddenly they were no longer in Suds Peterson's barn but out by Potter's Bridge, and the woods were scary dark and deep. Lester felt a fern of sweat start across his chest. He felt his head begin to ache, a tension headache, and he imagined, just for an instant, the sight of that woman standing up on the hillside looking down at him. A man, really, wearing a woman's clothes . . .

"Let him go," Lester said, even though it wasn't his place to speak. But he couldn't help himself, because Suds was creeping in through the doorway, doing a half-assed job of being a perpetrator, and what Lester really wanted to shout was that it was all phony, it wasn't this way at all, it wasn't this clear.

"Blue," Benji's owner said.

Then he dropped one end of the leash and Benji started.

"Blue," the owner said again. Blue was the attack color, they each had an attack color, because any John Q. Public could yell sick 'em. It was safer to use color—Goliath's was green—not sick 'em, or kill, or attack. Sick 'em wouldn't get any of these dogs started, but blue did, blue did so nicely as the Rottweiler took off in big looping strides that tightened and compacted when he was halfway across the floor.

"Monitor him," Suds yelled.

Which was another word for "follow." Which was what Lester should have done with Flick, he knew that now, except in the woods it was different. But Benji's owner followed drill, jogged after the dog, but not fast enough to call the dog off. The owner was only halfway across the floor when the Rottweiler coiled.

It all happened fast. Suds raised his arm—just what the average perp would do—covering his throat and screaming a little, but the Rottweiler didn't stop for a second. It couldn't stop, really, because it was airborne, flying, its big hungry mouth opening like the air scoop on a classic T-Bird. He hit Suds all jaws, a growl going up in his throat, and Suds stumbled backward, slammed against the barn door, swatting at the dog with his other hand as he went.

"Get him off! Please mister, get him off!" Suds yelled.

That was a sales job, Lester realized. It was Suds trying to make it all seem real in the middle of his sawdust-floored barn in Portsmouth, New Hampshire. He hit at the dog, although it was clear to anyone with eyes that the dog wasn't going to release his hold. The dog had him by the arm, was scraping his paws down Suds's fat middle while the padding made sounds like a sail luffing.

Benji was on Suds. Suds tried to push himself off the wall but Benji kept boring in, his height almost bringing him to Suds's neck. Lester noticed that Suds kept his chin tucked down, because Benji didn't know this was a game, didn't know shit except that he wanted a piece of this roly-poly fatso.

"Call him off," Suds yelled.

The owner did as he was told. He shouted "Down" about six times, but Benji wasn't having any. Suds—Lester could see this in the man's knees and wobbly legs—was getting tired.

"Call him off," Suds yelled, this time just a tinge of nerves coming into his voice.

On the seventh "Down" the dog finally dropped Suds's arm. Suds didn't move. Benji's owner hustled over, made the Indian "How" sign so the dog would stay down.

"Good," Suds said. "Lock him down."

"Wasn't that something!" Benji's owner said, squealy as a kid with a new bike. "That dog is powerful, huh? Isn't he something? The dog was wild, wasn't he?"

"He settled for my arm," Suds said. "I could have shot him or knifed him."

"Yeah, but—"

"He's going to have to go for the throat," Suds said, pushing up his catcher's mask. "Ask Lester. You got to get your dog to go for the throat. Right, Lester?"

Chimes went off in Damian Peule's mind when he stood on Ms. Fizz's front porch and found the door open. Of course there were chimes all around him. Metal chimes shaped like robins, a rooster chime that pecked at a glass ear of corn, a dog-and-cat chime, and so on.

But the door was open.

Damian, his hands red from scrubbing up after cutting the roast beef for Chucky, stood directly in front of the door, wondering what to do. He wondered, actually, what had already happened.

There was nothing to see from where he stood. An open door. Beyond it a dim hallway, sway-backed and floored with curling tiles, then some steps going up, and past the steps, the kitchen, the heartbeat of the house, the pleasure-center. He had visited it often enough over the past couple of years to know that Ms. Fizz, if she was anyplace, was probably in the kitchen.

So he called into the house.

"Ms . . ."

But he couldn't call out the name Ms. Fizz. That was ridiculous, sort of insulting. The woman had a name, for God's sake, but he didn't know it. He didn't know her name because her name had never come up. She had wanted anonymity as much as he.

"Hello? Anyone home?"

Wind chimes. *Clink, clink, clink.* The chicken pecked at the glass ear of corn and came away with nothing but sound.

At that moment Damian gave himself a little talking-to. This was not, he told himself, any of his beeswax. Maybe Ms. Fizz went out for a walk, or maybe she went out to pick up some milk, or maybe she ran out of Alka Seltzer on her last customer and she left in order to stock up. There was no reason in the world to enter her house . . . a dark, ugly house at that . . . and stick his nose in where it wasn't wanted. This wasn't some silly movie with the starlet ready to go down a flight of creaky cellar stairs, the whole audience screaming "Don't go down there!" just to find out that something terrible and hideous and undead was waiting to reach up from under the stairs and pull her into the next life.

"Hello?" he called again a little louder. "Anyone here?"

This time, for his efforts, he heard something drip. It wasn't easy to hear it, what with the wind chimes and traffic out on the street, but it was definitely something dripping. A faucet blipping slow and steady into something filled with water? A dishrack left to shed slowly into a sink? A drain just licking itself clean with a final swallow of soapy water?

He took two steps inside the house.

That, he told himself, is that. No more steps. Ms. Fizz ran with people who ran heroin and you didn't fool around with those fellows. People got very dead when they got very curious. It wasn't his beeswax.

What he really didn't want to think about, as strange as it was to him, was any sense of loyalty. He didn't want to think of Ms. Fizz the last time he had seen her, her cleaned-up face, her neat hair, the effort she made to take a peck of control over her life. He didn't want to think of her petting his donkey, saying hello to it, didn't want to recall that she had reminded him of home-baked bread and white aprons. She was just a whore, just a horse-riding, foam-mouthed—still, a decent woman. A woman who did what he asked, did it pleasantly, performed, and actually took pride in her work.

"I'm taking off now!" he shouted. "Anyone home?"

Someone was home. He would have bet money on it. The house was humming, like an accident scene, like a household where a man had just belted his wife, like the bedroom of a kid whose mom had just deliberately scalded him with cocoa. He knew that hum, had experienced it enough in his own life, and so he couldn't force himself to take off and leave the house still humming without knowing if Ms. Fizz was . . .

"Hey, last chance. Anyone here?"

Dripping and silence and the wind chimes clinking.

He started into the house, walking hard, banging his boots, because whatever was in the kitchen needed to hear him. He didn't want to go mincing down the hallway, sneaking past phony framed portraits of hunting dogs and partridges. Frightened people didn't make sounds, that was a fact, so he banged and hit things along the way, his blood rising.

"Hey, you in the kitchen," he shouted.

He rounded the corner and slammed open the kitchen door and saw, first thing, Ms. Fizz looking at him.

She was hanging from the kitchen sink by her right arm. She was dangling, naked, her knees bent, her eyes wide, her tongue out. She was lolling from the sink and spinning slowly as he entered. But she couldn't go far. She couldn't spin all around because her right arm had been stuck down the garbage disposal and the disposal had been turned on and she was stuck forever reaching down into the heart of her sink and pulling out a bloody stump.

She had also been scalped. He could see the ivory of her skull.

His stomach voided, he tried to cover his eyes from the blood on the ceiling, on the curtains, over the skin, blood sprayed like a broadcast of wheat seed across her face.

He started to back away. He backed down the hallway, then turned and sprinted. He ran onto the porch and banged into the chimes, banged nearly every last one of them, finding his voice at the same time.

"Help! Help me!"

The house, he felt, still hummed.

It was a bribe, but Barney didn't care. He knew what he was doing registered way up there on the lousy-father meter when it came to father-son relations, but it just didn't matter right now. He imagined he was probably causing a psychic scar, one of those events Seth would talk about twenty years from now on his analyst's couch.

"My dad promised to take me to the football game and give me a ride on Jaspar the Fighting Mule and buy me hot dogs but instead he took me to prison to interview a guy who had just discovered a murdered woman dangling from a garbage disposal."

So the bribe.

Seth wandered up and down the toy-store aisles, running at times, knowing full well that his dad was going to buy him just about anything he picked out. The kid was sharp, Barney gave him that. He had already nixed a plain rubber ball, nixed a Zorro costume, nixed a yo-yo and a glow-in-the-dark bat that bobbed on its own five-foot rubber string. Barney could see that Seth had already established a floor bid somewhere around fifteen bucks. Under that and the bribe wasn't going to stick. Over it, and Barney had a chance.

"How about an action figure?" Barney asked his son in Aisle 7, "GAMES, PUZZLES, MODELS, AND FIG-URES."

"No," Seth said, his eyes moving so fast over everything in sight that Barney wondered if the kid wasn't maybe close to having a seizure of some sort.

"How about a model?"

"No."

"Well, make a decision, partner, because we got to get going."

He followed Seth through the aisles, setting things straight when Seth toppled them. He glanced several times at his watch. It was past two and he had promised Giamoona to be down at the station house with the registrar's information on one Damian Peule, English major. English major on the seven, no, make it eight-year plan toward graduation. A fringe dweller, college-scene groupie who never got enough of frat parties and beer-stained kitchen floors and the occasional coed who was willing enough, or stupid enough, to follow him home. A guy who bounced checks, stayed enrolled in courses until the professors actually asked him to do some work, then came up with excuses—his file was full of them—about working night jobs, meeting payments, staying above water. Petition for readmittance. Petition granted. Petition to drop, petition granted. Actually, the guy had a classic profile for this kind of involvement. It was a Ted Bundy character profile: intelligent, undirected, poor follow-through, and access to many women of the soft and gullible kind. Access to three or four hundred women on two hundred acres of woodland.

"This," Seth said finally.

"That?"

"Yes."

"Do you know what it is?"

"Yes, Danny has one."

"Okay, partner."

It was a round beachball made of a tough rubber compound. You sat on it and bounced, if you were five-years-old, and somehow scooted around a room. You bounced and held onto a rubber handle that came up tight between your legs and probably goaded your genitals every other hop. It was called a Ride-em Balloon. It cost $22.73 retail, around $3.00 wholesale, and would no doubt last for at least fifteen or twenty minutes before it was punctured and useless.

"The Ride-em Balloon it is then, partner. You can call it Jaspar, just like the mule."

"Yes," Seth said. "Just like the mule."

A cease-fire, if not a peace treaty.

Barney never felt like a real cop in the presence of real cops. That was okay, at least at some level, because he wasn't a real cop and had never wanted to be. He was a security officer, which wasn't much like a cop when you came right down to it.

To be a real cop you had to look like Art Giamoona.

Giamoona was a cop's cop, a cliche that happened to be entirely accurate. He was big and hairy and street-smart. He had a stubble that was famous, or infamous, depending on how you looked at it. You could hang a sock on his cheek. You could play connect-the-dots with the food stains on his light gray suit. You could slap him anywhere and expect to feel a gun, or a radio, or a big bunch of keys.

He got a big kick out of Seth bouncing around the police office on his Ride-em Balloon, thought the idea of a ball, with a little rubber handle sticking up between the kid's legs, was really funny. He had actually tried it himself, bending down over it and pressing his ample buttocks onto the round arc of the balloon. He didn't bounce for fear of popping it, but he made it look like he had tried it and enjoyed the hell out of it. Which made Seth Barney one happy camper.

"We used sticks. You ever made a horse out of a broom stick, Barney?" Giamoona asked, taking his seat again and watching Seth bounce by on the linoleum floor. They sat at Giamoona's desk, going over the file Barney had pulled from the registrar's office.

"I guess so."

"This is better. See? He can make it bounce, just like a horse. You know, someone had an idea when he made that thing. Probably made him a rich man, a little thing like that," Giamoona said, turning in his seat to watch Seth bouncing off into the sunset.

Then he turned back and pulled the file closer. "So what do we have?"

"Marginal student, full name Damian Lavelle Peule," Barney said. "French-Canadian. High sophomore, almost a junior in terms of credits. A couple bounced checks, a couple dropped courses. Doesn't do the papers, skips classes, that kind of thing. Hangs around, works down at the Grocery Mart."

"He told us he worked there. Said they bowl the turkeys at the cans of creamed corn. You ever hear of such a thing?" asked Giamoona.

"Never did."

"Says the turkeys are softened up by it. The management doesn't care because the customers claim the turkeys are real sweet."

Giamoona closed the file. He looked once more at Seth, then slid the file into his top drawer. "You don't mind if I keep this a while, do you Barney?"

"No, we made a copy."

"I don't think he's our bird. They did a vaginal swab. No semen at all. They checked her mouth and found some dingus there. That was her speciality. This Damian kid even admits he was going over there for a"—Giamoona looked for Seth and saw he was back by the other desks talking to an officer named Doleman, before he finished—"a blow-job. But, you know, it doesn't fit. Why would the kid stick around and call for help? We checked his apartment. Some porn, but nothing too heavy-duty. Besides, the girl was on heroin, a regular user. She had a lot of ways to die."

Giamoona started to add something, then stopped and looked for Seth. Barney spotted his son still down the other end of the office.

"Go ahead," he told Giamoona. "He's talking to Doleman back there."

"He scalped her, too. Like the woman last summer. You heard that. What we're keeping quiet is that one of the glasses was coated with blood. Looks like he had a drink of it. Regular vampire, is what he is."

"He drank her blood?"

"Looks like it. It's possible, I guess, that some blood just spilled into the glass, but we got some lip smears from the rim. Either he drank before or after, so you tell me. This is one sick cowboy we're dealing with."

Barney felt himself going slightly light-headed. He wasn't a cop, after all. Nevertheless, the last thing in the world he wanted to do was appear a wussy in front of an office full of cops on a Saturday afternoon. But that seemed to be what his body was deciding to do. He felt himself getting steadily more lightheaded, and he had to consciously prevent himself from putting his head down between his knees and sucking air. He felt like grabbing his kid, his wife, and heading to somewhere safe, to Canada, maybe up to Cape Breton, somewhere north where the only crime was a couple of cockeyed lumberjacks knocking each other silly on a Saturday night. Drunk guys who maybe bit each other's ears off in a bar fight but they didn't eat the goddamned things.

Seth came bouncing back down the aisle.

Giamoona, good old Giamoona, leaned down to kid-level. "You got a name for that old horse there, Wyatt Earp?"

"It's not a horse," Seth said.

"No? What is it then?"

"A mule," Seth answered, and began bouncing backward.

Be careful, Barney wanted to say. Let's all be real careful now. But he didn't say a thing.

"You want to talk to this Damian kid?" Giamoona was asking.

"You wouldn't mind?"

"Me? No, the kid's coughing up his whole life history. No attorney, no nothing. He'd talk to the radiator if we let him. He's shook, major league. You go ahead, I'll watch your boy. Tell Henry to let you in. Tell him I said it was okay."

Barney stood, he didn't really know what he wanted to ask the kid. He wasn't Colombo. He wasn't Kojak or even Ironside. He wasn't good at tripping people up, catching them in their own lies.

He told Seth he'd just be a minute, that Detective Giamoona was going to stay with him, then went through a doorway into the detention center. Two walls of cells, maybe ten holding cells for penny-ante deadbeats. A swivel chair and an officer, Henry Camp, watching a Nebraska-Iowa game. Henry swung his big feet down and lowered the volume on the TV.

"How's the game?" Barney asked, surprised at himself for being able to talk on prosaic subjects.

"Cornhuskers are kicking ass," Henry said.

"Art said I could talk to the kid. Just be a minute."

"No problem," Henry said.

Barney followed Henry down the row between the cells, still wishing he were somewhere else.

George Denkin waited behind the door to his room until he heard Maslo finally flush the toilet. Maslo was a Yugoslav, a fat boorish man. It disgusted him to share a bathroom with a man like Maslo, but those were the conditions at Mrs. Cutrer's boarding house. Single room on the second floor, shared bath. Forty-seven dollars a week.

"Mr. Maslo, are you quite finished?" George Denkin called.

"Just one minute," Mr. Maslo called back, grunting to tuck in his shirt or hitch his belt.

"Your time is from nine until nine-thirty. You're using the bathroom during my time. It's eight-thirty-seven."

"You want me to do it on the floor?"

"I *want* you to respect my reserved time," George called. "I'll inform Mrs. Cutrer if this happens again."

"Hey, what are you anyway? You too good for everybody else?"

Suddenly the door to the bathroom was open. George Denkin stepped from his room, yanking his bathrobe closed.

Mr. Maslo wore shapeless pants, hitched by a wide leather belt, and a white Italian T-shirt. "You like your rules, don't you? Well, I'll tell you, I seen some things too, buddy boy. I also hear some things at night, maybe you don't want me to hear? You go ahead to Mrs. Cutrer. I'll have a few things to tell to her too."

"Just respect my assigned times for the bathroom."

"I respect you not this," Mr. Maslo said, snapping his fingers.

George walked past Mr. Maslo. Mr. Maslo snapped his fingers again, this time bringing them close to George's right ear. George did not react. Mr. Maslo was already dead, and didn't know it.

He closed the bathroom door behind him, deliberately breathing through his mouth. He reached to his right and switched on the exhaust fan. The sound covered the faint scraping of Mr. Maslo's slippers as he went back to his own room.

George placed his shaving kit on the sink. His breathing was unsteady. He reached to his right and turned on the water in the bath. He cranked both handles full, hot and cold, and let the water pound down in the old claw-footed tub. Then, moving with more assurance, he turned on both faucets in the sink.

He stood for a moment in the center of the bathroom, examining his face in the mirror. He was changing. He could see himself growing more powerful. It was only a matter of time before others began to see it as well, then he would move on.

He reached behind him to slide a thin bolt home above the lock, then tried the doorhandle. Secure. The hot water pushed fog at him from the bath and sink.

He went to his shaving kit and took out his razor. It was a straight-edge, a present from his grandfather. He shook a can of Noxema until it gave him a decent foam, then slowly covered his face. He shaved quickly, hurrying to finish before fog closed off the mirror.

Afterward he removed his bathrobe and hung it from a hook on the back of the bathroom door. He stepped into the bathtub and began ladling water over his body. Next he lathered his underarms, his legs, and his chest. The hair on these parts was little more than stubble.

He shaved himself with his right hand. He trailed his left fingers over the shaven parts, checking to make sure they were clean. He rinsed himself, then shaved again, this time cutting closer to the skin. His left hand, searching after the razor, found no friction whatsoever.

The fog was thick in the room now. He let the water run while he lathered his pubic hair. He concentrated as he started to shave, shaping the hair into a triangular patch. The outlines of the patch were clear and long established. He shaved the insides of his thighs, his hips, his buttocks. He rinsed again, then stepped out of the tub.

He did not look at the mirror.

He stepped to the door and listened. Nothing. He stepped back toward the tub, his penis getting hard. He closed his razor, held it by one end of its ivory handle, then smacked the tip of his penis with the dullness. When his erection did not fade completely he smacked it again. This time it curled down.

His blood moved faster. He opened his mouth slightly to ease his breathing. He lifted another item out of his shaving kit, a small pair of Chinese handcuffs purchased by the dozen from any gag or magic shop. This one was made of purple paper.

He held his penis steady and slipped one end of the handcuffs over the glans. He inched the handcuffs up, gathering a full inch and a half of his penis into the purple intestine. He tugged on the cuffs to make sure the purchase was secure, then squatted. He bent the free end of the Chinese handcuffs backward until he caught it between his buttocks. He adjusted the tension by lifting it slightly higher in his backside. When it was adequately clamped, he stood.

His penis was gone. In its place was a nub of flesh tucked backward. The triangle formed by his pubic hair had become a vagina.

For a few moments he could scarcely breathe. He still resisted the temptation to look in the mirror. Not yet, he told himself.

He walked to the toilet, his hips swinging slightly. He felt the rear end of the Chinese handcuffs wedged between his buttocks, the tip tickling his anus. He lowered the lid of the toilet, then stood with his hands on either side of the rear tank. He was too excited for a moment and forced himself to straighten. He took three deep breaths, then, moving more confidently, coughed loudly, using the sounds to cover the noise he made removing the top of the tank.

Almost, he thought. A minute more.

He set the top of the tank down on the closed lid of the toilet. Then he reached into the tank and lifted out the whore's scalp.

Water fell from it, splattering the wall behind the tank. He twisted it lightly in his hands, wringing it gently, pleased that most of the blood was gone. He bobbed it two or three times above the water in the tank, each time gratified to hear less water released.

He unfolded the scalp and placed it on his head. At first the hair was unruly, although the skin helmet fit perfectly, and with two swipes of his hand he managed to push the hair away from his face. He took up a comb from inside his shaving kit and ran it through the hair. Straight hair. Beautiful hair. He stepped to the mirror, wiped it with his forearm, then parted the hair on the right. He parted it exactly as the whore, Mary, had worn it.

At four o'clock in the afternoon Zelda Fitzgibbon heard the first phone call. The ringing brought her head up from the desk, made her stare at the dull sunlight, the waves of trees stretching back and away from the dorm, the ivy wands just touching the edge of her window. She had been deep in Emile Durkheim's *Suicide* for her Psych 112 class with Professor Farley Simon. She had been thinking about the end, why people took the final step off the bridge, why they gave little razor grins to their wrists, all of which somehow made the ringing sound like a knell. Or perhaps that was a bit heavy-handed, a strained image, but the sound *was* haunting. A knell. The church yard calling the congregation to services. A northern graveyard beside a fieldstone church, an Irish priest holding his hands open, the ground bright with new dirt, and above them all the wicker of a crow's wing and a bell, a bell ringing through generation after generation.

Give me a break, she told herself. She was getting carried away because she had spent too much time sitting inside on a beautiful day bending over a book on suicide, for God's sake, and the phone was going to make her crazy if she didn't go out to pick it up and rejoin the land of the living.

She checked herself in the mirror, straightened her sweater, then opened the door. The volume of the ringing increased at once. She heard it clearly now. It was no longer muted from sifting through walls. It rang straight down the hallway, a single pay phone over by the steps where there was a small commonroom, a Coke machine, and an ancient ping-pong table that had been folded up, pushed against a wall, and now served as a message board for in-coming calls.

"I'll get it," Zelda said aloud.

Speaking aloud was partially a joke, more a reaction. As she said it she realized she was probably the only one on the floor, and that, for an instant, didn't seem very funny. She felt like she was ten-years-old and had been home all day faking a bellyache and now it was time to go out to the kitchen and convince her mom she felt better. The kids would be coming home from school, and really the bellyache was better and the rooms had begun to seem awfully dark and quiet and there were no good TV shows on, she had read all the magazines in the house . . .

The phone continued ringing.

She was well on her way to the phone, stepping purposefully, consciously rejoining the land of the living, when a thought occurred to her. It was a less than cheery thought but it came with such insistent practicality that she couldn't ignore it. It made her stop, it made her listen. It made her realize people don't let the phone ring twenty or thirty times unless there has been a death in the family and they have to get in touch with someone and even then you could call security and have them hunt the person down. Call the R.A., call residential services but don't call the dorm and let the phone ring and ring and ring.

At the same time she became aware that the dorm was indeed quiet, was preternaturally silent, and that she was standing perhaps twenty feet from her open doorway and the hallway was not well-lighted. She looked backward and forward, trying to determine if the lights had simply not come on, if it was just a dark afternoon, or if a bulb had blown somewhere.

Or if, for some reason, someone wanted her out of her room.

That, too, would be an excellent reason to ring the phone long and steady on an October afternoon. If someone was checking to see if the floor was empty the phone might work very nicely, since it was a well-established fact that the girls on the floor were always anxious to hear from their beaux and families and they didn't let the phone ring too long without somebody stepping up to it, taking the message, and shouting down the hallway that there was a call for Jane or Mary or Sally.

Before she could come up with an answer, come to any conclusion, the phone stopped ringing. It stopped and a moment later she heard a door open and shut. It was a heavy door from the sound of it. She didn't know, she couldn't be certain, but it sounded like a fire door swinging shut on the fire stairs at the other end of the hallway.

Which was odd because the entire dorm had received several warnings that the fire stairs were to be used only in emergencies. You could not go through the doors without triggering an alarm, but someone had stepped through without making much of a sound. Certainly no alarm had gone off. She could hear, just faintly, a person using the staircase. A person coming down the steps, slowly. The phone was no longer ringing, but that silence was a sound too in its way, an absence of sound that meant whoever was on the staircase might be listening.

She felt herself getting giddy. It was not a glad-giddy but a fear-giddy, and it was probably nonsense, probably just the product of a long afternoon with Durkheim and his *Suicide*, but the feeling was undeniable, and it grew with each footfall from the staircase. Nobody was supposed to be on the fire stairs unless the building was on fire.

She took a step back toward her room. She took several steps. The phone wasn't ringing, and there was no reason to stand in the middle of the hallway. She was supposed to be studying, and maybe Mom was right, maybe it was better to stay inside with a bellyache. She was certain there was an explanation for whoever was out on the fire stairs. It would probably be one of those awkward moments when the door opened and she would give a little yelp and it would be the cleaning lady or a security officer or even a fire marshal.

Only the cleaning lady didn't come on Saturday.

Saturday was a holiday, and if she had any sense she should have gone out to the football game, sat through a pretty afternoon watching young men in tight pants, been part of a crowd.

What made her run was the next thing that happened. She saw the light in the staircase go out. Suddenly the hallway grew a little dimmer. She didn't wait, she didn't question any further. She hustled down the hallway, shuffling her feet for traction, reaching out with her hand to hook it around the doorjam and swing herself inside.

By the time she got there she was breathing hard, she felt a trembling enter her limbs, which made it difficult to close the door softly.

Nobody here but us chickens.

Nobody here at all. As her door clicked shut, as she spun the lock, she heard the door to the fire escape open softly, the creaky yawn of it like an animal panting.

The guy in the woods wasn't a vampire, Tony Corposaro told himself.

Then, just as quickly, he thought, but he might be.

That was Tony's private debate as he watched his bone-headed pal Jimmy Ryder crawl under the Colbin College bleachers. Tony knew what Ryder was looking for. He had done the same thing himself throughout the previous football season, netting, if he remembered, six or seven clear panty shots, four or five glimpses of pantyhose, and one or two eyeballs of infinite inviting darkness. Mostly, though, the bleacher seats blocked everything interesting so that you had to crawl around for maybe the whole second half just to get a decent peek at anything.

And, really, the peek was gone in about two bat-seconds. Gone and covered by a prim set of hands coming down to fold her skirt up against her fanny. In the meantime you ran the risk that Mr. Bull, the ticket-taker at all the home games, might wander by and see you. That was bad news because Mr. Bull was a Bible-smacker who didn't forgive boyish pranks that hinted of s-e-x. He'd give your folks a stiff-throated phone call later in the afternoon. Say your kid was down here with his nose up in the air, sniffing around like a randy dog. Say your kid was a pervert and an offense to the Nazarene. It had happened to Scotty Benbow, and Scotty was now in therapy with some geekster from Peterborough getting blabbed at three times a week about his sexual identity. Of course Scotty Benbow snorkled around under the bleachers with a Kodak Instamatic up to his eye, but it was still pretty much the same thing.

It wasn't worth it.

Besides, they had a vampire to kill.

"Come on," Tony whispered now to Ryder. "Come on, come on, give it up."

Ryder only stopped, looked at Tony, pointed up, made a classic outline of a woman's figure with his hands, then turned those same hands into goggles and stood staring above him. He kept standing there, probably seeing something pretty good, Tony imagined, because Ryder didn't budge. He didn't make a joke out of anything at all and he didn't move an inch because he didn't want to cause the woman above him to sit down. The whole crowd was on its feet, the game was almost over, and it was prime time to be shooting the proverbial beaver.

But the vampire would be moving soon, Tony thought.

So he leaned under the bleachers, put his hands to his mouth and whispered to Ryder, "Mr. Bull's coming."

Ryder came flying out, tripping once on an empty soda can but righting himself fast. His bald head, his whole body was in a panic. He came out and grabbed Tony, yanked him to the left, and began beating it back to the woods, down toward Cooly's Stream, before Tony could get out that Mr.

Bull hadn't been coming and they didn't have to run.

"You're a wicked dinkster," Ryder said when he finally understood, after running a good thirty yards into the
woods along a game path, that Mr. Bull was not high-
tailing it after them. He stopped, seemed to consider, then
judiciously punched Tony once on the arm. Then he must
have decided he needed to wrestle, because the next thing
Tony knew Ryder had him in a headlock and was dragging him deeper into the woods, administering noogies as
he went. It was sort of a joke, but also a little bit serious, which was always the weird thing about Ryder. You
couldn't always tell which side of the line he was on. Even
now his headlock was a little tighter than it had to be, tighter
than it should have been if they were just grabassing. Tony
didn't do anything except go along because if you did maybe grab Ryder's hand and try to pry a finger loose it might
just get Ryder going a little more. He might just look at
you with that bald head, those ridges (where old Doc Syvak
pulled him into this life with forceps) running right from the
points of his forehead like two rain gutters, and you would
know he might come at you not because of anything you
had done, really, but because his dad was a shiny-headed
dimwit who worked over at the military base during the
days and came home at night with one powerful thirst. A
thirst that didn't quit after one, six, or sometimes twenty-
four Pabst Blue Ribbons. A thirst that was quenched by
Jimmy Boy running back and forth to the kitchen, doing
it sharp and lively, because if he didn't, if he didn't play
Gunga Din the way Pa wanted, well then Pa was just as
likely to work up a second thirst whipping the sluggish tar
out of sonny boy. That was why you didn't cross Ryder too
much, and Tony understood it.

"You got me so scared I was ready to pee in my pants,"
Ryder said when he finally released the headlock. He
punched the neck of an aster, then punched the head and tore
the plant loose from the ground. "If my dad caught me under
there looking up at all those little panty monsters . . . oh, you
should have seen her, Tony. Some decent, let me tell you."

"We got to get the stakes if we're going to kill him. It's
getting darker," Tony said.

He looked square at Ryder, which was what you had to do to change his channel.

"We'll get the stakes," Ryder said, becoming serious. "Don't you worry about that. You bring any garlic?"

"I stashed it out at the blind. We better get moving."

"Wait till you see what I put out there," Ryder said, breaking into a slow trot. "Come on, Daffy."

"What is it? What do you have."

"You'll see. Just wait. It's wicked decent, you'll see."

Tony ran east, falling into the easy dog-trot they always used when they wanted to make time. Near Egg-Head, a huge granite boulder they used for a landmark, Tony passed Ryder and took the lead. It was an unspoken exchange of authority, one neither of them thought to question. He followed a game-path that zigzagged through puckerbrush and hardhack, guiding them toward the Kon-Tiki deer blind. On a different afternoon they might have stopped to examine deer scat, or some of the rubbings the rutting bucks left on the trunks of young alders. But this wasn't an afternoon to stop, because the sun was already sitting on the rim of Gobble Hill, and Tony knew from reading the tide tables in the Coldbridge *Chronicle* that true sunset was at 6:03 that evening. Until then, the vampire had to wait. The vampire had to be dead, not un-dead. If they came on the vampire before true sunset there was nothing to it. You hammered a wooden stake through his heart, chopped off his head, and stuffed the mouth with garlic. That was standard procedure when it came to disposing of vampires, and Tony was steeped in the tradition. Follow the rules, the vampire turned to a skeleton, then to dust, and finally to molecules. Tony knew what he was about.

If they had been running on any other afternoon, at any time later in their lives, they would not have believed in vampires. They would, for example, have been amazed to find out what the detective had discovered about the killer drinking Ms. Fizz's blood. Even now, on this particular day, they did not wholly believe they were going to kill a vampire. If they had, they would have left themselves more time. They were running, actually (although of course they didn't know it), at the end of their long leash of childhood.

They still possessed the peculiar childish ability to make believe. The belief was acutely real to them; it was also, simultaneously, fissured by an increasingly rational understanding of the world, a world that had killed off Santa Claus, the Easter Bunny, and, although they couldn't have named the artist, the happy clutter of Norman Rockwell's vision. They held onto a belief in vampires because they had a mind for monsters, but also because, with the increased knowledge of the world, it was easier to believe in evil than in a fat old man who slid down chimneys and worked all year just to make children happy.

Tony was still in the lead when they reached the deer blind. Almost reached the blind, rather, because before they could make it he felt something *whap* against his shoulder. Whatever hit him wasn't so hard but it was solid and Tony couldn't help himself from falling down and rolling. It was like an army move, something out of Rambo, and he was not a little proud that he had performed it instinctively.

"Look out!" he yelled to Ryder.

But his shout wasn't necessary. Ryder was already down on the ground beside him, crawling on his belly through a wedge of cattails and stag-horn sumac.

"It's Wayne Steele and his a-hole buddies," Ryder said, yanking himself forward on his elbows. "I saw the peckerhead. Him and another guy."

"What are they throwing?" Tony asked.

"Mud cakes, I think. Mud pies."

As he finished, two more clods of dirt came flying into the bushes beside them. The clods sounded heavy; they broke grass stems as they landed, then scattered like shrapnel. Another clod came from behind them, this one following the exposed spine of the trail. It smacked against Ryder's leg and disintegrated on his back. Tony turned just in time to see loudmouth Richard Cloutier duck into the bushes for cover. They were pinned down. They had walked into an ambush.

"Cut it out, Wayne," Tony shouted.

"Cut it out, Wayne . . ." echoed back to him. It was Wayne, who had made his voice high and petulant so that it sounded like Tony had been pleading with him. Tony listened, trying to determine direction, but it was hard to do.

"Wayne, you a-hole . . ." Ryder started to say. But just as he began to speak someone ran across the trail, threw three quick clods at them, then sprinted off into the bushes once again. Ryder jumped to his feet, ready to attack, but then Richard Cloutier bombed them from behind again, two clods bouncing squarely off Ryder's back. Cloutier was gone in an instant, diving and scrambling off through the woods so that even Ryder knew it was no use chasing him.

"Succotash now, you fucker," Wayne shouted from somewhere in front of them.

Then they were gone. Or at least, no more mud pies came bombing through the tall grass. Tony figured they might have run out of ammunition and had made a retreat to Cooly's Stream to load up. A few seconds later, though, he heard whoops going in the opposite direction, heading back to the center of campus.

"Crazies could put our your eyes," Ryder said. He stood in the middle of the trail, crouched. "How you think they found us?" He walked in a small circle, almost as if he expected to find one of the attackers under a clump of weeds nearby. Tony dusted himself off. He checked the deer blind. It was still in one piece. He doubted Wayne and his followers had even seen it.

"I don't know. Followed us from the game maybe. They know we come down here."

"We got to get some ammo," Ryder said.

"We got to kill the vampire."

For a second Tony saw that Ryder didn't believe in the vampire. Ryder was only playing along because Tony had made it up, because Tony was good at making things up. In that moment there was a small test of wills. Tony didn't doubt he'd win, but they stood for a moment staring at one another until Ryder finally looked away. It wasn't a complete victory, because Ryder shook his head and tramped past, muttering loudly enough to make his point . . . "Ain't no such thing as vampires," he said.

"Well then, what about the smell? What about the vault? You got any answers, smart guy?"

Tony realized he was still rattled from the attack, but he also held to the fact that there *was* a smell coming up from the ground in the middle of the colonial grave-yard and vampires were notoriously smelly creatures . . . It wasn't George Washington down there, that was for sure. It was something new dead, something hungry and ugly, something that didn't floss for the last thousand years or so.

"Wayne's an a-hole," Ryder said, picking up a broken clod and winging it down toward Cooly's Stream. They both listened to it crack through the trees. Its final sound, as it broke apart, was like snow hitting old leaves.

"You want to or not?" Tony said, pressing the advantage. "You want to kill the vampire or do I have to do it myself?"

"No one said you had to do it yourself. I'm not chicken, you know?"

"I know."

"All right then, let's just do it."

It wasn't exactly the attitude Tony wanted from his fellow vampire-hunter. It made a certain amount of sense, however, because everything he had ever read about vampires told him vampires were able to create confusion among their pursuers. They tried to mess up plans until sunset when they could take care of business themselves. Tony knew that.

"If those bastards come back I'll give them something they won't forget," Ryder said, chucking another clod of dirt, this time smack against the deer blind.

"Okay," Tony said. "But I think they took off."

And really it wasn't the same, even though Tony attempted to persuade himself that it was. He didn't know what had been sucked away, but he was aware that the whole thing was starting to feel like a phony sort of adventure. This was just Coldbridge, New Hampshire, Colbin College campus. It was Cooly's Stream on a late Saturday afternoon.

That's the vampire talking, he told himself, but it didn't work. His imagination felt sparked out. He walked slow-ly over to the deer blind, following Ryder. He was about to call the whole chase off—he knew he had the power to do it, because Ryder would go along with most anything—when Ryder made a grab behind a blow-down and came up with a three-foot-long machete.

"What did I tell you?" Ryder said, whistling the knife around in front of him. "How's this for a booger picker?"

"Where'd you get it?" Tony asked.

"My dad keeps it up in his old war chest in the attic. I snuck it out last night, then brought it down here this morning. He took it off a gook who took it off a G.I. See this?" Ryder asked, holding the handle out to Tony. The handle was made of some sort of black plastic. It looked like the grip of a power tool. "Blood," Ryder said. "This baby was used, Tony-o-Bony."

"That could be any blood, you know. It doesn't have to be human blood."

"Could be, but it ain't. We'll chop the Count's head off with this thing, you'll see."

It was 5:23, a little over a half-hour to sunset. Tony put Ryder to sharpening stakes, then climbed into the deer blind to retrieve his garlic. He only had three cloves, which were all he could requisition without tipping his mother to his plans. He had taken them one by one over the course of a week. Now he put them in the pocket of his jeans and climbed back down. Far away, and to the south, he heard someone shout. It was Wayne, he figured. Wayne and the boys.

"Hear them?" Ryder asked, holding up two stakes. The stakes were hunks of pine sharpened into points. They reminded Tony of the logs used to build a cowboy fort.

"I hear them. They won't bother us. You ready?"

"All set."

"Let's go," Tony said. "Let's kill us a vampire."

Tony knew the way to the colonial graveyard, but the odor would have guided him in any case. He smelled it every time the wind came to them.

Ryder ran with the machete in front of him, held against his chest. Tony carried the two stakes across his left arm.

In his pocket he felt the garlic wedged against his skin like round wads of gum.

They jumped Cooly's Stream. It was just a pool of slack water and croaking mud this late in the season. A path had been beaten up the other side mostly by deer hooves. They had to go down on all fours to pass under the low canopy of thorns. Bending that close to the ground, Tony saw coon prints and a few smeared tracks of something smaller—mink maybe, or woodchuck.

"You smell it? Wicked bad, huh?" Ryder asked when they were on the other side. He stopped and turned around. Tony ducked back to stay clear of the machete.

"It's him. The vampire," Tony said, breathing hard.

"You think?"

"What else?"

"You think maybe we should make some crucifixes? We could use sticks?"

"No time. It's almost quarter to six."

Ryder didn't move. It was getting dark. That was one thing, Tony realized, he hadn't thought through. They didn't have flashlights; they didn't have candles. They would need them before it was finished, because if the woods were dark, the vault itself would be that much darker.

Tony took the lead, pushed through the last of the soft-woods and stopped at the edge of the graveyard. It was just a dark bushy field in the middle of the forest. Overgrown weeds, brown headstones flaking to rusty piles of mineral dew. At the northeast corner, on the other end of the cemetery, he saw the single hump that marked the vault. From behind, the hump looked like the neck of a gorilla peering away from them.

"You ready?" Tony asked.

"What time is it?"

"Five-fifty. We got fifteen minutes."

Not quite. Tony knew it was more like thirteen minutes, and even that was so only if his watch was accurate. If his watch was a little slow, that meant sunset was even sooner. It meant they could be opening the vault door just as the vampire was waking. They might arrive in front of his door like two Girl Scouts selling cookies.

"You think—?" Ryder started.

"We got to," Tony cut him off. "We've come all this way."

"It's awful dark all of a sudden. Stinks to high heaven, that's all I'm saying."

Tony nodded. He didn't look back at Ryder as he started across the graveyard. The grass was high and pocky. It snagged at the shins of his blue jeans; it made a whistling sound. Tony walked with his legs bent, ready to run if it came to that. The soil beneath him was rutted and broken. The vault, the gorilla neck, was covered with a ridge of hair raised as if on the animal's spine.

It only took a minute to cross the graveyard.

This was where he wanted to be, this was what he had been plotting for, but Tony had a sudden pull. Vampires seemed very real to him in that moment. Vampires seemed more than real . . . they seemed obvious, like the answer to an algebra problem after you got it. They had to exist. Angels existed, and God existed, and the Devil and Count Dracula, and the Wolf Man and Abbott and Costello, all of them existed.

"Here," Tony said, digging in his pocket for garlic. "Put some of this in your pocket. "It'll protect you."

"We should have made crucifixes."

"Well, we didn't, did we?"

Hurry up, he told himself. The vampire is trying to make you late. He felt an impulse to run away as fast as he could. He knew he wouldn't care if he ran into bushes, was smacked by tree branches, because any place was better than standing on the hump of gorilla neck, waiting to scramble down, wedge the door open, and step inside.

"So?" Ryder asked.

"Come on."

It was 5:57 by Tony's watch.

He went down the left side of the gorilla neck. Ryder came down the right side, holding the machete out and away from his body. They came together at the bottom, in front of the vault door. Ryder stepped forward with a scrap of rock in his hand and drew a cross on the door.

5:59.

"Use the stakes to pry it open," Tony said, then realized he held the stakes himself. He also realized his breathing wasn't right. Air wouldn't come. He fitted one of the sharp points in the crack and started to pull, but Ryder stopped him.

"Look," he said, pointing to an arch of squashed grass. "It's been opened."

"Holy shit," Tony said.

"What time is it?" Ryder asked.

"Six o'clock."

They looked at each other. It was dark. It was almost completely dark.

Tony put the stake down at his side and pulled at the door. It shifted its weight, as if shrugging onto its hinges.

Then it began to open. And it brought the smell with it. It was impossible not to inhale it because it covered the entire doorway, seeped out at Tony's knees, and flew up above his head. It exploded, was what it did.

Now, Tony told himself. Now before it's too late. And was amazed to find himself stepping inside. He was conscious of stones, old stones, and lime, and spider webs, and grass and vines breeding on the walls. The vines looked like hair. It was all dark, and he glanced at his watch, seeing nothing at all except the vague glow of phosphorous.

Beside him, he heard Ryder's machete clang against the steel frame of the doorway. Tony bent down, hoping that lowering himself would somehow provide more light, but of course he couldn't see any more that way.

I am under earth, he thought. I am under the earth and this is what it will be like when I die, only I won't know it.

"Oh, Jesus," Ryder said.

Tony heard Ryder inhale in a short gush, grabbing for air. Ryder was going to scream, he was going to do something nutty, but there was nothing Tony could do to prevent it, because he found his own chest waffling down, sucking in for the big blast.

I'm going to scream, Tony told himself, realizing this scream had been building for a long time. I'm going to scream my freaking head off.

Tony heard Ryder open his mouth and start to gargle up a sound, but he couldn't see a blessed thing. Then he felt Ryder's arm come around his shoulders, felt himself pulled to one side, and then, at last, he saw the woman hanging from a beam at the top of the vault.

"Mother of God."

But in the darkness the woman changed and became only soil, became only the wavy grain of the cement wall at the rear of the vault. It was nothing, nothing at all, until another breeze touched her and rocked her slightly forward. Then Tony really saw her . . . she was swinging . . . she was hanging from her hair, which gave her enough slack to lean forward, her arms chafing stiffly against her hips and sides, reaching out in a leathery welcome.

Tony screamed until he thought his throat would rupture. Her feet touched the floor as she leaned forward. She looked like she was stepping forward, looked like she was *flying* forward, and all he could see was her mottled skin, her sloppy eyes, her grin of black teeth.

"Tony . . . Tony!"

"Let's get out of here," Tony said.

Before he could get anything straight, he saw Ryder fall forward, tripping in his mad rush, the machete up above his shoulder, ready to strike. What he would have said to Ryder if he wasn't under the earth and the darkness wasn't all around him was that the woman was not a vampire. It was not a vampire at all.

He heard it move. He heard its steps. And he felt—this was clear—something coming at them, something moving from the wall at the back and stepping forward. It was coming to meet them, coming with its own hands ready, and Ryder was just rushing into an embrace, into his own foolish death.

Sufferin' succotash, Tony told himself. Run, he told himself. Finally he did. He turned and ran back through the doorway, ran for all he was worth, because he felt whatever it was had already dispatched Ryder. It had killed Ryder as fast as any vampire might have, but this wasn't a vampire, it was a half-rotted woman rising up from the lime walls of her own crypt.

He ran straight into the woods, ran with such force that his shoulder hit a sapling and spun him almost all the way around. It was dark, but he continued to run, his hands out in front of his face, the knowledge slowly working into him that he was making too much noise. He would be tracked, the woman would follow him, so he ran another ten or twenty feet and then dropped to the ground and rolled under a bush, clutching the stems of the bush, and it was wet underneath him, dark above.

He opened his mouth and breathed carefully, because he heard the woman enter the woods after him. He heard her crashing through the woods until she apparently lost his sound. She stopped and did not move again for some time. He understood any move now on his part would be his death. Any move and she would come to him, pull up the edge of the bush, and swing toward him, her teeth gone, her cheeks tight, her eyes moving rapidly through the empty sockets.

It was quiet. Tony lay on his belly, clutching the plant roots to his stomach. He was curled around the plant, he was in the plant, and something was crawling on his face. Probably a daddy longlegs, but it was an eerie feeling, a strange feeling, so he slowly lifted his hand and flicked it, by mistake, down his shirt. He brushed again and felt the spider smush. One of its legs still pawed at him, and he brushed it again.

Be still, he told himself. Be still because she's out here in the woods and she'll wring your stupid neck.

He was accustomed to hiding, though. He was the veteran of ten thousand hide-'n'-seek games, and it was nothing at all to remain coiled against the bush as long as he needed. He looked up once, even though he knew a man's face was the most visible part of him in the dark, and saw nothing but branches.

He was still looking up when he heard someone crashing through the woods. It was an old trick, a hide-'n'-seek trick of trashing some bushes hoping you flushed someone out of hiding. He had caught dozens of kids by using it himself, because when someone came close it was hard to believe he didn't see you.

Tony got up onto his knees even though he knew it was a trick. A dumb thing to do. A stupid thing, really, but he didn't care, he had to make a move. On his knees he was able to orient himself better. The cracking sounds came from his right, which meant they were fairly close to the cemetary. Someone was probably smacking the bushes all the way around the ring of trees circling the cemetary, trying to get him to move.

"Hey, Tony! Hey, Tony-Bony, you freaking chicken!"

It was Ryder. Only Ryder was dead. Ryder was killed by the vampire, by the dead lady dancing toward them. It was just a voice, and that didn't necessarily mean it was Ryder. It could be someone who had pinned Ryder down, forced him to reveal the name of his companion, then the guy had come out looking.

"Hey, Tony, where are you? This guy's got a woman's head hanging in there. Come on out. Where are you?"

Tony didn't answer. Instead he put his hands together, puffed them out, then hooked his lips over his thumb joints, and blew into the hollow between his palms. The air pushing through his hands made a sound like an owl. It was a sound Ryder would recognize. It was a sound, in fact, that Ryder could answer, so Tony waited, ready to dart under the bush again.

Then the answer came—an owl call like his own. It made Tony get up on his feet, made him start running back toward the cemetary.

"Tony, come on," Ryder called.

It was dark and his shoulder hurt. Tony slowed when he came close to the cemetary. He stood for a moment on the edge of the clearing, watching Ryder flailing at the bushes with his machete. Tony raised his hands and gave the owl call again.

"Where did you go?" Ryder said as soon as Tony stepped into the clearing. "Some partner you are. You motored."

"Let's get out of here," Tony said.

"The guy isn't around."

"Are you nuts?" Tony said, moving closer.

It was completely dark now. Tony could just make out the open vault fifteen feet away. Ryder came toward him, the machete wagging back and forth in front of him. Ryder had the bone-head look on his face, and Tony told himself to go easy.

"Come on," Ryder said. "This guy has a woman's head or something hanging in there. He's got it hanging from her hair."

"Let's go."

"You chicken?"

"I'm chicken, okay? The guy *killed* people, don't you get it, Ryder?"

"I thought you wanted to kill a vampire."

"That isn't a vampire, you dumb ass."

Tony saw Ryder switch the machete from one hand to the other. It was weird, the whole thing didn't seem to be sinking into his bone head. Ryder wanted to stick around while every nerve in Tony's body said it was time to make tracks.

"Come on, Ryder, let's go," Tony said.

"You ran out and left me in there."

"I'm sorry. I was scared—"

"So was *I*."

Ryder was pissed about being left alone, and that was okay, he had a point, but Tony sensed it went deeper than that. It had something to do with his dad and dark places. He seemed to remember that Ryder had once told him a story about being locked in a closet all night for punishment, but that wasn't the issue right now, the issue was they had to get going, they were done, they had to get the hell out.

"You didn't give a damn about me!"

This time Tony took two steps back because Ryder came at him with the machete over his head, just like he had gone after the dead lady. But then Ryder turned at the last second, wheeled, and hacked the machete as hard as he could against a fir tree. It made a white slice. He slammed it again and it made another slice. On the second slice he had to put his foot up against the tree to wedge the machete loose. He had to yank it all to hell, and Tony backed away a few more steps, because Ryder was in the middle of some kind of tantrum, was hacking at someone who wasn't there.

"Don't you ever get me in something like that again and then bug out, you hear me?" Ryder said, panting. He had the machete in his hand.

"Okay."

"I mean it."

"Okay."

Ryder turned once more and hacked at the tree. A piece of bark flew up, turned once in the air showing its white underside, then clicked twice as it rattled through a bush beside the tree.

Tony felt like Ryder and the dead woman who walked somehow made a pair. But he kept the thought to himself.

The way Barney understood it, a woman named Mrs. Grace Corposaro called Art Giamoona down at the Coldbridge Police Station when her son, Anthony, also known as Tony, didn't come home from the Colbin College football game at a reasonable hour. She called Art specifically because he was Italian and she knew his family through Art's aunt, one Tilly Jo Semina, with whom Grace Corposaro played bingo on alternating Tuesday nights over at St. Thomas Aquinas in Dover. Tilly frequently bragged about Art, informing Grace that if she ever needed anything done—policewise— she shouldn't hesitate to call her big-wheel nephew Art Giamoona. Mention a name, get an answer, that was Tilly Jo's motto.

So on this early Saturday evening, when Anthony didn't show up for dinner, didn't call to check in . . . when all her phone calls to Anthony's usual pals turned up nothing, she had decided to call Art Giamoona. She was alarmed, but also collected, according to the report Barney eventually received. She was insistent that this situation did not fit her son's pattern of behavior. Tony wasn't the type of kid to ignore curfew; they had made no arrangement about him going to a movie, or skipping dinner; Tony was a fairly studious boy who kept to regular routines, one of which was to watch reruns of his favorite TV program, *Kung-fu*, while eating hot dogs and Cape Cod chips every Saturday evening.

Naturally Art Giamoona wasn't in the one time Grace Corposaro decided to use her bingo connection. He was, Barney seemed to recall, over at Seabrook playing the dogs. As a result the phone call was passed on to Henry Camp, the same man who had let Barney into Damian Peule's holding cell earlier in the afternoon. Henry Camp had taken the information from Grace Corposaro, said he would send somebody over, then called the college security office to see if they had any poop on the kid. In a final little bend of authority and happenstance, Barney was back on duty after taking Seth home to Matty. He always worked Saturday nights, because that was when the frat brothers howled. That was when the local tavern, the Mule Barn, took in five or six fake I.D.'s. And that was when chances were highest that some homesick freshman would decide he couldn't hack it any longer and went to sleep with three quaaludes and two six packs pumping the long sleep into his bloodstream.

That kind of thing.

When Henry's call came in, Barney took it and told Henry he would swing by the Corposaro home himself. He agreed to do so for two reasons: first, he knew the campus better than the police, and therefore might be able to track the kid better. Second, Art Giamoona was a friend and the story of this kid had a tingle about it.

It was too early to know if it was the same kind of tingle as the one surrounding the girl at Potter's Bridge, the same kind of tingle humming around the lady with her arm down the garbage disposal, but as he rode over toward the Corposaro's house on Dunbarton Road he found himself oddly reluctant to arrive. Not that he lallygagged or stopped to shoot the breeze with anyone, but he also didn't hit the accelerator on the straight sections of roads. He didn't proceed with any sense of urgency, which was probably unfair to Mrs. Grace Corposaro, inconsiderate of a mother's feeling for her son, but right now he didn't like the kid's odds, because the football stadium abutted the woods, and it would be natural for kids to wander in the woods, maybe work their way down to a stream or hollow, maybe even to a woodland fort, and in those woods . . . The woods are scareyy dark and deepp, Barney remembered Jam saying.

He finally swung into the Corposaro's driveway and parked behind a green Mazda pick-up. There was another car—a VW Golf—beside the pick-up. On his way up the front porch he passed a small statue of the Virgin Mary. She stood in her own bandshell directly under a bay window surrounded by pots of mums covered with shiny tinfoil. Beyond the mums, in a semicircle around the Virgin statue, someone had scattered scraps of bread. It took Barney a second to understand. Cast your bread upon the waters. Someone was calling Tony back by placating the Virgin, someone was making an offering.

Mrs. Corposaro had the door open by the time he climbed the three slate steps at the end of the walk. She was dressed in a cardigan sweater and black pants, a white blouse and a large crucifix. Her hair was pulled back into a ponytail, a style somewhat too youthful for her face.

"Mrs. Corposaro?"

"Yes. Are you Arty?"

"No, Art is out this evening. I'm Captain Len Barney. I'm in charge of campus security."

"I called the police."

"I understand, but in cases around the college our force has a better understanding of the campus, where the boy . . . Tony . . . might have gone. Believe me, we will be every bit as thorough as the police."

She didn't like this. He could almost see her calculating taxes, wondering what in the world she had been paying for all these years if the one time she needed something back from the City of Coldbridge it couldn't send its police force. Watching her, Barney wanted to say that he understood, that he could see her point, but really he was the man for the job.

She pushed the door a little wider and let him step inside, then led him into the kitchen. No welcome, please sit down or follow me. She went into the kitchen, pointed to the kitchen table, then poured two cups of coffee. Barney sat in a captain's chair across from what was obviously her command center. The phone was pulled onto the table beside an open address book. There was also a yellow pad of paper with names checked off. The woman, Barney realized, was worried, but she was not being stupid.

She handed him a cup of coffee, pointed to the cream and sugar already stationed on the table, then sat down at her command center.

"He should be home by now," Mrs. Corposaro said.

"He went to the game at what time, Mrs. Corposaro?"

"Oh, two or three o'clock. I don't remember exactly. It's just up on the campus. Well, you know where it is."

"Did he go with anyone? Any of his friends?"

"He went with Jimmy Ryder. I called Mrs. Ryder. Jimmy's not home but she doesn't seem worried. Jimmy has a freer leash, if you understand me."

"I do."

"I called Tony's friends. The ones I could think of. I called Mrs. Ryder and got a list of Jimmy's friends. No luck there, either."

"Did Tony play in the woods behind the stadium? Do you know the area?"

"He played down at Cooly's Stream. He and Jimmy were building a fort down there. I don't know where exactly. I told them a thousand times they were not to go into the woods."

Barney wanted to call Matt Bull, the ticket-taker out at the games. Maybe he had seen the kids. There was also a chance that Tony was having his first bender, slopping down beer, maybe smoking a little grass, because kids these days started early, started at the tag end of elementary school. Maybe Tony had a snoot full and he was on his way home when he decided to sit down against a tree, maybe take a small snooze, and he had slept like Rip Van Winkle drunk on bowling and frothy ale.

He was about to ask Mrs. Corposaro if he could use the phone to call Matt Bull when he heard a door slam at the front of the house. He heard someone flicking the locks closed, and then he heard a chair dragging across the floor. Grace Corposaro was on her feet and started out into the hallway leading to the front door. But before either of them could make it out of the kitchen a young boy came running in, his hair matted and covered with grass seed and sticks, his clothes filthy.

"Tony!"

The boy didn't seem to hear. He didn't seem to see anything. His head kept twisting around, straining to watch the front door, looking, it seemed to Barney, as if he wanted to keep running.

"Tony!" Mrs. Corposaro said again. This time she managed to grab her son and hug him to her.

This boy had obviously been running for miles, and he could have arrived in no better place than in the capable arms of Grace Corposaro.

Goliath was on overload. The dog was rearing up against his lead, waving his paws in front of him. Goliath wanted inside the vault, but Lester didn't want to let him go.

Lester also didn't want to go himself. He stood beside his car, the lights pointing directly at the vault door, watching Captain Barney and about fifteen other men getting ready to open the door. They had their guns out and a few of the men had put bandanas over their noses. They looked, in the light, like a bunch of old time bank robbers getting ready to blow a safe.

"Easy," Lester said to Goliath.

But Goliath wasn't going to be easy, that was the whole point of training him with Suds Peterson over in Portsmouth. Flick had been an easy dog and Lester didn't have to think long to know where that got her. So instead of telling Goliath to be easy again, he bent down next to him and whispered in his ear.

"You kill when you smell that, you hear me? You sick 'em, boy, because that's a dead smell."

Goliath whined, yanked harder against the leash, and scraped his paws in the mulchy dirt.

Lester saw Barney wave that it was time. At Barney's signal he pulled Goliath back behind his car and drew his own gun. He watched Barney get a good hold on the door, his legs wide, his weight back. The men, seeing the captain ready to spring the door, fanned out. They had their instructions, fan out and keep low, don't shoot if you can help it.

"Ready?" Captain Barney shouted.

No one answered. They were as ready as they were going to be. Lester raised his gun. He saw cops all around him raise theirs, each sighting in on the vault door. There was a guy laying on the ground; another, brave if not too smart, was up on top of the vault ready to shoot straight down at whatever came out. The guy was set up for a cross-fire.

Lester heard the door begin to open, the hinges braying and rasping. Barney started running as soon as the door gained momentum. He ran to one side, leaving the cops a straight shot at the interior of the vault.

"Oh Jesus," Lester said when he saw the inside of the door.

A human head was riding the door.

A human head nailed up to the top beam. It was nailed by the ears, like a doorknocker, so that the shake of the door made it appear to be nodding. Made it appear to be saying hello, grinning and nodding. There was no telling if it was a man's or a woman's head, it was just a hairy hunk of flesh nailed up there.

Before Lester or anyone else could say anything, there was a shot. Someone shouted to stop. The shot kicked the door back, slammed it against the bunker, giving the head a faster ride. It swung shut with the door, then bounced again out toward them. As the door shook from the impact the head came back to them, dancing, shaking. It rattled against the door until one ear gave, or the nail slid away, and the head swung down, the skull rasping against the metal.

"Stop!" someone yelled, at the head more than anybody with a trigger finger.

But the head hung there, shaking gently, the skull pattering lightly on the door behind it. It hung there looking at them sideways, looking at them as if it wondered why they had come so late.

He was thinking of Seth in his pajamas. Seth's hair, especially around his ears, would be wet from his bath. The kid had a game he played in the tub. He sat in the water for a half hour, plastic coffee scoops floating around him, trying to sink the scoops by bombing marbles at them. It was some sort of navy game, a game that really—Barney wasn't just being a proud dad, he didn't feel—was almost too sophisticated for a kid Seth's age to invent. So Seth would plunk away in the tub and the upstairs would smell like steam and powder, maybe a tinge of perfume, and Matty would be combing out her hair getting ready for bed. It would be quiet and calm, peaceful, just lamps on now, and his family's skin would be tan and soft, the color of healthy boots worn quietly and well through two or three winters.

That was what Barney was thinking about.

Because the task at hand was a stroll into the vault, and that did not bear thinking about. Better by far to let the mind wander. Better to let it search for a happier tune, because this particular dance number was becoming too much.

"Okay," an officer near him said. "We're all ready."

Barney nodded. He told himself to buck up, to square his shoulders. A generator hummed to provide light, and some G.I. cop had pumped a gas canister into the vault to chase the killer out, and the smell of the gas and the body parts had turned the graveyard into a strip of the New Jersey Meadowlands.

And no matter what he did, no matter where he looked, his eyes eventually returned to the head hanging on the door.

"All right everyone, stand ready. I don't think anyone could stay in there with the gas, but be ready."

This from a heavyset cop named Wilbur Chase, a detective from over in Henniker. He was in charge, a chubby Wasp, the kind who wore neckties with little figures of dinosaurs or a miniature map of Martha's Vineyard on them.

"Captain Barney?" Wilbur said near him.

"Okay," Barney said, testing his voice.

"We'll go in, take a look, and then let the teams in. We've got a mobile lab from Concord on the way."

"Okay."

Just the two of them. Gunfighters, only Barney didn't have a gun. He had a walkie-talkie at his side, a notebook, nothing else. That was probably okay, because Wilbur drew a gun that looked to be about three feet long. Wilbur stuck it in front of himself, waist high.

"I'll go in first. Not that I expect anything," Wilbur said.

"Okay."

Wilbur led the way across their half-circle of lights and cop shadows toward the vault. The vault was wide open, a hinge apparently sprung, the door dangling back and away. The head still stuck to the door, but only one ear held it, and that ear, it occurred to Barney, stretched like a played-out washer.

"One crazy son of a bitch, huh? To hang a head like that?" Wilbur said.

Barney nodded. He didn't trust his voice anymore. His stomach felt like it was glued to his ribcage. Every breath brought a flutter down under his belt.

"Anyone in there . . . come out now," Wilbur shouted when they were finally close to the door. He held his gun out.

The head was just a few feet away now. It was flyblown, old. The eyes were gone; the lips were retracted back so that the gums were bared.

Barney stepped into the smell. A little of the gas remained in the vault so that his eyes began to sting and water. He saw there was no lady really, just a scalp hanging from a beam in the ceiling, a scalp pinned to a styrofoam head pale white.

Like a moon.

"Christ," Wilbur said.

Six styrofoam heads hung from the bowed rafters of the vault. *Six.* He could account for two. Where did the other four come from? Each was made-up with eye shadow, lipstick, and rouge. Each was topped with a female scalp.

Not all the scalps looked dry.

Wilbur said, "You think this guy wears these things? See that big mirror over there? You think he tried them on like wigs?"

Barney nodded. That made sense, that tied it together. The strangeness of it was, Barney suddenly felt tremendously sad. He felt sad for the dead women, felt sad for the person whose head hung on the door, but he also felt sad for the sick creep who had brought them there. He saw a kerosene lantern set up on a stump of pine. A smaller pine stump had been arranged beside it for a stool. It was just what that psychology professor had predicted. This was a playroom, a dress-up room, and the sad sick character came here and *sat* with the dead people. Sat in a hole under the ground, putting on lady's hair sometimes, sometimes just sitting by himself at his little Alice-in-Wonderland tea table, talking with his friends.

Wilbur poked the head hanging on the rear wall. She swung slightly, turning and curling from a natural list in the way the scalp had dried. Her hair was knotted to hang over a flat-headed spike hammered into an overhead beam.

"I've seen enough," Wilbur said.

Barney followed Wilbur out. He stepped into the lights, consciously bellying around the door and the head. He tried to take even breaths. Wilbur said something like "all clear" to some of the cops, who came to meet them. Barney didn't say anything.

CHAPTER SIX

HERE, KITTY

PRESIDENT MATHEWS'S BACK HURT. IT HURT LIKE HOLY hell. He suspected it was a disc, but an MRI test had come up blank. No soft tissue problems, no rupture, no skeletal irregularities except for a slight scoliosis. He had spent six hundred dollars the day before, had walked around in a hospital johnny for two hours, had allowed himself to be shoveled into a tube to be microwaved, all in order to find out that he had undiagnosable back pain. Nothing there, Doc Sacks had told him. Don't see a thing. We'll keep you on muscle relaxers, see how you do on those.

His back was killing him. That's how he was doing on those.

Which was only part of the problem. His main problem, right at this moment, was trying to wheel his kneeling chair into the board room. The damn thing spun whenever he thought he had it going in the right direction. Naturally he couldn't bend over and carry the chair in like a normal human being. He couldn't risk picking up something that must have weighed all of fifteen pounds. As a result, he corralled the chair forward, shoving it with his feet, herding it closer and closer to the door.

He had the chair halfway into the board room when he saw Captain Len Barney. Barney already sat at the table, a file folder opened in front of him. President Mathews knew the contents of the folder, he carried a duplicate copy under his own right arm. The title was stencilled across the cover: "Security Report on Potter's Bridge Incident."

"Barney . . . could you?" President Mathews began.

"Certainly," Barney said.

It was humiliating to stand by and watch Barney carry the chair in for him. He might have said something, might have tried to make a joke, but then he caught a good look at Barney. The man looked sick. The man looked positively cadaverous. His cheeks were drawn, his eyes rimmed and worn out. When he smiled, his lips pulled back a tad too far.

"Thank you, Barney," President Mathews said, still looking at the captain.

"No problem."

"Are you feeling all right, Barney? You look exhausted."

"A little tired, is all."

"No, I mean it. You're putting in too many hours on this thing."

"It's got me going, it's true," Barney said, returning to his place at the table.

President Mathews knelt carefully on the chair. It was a chair made in Sweden or some Scandinavian country. He had ordered it out of a catalog, hoping it would bring him some relief. But now, as he slowly settled his weight on his knees, he felt his backbone grinding.

He ignored it as well as he could and opened the file in front of him. It reminded him, for some strange reason, of opening a menu. He even felt a momentary yearning for Chinese food. Beef lo mein, maybe a side of spring rolls with Chinese mustard, no, make it horseradish . . . anything hot enough to distract him from the pain in his back. He wondered, at the same time, how he was going to hop up from his kneeling chair when the members of the board started to arrive. Couldn't show them any weakness. Couldn't show them the president of Colbin College had to ask his wife Agnes to tie his shoes in the morning.

The only man squarely on his side was Barney. And Barney looked like a fellow shacking up with two licentious seventeen-year-olds. He looked at Barney.

"It's not my business . . . but are you getting enough sleep, Barney?" he asked.

"I look that bad?"

"You look haggard."

"I've been pretty flat out," said Barney.

"Well, you're not going to help anyone that way. No use getting sick yourself."

Barney nodded. President Mathews nodded. President Mathews also felt his backbone slip and tip a nerve. The nerve sent a message down his leg and back up again. President Mathews smiled, smiled wide, because it was either smile or shout.

"I wanted to get everything prepared for the meeting. We have the tests back from the vault," Barney said.

"And?"

It wasn't much of a response, Mathews thought, to give a man who had obviously been working himself to death on the school's behalf, but the pain had cracked into his jaws, into his neck and shoulders so that he could barely speak. He considered taking two of the pills Doc Sacks had prescribed but that would involve movement. At the moment he had to be perfectly still.

"Where do you want me to begin? Do you want me to wait for the rest of the board?" Barney asked.

"No, you might as well tell me now."

"I should tell you first of all that the state is thinking of asking the F.B.I. to come in. The F.B.I. has a task force for this kind of thing. They do a psychological profile from the facts, the way the women were killed, and so on."

"Admissions will die if we have the F.B.I. floating around the campus."

"I know."

"All right, so tell me what the results said."

"Well, one of the scalps belongs to Toni Glennon, the girl killed under Potter's Bridge. The freshest scalp is from the prostitute who lives in town. Ms. Fizz, the one I told you about."

"The blow-job lady?" Mathews was no prude.

"Right. There are four more, all of them on those styrofoam heads I told you about. Make-up, the hair combed neatly, the cap of skin still in place. The state lab says the other four scalps are at least four-years-old, maybe older. They seem to think the fellow has been in the business for a while."

"Here at Colbin?"

"They don't know. They're testing soil samples to see if the dirt and dust in the hair is consistent with the dirt near the vault. It's possible the guy brought the scalps with him from somewhere else. Maybe he stays until things start to heat up, then moves on."

President Mathews tried and failed to find a comfortable position on the kneeling chair. "What else?"

"They're putting a bulletin out for any scalping victims. They also found one corpse buried in the floor of the vault. It was a woman's body, decapitated, badly decomposed. The head was hung on the door. They don't know why that particular head. They don't know why he hung the head up. Some of the lab guys were guessing that that was his first victim. He killed her before he really understood what he wanted from her. He got into the scalping a little later."

"So he's been here at least for . . . ?"

"At least a year, if not longer. He's not stupid, whatever else he might be. When the state troopers searched the immediate vicinity they found a number of booby traps. The kids who found the vault were plain dumb lucky they didn't stumble into one. He had trip-wires set up to warn him if someone was approaching. He also had three pits set up with fake surfaces. Step on them, you go down onto some stakes. He has sort of a siege mentality."

"Go back for a second. The head on the door is the oldest, then?"

"Apparently."

"And he was just wearing the scalps, is that it? Playing dress up?"

"They don't know. He ate meals there. He could probably make tea. There was a terrible stench down in the vault. What some of the lab guys believe is that the body, the first body, was sometimes pulled out of the ground."

"Are you *serious?*"

"The soil wasn't packed solid, if you know what I mean. The grave wasn't deep. One of the guys at the lab was saying he had heard of something like this once. A guy buried his fiancée in his basement but couldn't stand to think of her down in the ground, kept pulling her up, then the smell got bad and he put her down again. I'm going to see Farley Simon—the psychology professor here on campus—a little later to see if he has anything to add."

"Christ almighty, it's grizzly."

"The state wants to talk to you about bringing in the F.B.I."

"Do we have a choice?"

"Not really. Not once they decide to act. Maybe you can stall them but eventually they'll start their own investigation."

Before Mathews could ask anymore he heard his secretary, Mrs. Krebs, leading a board member through the outer office. He heard her laughing and heard a deeper male voice.

"Keep on it. Keep me posted on anything that comes up," Mathews told Barney.

Mathews tried to stand. He had to use the table to hoist himself to his feet. He managed to let the grimace that crossed his face turn slowly to a smile when he greeted John Aureback, the first member of the board to arrive.

George Denkin carried a book bag when he fell in behind Zelda Fitzgibbon as she walked through town. He wore jeans and Timberlane boots, a flannel shirt and a burgundy windbreaker. He looked, he felt, exactly like a student.

Zelda Fitzgibbon was only five or six yards in front of him. Other people crowded the street, he hardly noticed them.

He followed her on her morning errands. She stopped first at the CVS pharmacy. He went inside with her and watched as she bought cotton puffs, Vaseline skin conditioner, and a tube of lip balm. For himself he selected a pack of Dentyne and a box of cough drops. He stood directly behind her in the check-out line. He paid for his purchases as she propped her bag on her right thigh and shoved the purchases inside.

"Either I need a bigger purse or less books or something," she said to the counter clerk, or maybe to him, or maybe to herself.

He didn't want to talk to her.

He never wanted to talk to them until he was certain of their answers. Then he talked their ear off.

He paid and went out of the CVS ahead of her. He bent down near a parking meter and untied his shoe. It was an obvious dodge, but he did not believe she would be thinking in that way. They never did. That was one of the intriguing things. They could be walking beside him and not know.

He heard the pharmacy door open and turned after counting to five. She walked north along the street, stopping before she had gone twenty feet to check a window. He finished tying his shoe, then hoisted his bag and followed her. He walked carefully, pretending as he went to be looking across to the other side of the street. He wanted her to imagine he was searching for someone. He did not want her to see his eyes, because that sometimes sent them away.

She went into Clay's Stationery. It was a card shop mostly, and he hesitated in the street outside, wondering what he could buy that would make sense. If she ran into him again in this second store she might get nervous. The whole town was nervous anyway. He knew that. It was not safe for him any longer, not since they took away his things. He would have to move, but first he needed something wet with which to start the new beauty shop. That was why he followed her.

On the spur of the moment he decided to cross the street and wait for her to emerge from Clay's. It turned out to be a good decision, because when she came out four minutes later she crossed the street herself, her book bag over her right shoulder. A pad of paper stuck out the zipper of her book bag. She walked with wide steps, walked as if she were finished with her morning errands.

He followed her, keeping a good twenty yards behind.

He watched her hair as she walked. It bounced and waved in the sunlight. She seemed to be in an excellent mood. She waved to someone, but he couldn't tell from his vantage point if the person returned the wave. He speeded up to be closer to her. She was heading back to her dorm, which was too bad. She was studious and tended to sit for long stretches in her room. He had seen her more than once up in her window, her hair hanging down to cover her face as she bent over her books.

A few Saturdays before, when he had phoned from the floor above her, he had watched her for an hour before finally deciding to try it. She had made it back inside her room just in time. He had returned to his position outside the dorm and watched her block off her room door, protecting herself from him while he stood and observed her. It had been an exciting and involving episode.

This morning, however, luck was with him. She no sooner went inside Sheppard than she stepped back outside without her book bag. In fact she reappeared so quickly that it almost forced him to speak to her. She looked around, zipping up her jacket before she began walking, and her eyes came dangerously close to meeting his own. She smiled anyway. He was fairly certain, at least, that she smiled. He could not be positive that she had smiled because he kept his eyes down. He had no option but to continue walking, acting as if he had business in Sheppard himself. To veer off at this point, to pretend he had forgotten something, would have been transparent.

As a result, he passed within a foot of her. He shifted his book bag and tried to appear preoccupied. He continued looking down at the ground as he pushed through the outside door, at which point he turned slightly and allowed himself to glance back at her.

She was walking, hurrying along toward the north. It did not take him a moment to decide where she was headed.

He knew her habits.

She was going to the barn.

Farley Simon stood in front of a tubby blue-and-white mailbox inspecting a brown envelope he was about to drop in the slot. The envelope was addressed by his own hand in careful block letters. The stamps were perfectly squared with the corner of the envelope. Farley had made certain there could be no question about the sender's state of mind. The precision of the envelope—and the article inside, Farley reminded himself—represented an effort by someone experiencing a psychological moment of achievement and well-being.

A moment, in other words, ripe for publication.

That was what the envelope suggested as it slid down the throat of the mailbox. It was regrettable, Farley felt, that his was not a performing art. He looked up from the mailbox and saw no one. Not another person on the street, not one living creature to applaud the exhaustive research that had gone into the article. In fact, the whole thing had been done with what almost amounted to deliberate secrecy. He had directed the manuscript to Harry Nell, a fellow psychologist and former classmate, who now worked in New York City at the Truman Clinic. Harry had promised to pass the manuscript along to Barry Sauer, a contributing editor at *Vanity Fair*, who would in turn assess the manuscript, then decide if it was worthy of being passed along to his own friend, Sharon Fey, who was currently the articles editor for *Psychology Today*.

But applause or not, Farley Simon felt restored. He felt like a man whose profession was suddenly exciting to him once more. He slapped the side of the mailbox with his gloved hand, then, on impulse, stepped to one side and gave the box a solid kick in the flank. The box made a hollow grunt.

"Go," he said to the manuscript inside the box.

For the hell of it, he kicked the box again.

That might have been one too much, because he spotted a security officer walking toward him. The officer had appeared from the Hampshire House, had come quietly down the walkway, and had caught him booting the mail-box.

"You lose something, Professor?" the officer asked.

"No, just the opposite."

Farley Simon pulled his overcoat around him. It was a camel hair overcoat, quite a good one in fact, and Farley felt it made him look competent, even successful. He was conscious, furthermore, of ruffling himself like a grouse to prepare for a reprimand from a security officer, when he realized the officer was none other than Len Barney.

At least he thought it was Len Barney. If it was Len Barney, the man who had come to his office several weeks before, something had been at the man's soul. Len Barney looked gaunt and sharp-cheeked. His eyes looked empty and his lips were thin and undernourished.

"Captain Barney?" Farley said.

"How are you, Professor? Something stuck in the mail-box?"

"No, actually I was kicking the thing for luck. I'm sending off a manuscript. A kick for luck."

To Farley's surprise, Barney stopped near the box and kicked it himself. He kicked it hard, harder than Farley had. The box grunted again and some mail apparently slid into a more solid pile in its stomach.

"Double luck then," Barney said, smiling.

It was an effort for the man to smile. Farley was astonished at the transformation in the captain.

"I was wondering if you had a moment, Professor? I was on my way to see you. Are you going anyplace special? Perhaps I could walk you?"

"Actually I was thinking of having a drink. I'm finished for the Thanksgiving break. I'll buy you one if you like."

"Maybe I'll just walk along with you, if that's okay. Can't drink on duty."

"Not even coffee?" Farley began walking, not sure the captain intended to join him. Apparently the captain wasn't certain himself, because he waited a moment before he left the mailbox.

"You look tired," Farley said when the captain was along-side him.

"I am. This campus killer thing has me going."

"Terrible, what I read about it. You found the fellow's playroom, didn't you?"

"Yes, I guess we did. You were right about that."

Farley knew where the conversation was headed, but he didn't feel like discussing murder and social deviants five minutes after sending out his manuscript. He stopped. They were on Hudson Street, still two blocks from the center of Coldbridge. There was no point, after all, in making the captain accompany him to Molly's Luncheonette.

You poor bastard, he thought, looking at the man. You've got a bone in your throat and you can't choke it down or cough it up.

"Ask your questions, Captain," Farley said. "I'll answer what I can."

"I hate to bother you."

"But you're going to anyway. So fire away."

"I want to know now that we have his playroom, if maybe he's done here. Do you think that means he's—?"

"He's left?"

"Left or stopped?"

"He won't stop. He might have left. These people are often transient. Ted Bundy was from Oregon, wasn't he? Eventually caught in Florida. It's hard to predict their movement."

"And if he stayed here?"

"Well, that's difficult to say. You found his playroom, so for a time, at any rate, he's dislocated. Disenfranchised, I guess is the word. Maybe he'll try to reestablish a room somewhere. If he's schizophrenic, perhaps he's in remission. Maybe he's on some medication. He probably isn't stupid, so he knows the authorities are after him. I'm just guessing, at best speculating on all this, Captain. Exams are coming up. He might even be studying if he's a student."

"Would he care about his grades?"

"Who knows? If you're asking me if it's safe to assume he's gone, I can't reassure you. He might be right where he's always been."

"I see."

"I'm not an expert, Captain. I told you that."

"I'm just checking however I can. And you were right about the playroom."

Farley continued watching the man. They weren't at the bottom yet. Farley didn't know what the bottom might be, but he was certain they hadn't arrived. He decided to wait, to shut up, because the easiest thing to do in a situation like this was to talk all over the man. To protect yourself by talking, because if you decided to listen instead he could possibly come up with something you weren't going to like.

"The guy scalps his victims," Barney was saying. "He had six styrofoam heads, you know the kind, hanging from the rafters of the burial vault. The kids said the heads were moons and I know what they meant. Each of the styrofoam heads was made up to look like a woman. Eyeliner, lipstick, all that. The scalps were pinned to the heads. The hair was combed, too. We can't identify for sure any of the scalps except the one from under Potter's Bridge—she's got an ear missing—and the other one, the one from the prostitute. He had a head nailed to the door that must have been, they aren't sure about these things, five- or six-years-old. We have no idea where that came from. It seemed like sort of the gargoyle for his little cathedral."

"I wouldn't be surprised to find one was his mother's," Professor Simon said, thinking aloud.

"Are you kidding?"

"Just a guess. Maybe not his mother, but someone who reminds him of his mother. A substitute figure."

Captain Barney stopped. His breath made short puffs in the air. The snow fell a little harder.

"Do you think he carries them around?" Barney asked a moment later. "Goes to a place, commits a murder, scalps the woman, then adds it to his collection? Something like that?"

"Maybe. It would be difficult to kill six women without arousing suspicion. Any idea what he does with the scalps?"

"He had a big mirror in the corner of the vault. Must have been a job getting it to the vault. The roads are all grown over, so he must have carried the thing. But I wanted to ask you about something else. Some of the state investigation team think that he buries this same body over and over. Puts it underground, then pulls it back up. Have you ever heard of anything like that?"

"Well, yes. It's called the Pygmalion syndrome. It's more common than you might think. Pygmalion went to Hades to bring back what was her name? It starts with an E-u-r . . . it doesn't matter. He went to Hades to retrieve her when she was taken from him. He was allowed to bring her back to earth, and life, if he didn't look back at her to make sure she was following. Do you remember the story?"

"I don't think so."

"Anyway, it's a fancy name for an abberation. Hamlet jumps in Ophelia's grave. Romeo goes to the Capulet vault to join Juliet. Nowadays an Irish mother might throw herself on her darling son. Its roots are simple enough. The remaining loved ones can't bring themselves to say goodbye to the parted. Sometimes it can grow to macabre proportions. Necrophilia, love of the dead. It can turn sexual because sex is the vital force. The person may believe he can actually— I don't know how else to put this, Captain Barney—can actually screw the dead person back to life."

"So he's pulling the body out to have sex with it?"

"I have no idea. I'm just throwing out theories. You're going to have to see if one fits."

Barney's eyes were watery. The notion of the killer sitting in a dark burial vault trying on hair got to the captain. It was disgusting to any sane human being, but Farley knew this particular deviance climbed right down Barney's pajamas.

"Why? I mean, I know you don't have all the answers, Professor, or the motives for this kind of thing, but it seems so damn crazy."

"Not to mention perverse," Farley said.

Farley looked at the snow again. He wanted a drink. He wanted to sit in Molly's Luncheonette, drink a warm buttered-rum, and perhaps bum a cigarette or two from Molly's bar pack. He didn't know what Barney wanted. Or rather, he knew what he wanted—he wanted reassurance, wholesomeness, cleanliness. He wanted to know why the murderer happened to turn over this particular stone. Why anyone wanted to glimpse all the lizards and beetles, and the roots turned white from lack of sun.

"I don't have the answer, Captain. No one really does. Some babies are born without arms, some without a nervous system. I don't know why that happens either . . . I'll give you something else to think about. Maybe he didn't kill them all. Maybe he dug some of them up."

"Are you serious?"

Farley shrugged. He needed a drink. He waited a second more to let Barney absorb this last notion. When the captain spoke again his voice was barely audible.

"What will he do now?"

"Find more scalps, Captain. That's probably what he'll do."

Zelda Fitzgibbon fitted her key into the door of the barn. She turned the key until she heard the lock click. It clicked smoothly because Mr. Kim paid attention to such things. It left no doubt about being open.

The large wooden doors moved easily as well. The right-hand portion slid open on its runner, gliding as she pushed it aside. She walked the left-hand portion of the door to the wall and made sure it was willing to stay in place. On a better day, on a day with stronger light, the open doors would have let in a fine square of sunshine. But it was cloudy and cold. The weather report called for snow, the first of the season, and as she stood in the doorway she felt a brisk wind at her back.

She took two steps into the barn.

"Mr. Kim?"

No answer, but that was okay. He was gone, she knew, to a conference in Brattleboro, Vermont. He had gone to hear a paper on Lyme disease, which was the hot new topic, the topic everyone wanted to hear about. "Deer Ticks and the Threat to Humans," was the title of one of the papers being read at the conference. Mr. Kim himself had not been particularly excited to go but he was part of the biology department, a shuttle van was chartered, and it was his professional duty. So he had gone, arranging with Zelda to check the animals in mid-afternoon, his conscience, she understood, made lighter by the fact of her dependability. Charlie Summers would be in at six to put the animals to bed. Until then, she was in charge.

"Mr. Kim?" she called again.

There was no need to call, actually, because Mr. Kim was not the sort of man to change plans at the last minute. She knew that. But it was reassuring to check the barn with her voice, to give him a chance to answer in case he had returned unexpectedly.

"Not here," she said out loud.

It felt surprisingly good to hear the sound of her own voice. The barn was isolated. She had noticed this, as if for the first time, as she walked to it through the quiet afternoon. The barn was set back off Dunbarton Road, set back maybe a fifth of a mile, and there was nothing at all behind it except pine trees and hard woods and the neglected fields that now served as pasture for the mare and Jaspar. In the afternoon light the barn had resembled a New Hampshire homestead, a stark white structure looking out on what must have been miles of unmarked fields and streams and small dirt roads. All it had lacked was an accompanying farm house, a curl of smoke rising out of its chimney and a farmer standing outside cutting firewood.

The wind came up behind her once more, and she stepped farther inside to be away from it. It was warmer away from the door, but by no means snug. The barn was hardly airtight, and as she moved down the center aisle, watching the animals lift their heads as she passed, she saw their breath spout out in expectant vapors. A draft came from high up in the barn, sifting through the cracks and chinks and falling on the animals from above. A few of the beams in the barn roof were already coated with bone-white frost.

"Hello, everyone," she said to the animals.

It felt good to have the company of the animals, to have their attention. The animals were friends and companions, and they made the barn seem less isolated. She turned at the rear wall and looked back through the barn. The door was a square of light, an almost perfect square, and outside the sky was getting darker. She squinted to see the air beyond, squinted to see the pine trees, because if the snow began to fall she expected to see it first against the green fir boughs.

"You smell it, don't you?" she asked the animals. "Snow's coming."

She sat on the small bench at the rear of the barn and pulled on her muck boots. Then she lifted a pitchfork and walked back up the center aisle. Jaspar the Fighting Mule put his head over the edge of his stall. She stopped in front of him, put the pitchfork against the railing, then scratched between his eyes. He opened his nostrils wide, flicked his head slightly and tried to nibble her sleeve.

"You're a bad boy," she said, rubbing him harder.

She looked again at the open barn door, her hand slowing on Jaspar's head. And it was probably her imagination, it must have been her imagination, but she felt Jaspar's head swing purposefully away from her hand. He moved gently, not alarmed, but he turned to follow her gaze, turned to see the barn door himself.

As he moved, his chin knocked against the top rung of his stall. She tried to find his head with her hand without turning from the door. He had moved slightly, leaning to his left, quartering to face the square of afternoon light and the barnyard and the right-hand portion of the barn door sliding closed.

"Easy," she said.

She didn't know if she spoke to Jaspar or to the door itself, because it continued closing, wobbling slightly on its tracks, shaking and rolling forward, cutting light inch by inch. The barn was becoming dimmer by half, by more than half, because the sun was low and to the southwest, and that meant it came in primarily through the right side, not the left. If someone wanted to cut off light that was indeed the proper door to close.

"Just the wind," she said.

She turned to look at Jaspar. His ears stood upright on his head. His right rear hoof lifted an inch from the floor, cocked slightly, almost as if he were nervous. Almost, she told herself, as if he wanted to run. But that was ridiculous, it was just nerves, except the other animals, the mare and

the pigs, had also gone quiet and the door was still sliding, still rolling on its runner. She had checked that door,
had made sure it was steady, and there was definitely an
explanation, certainly a logical explanation that would tie
up loose ends because doors didn't simply shudder closed
under their own power.

Not in Mr. Kim's barn. In Mr. Kim's barn things stayed
put. Locks worked, doors slid on greased runners, the floor
was swept daily, the oats were in a bag and you cleaned up
if you messed up, that was the rule.

But the door kept jiggling forward.

"Hello?" she called.

And that, after all, was probably not the best thing in
the world to do. It wasn't a great idea because her voice
sounded awfully small. It sounded, to her surprise, awfully
frightened, but it could be Charlie Summers arriving early,
could be another student coming to cover for Mr. Kim.

Or it could be Mr. Hotchkiss.

"Stop it," she whispered.

Her voice made Jaspar shake his head. She grabbed his
left ear in her hand and stroked it. She stroked it three
or four times, because Jaspar was a dear old pal, a good
chum, a heel-kicking, teeth-gnashing, fighting mule. And
she stroked his ear because the thing to do, of course,
was to walk to the barn door, check to see if anyone was
around, then block it open with a feed sack or a chunk of
wood. That was the sensible response, but the barn suddenly seemed darker, was darker, and the aisle between the
stalls appeared awfully exposed. It appeared, really, when
you thought about it, like a bowling alley or a dance floor
or the hallway in Sheppard when the fire door panted open
and there was no one there, not a soul.

"Hello?" she called again.

Just a little lilt in her voice. Just a little fright and curiosity mingled, not unlike the voice of, say, a woman alone
coming awake late at night to hear the tinkle of silverware
down in her dining room. Just a tad of worry coming in,
and she couldn't straighten it out, couldn't iron the thing
down. For a second she wanted her dad to grab her hand
and walk with her back to the overhanging tree, to use his

flashlight to inspect the branches, because there had really been nothing at all, no Mr. Hotchkiss, no crazy man asking her to step closer, just empty limbs and his flashlight sawing at the bark.

"Okay," she said, testing her voice.

She released Jaspar's ear and stepped to the center of the aisle, lifting the pitchfork in front of her. The pitchfork was heavy and tried to daub forward like a dousing wand. She hoisted it again, angling her elbow under it and against her waist for support. She kept her eyes on the left-hand portion of the door, squinting to see. The light there looked milky, looked like it was teased with snow.

She gripped the pitchfork tighter and started forward. The pigs grunted as she passed them. A draft suddenly caught her from above, slipping under her shirt and down her vest. She kept her eyes on the doorway, specifically on the left-hand portion because the light coming through it was welcome. The light coming through was very welcome, as a matter of fact, because the barn didn't have much in the way of electrical lights. Two small bulbs dangling on old cords, that was all she could recall at the moment. It was important that the left-hand side stay open because if that door started to close, then she'd be all alone in this barn and there wouldn't be any light except a few sunbeams way up near the roof.

She went up on her toes when she passed the mare, Charlotte. She tiptoed past the harness rack and an old mower blade. She bellied to her left, raising the pitchfork slightly higher. The pitchfork felt solid in her hands now. A tiny snag of adrenaline bumped into her blood stream, and she realized she was alone, the day was ending, and no one knew where she was except Mr. Kim and Charlie Summers. No one knew where she was except maybe Martha, who was doubtless already packing for her trip to Richie's over Thanksgiving.

The door was only six feet away now. A body length. She stopped and came down off her toes. It was snowing outside, just spitting, the clouds wisped into mares' tails. She looked at the closed section of door hoping to see some explanation, but there was nothing there, nothing unusual, so she stepped forward, drawing in her breath at the same time, squeezing the pitchfork in her hands.

Her momentum carried her through the door in one hearty gush, and she wheeled to her right, ready for anything, the snow sugar on her eyelashes. There was nothing there, nothing at all, and she nearly convinced herself of it, nearly lowered her pitchfork, when she happened to look at the ground. Even then she tried to talk herself into a rational explanation, because they were just tracks near the door, just imprints from someone in boots. And that could have been Mr. Kim, could have been anyone at all, since the tracks weren't necessarily fresh.

But the tracks went around the corner of the barn, back toward the manure piles. Back toward the rear of the barn, back to where a small door opened into Mr. Kim's office. Back, she noticed, to where Jaspar was now looking, his ears still high on his head.

Close the door.

That, Zelda figured, was far and away the best plan. Close the door from the outside, lock it, prop the pitchfork against the side of the building, then call it a day. Tell Mr. Kim, if he ever asked, that she had checked the animals, the animals were fine, and that she had been obliged to return to Sheppard Dorm in order to study for an exam, finish a paper, do the laundry, or all of the above.

Just close the door.

It really didn't matter what was going on. It wasn't her job to figure out if the tracks were left by Mr. Hotchkiss, or were actually old footprints that had been left during the fall rains by Mr. Kim or Charlie Summers. The tracks did look suspicious with snow outlining them, but it wasn't anything she could be sure about. She couldn't be positive one way or the other. Well, there was no way on earth she intended to go back inside the barn. Not today, not alone.

So it was simple.

Just close the door.

She could even feel her body straining to get started. The only problem was that to close the barn door meant putting down the pitchfork, sliding the right-hand portion closed, then locking it. She wasn't positive she could make her hands steady enough to fit the key to the lock. If she approached the door, if she fumbled at all, it would give him a chance to . . .

Forget the door, she told herself. Just buzz off.

But that advice was not altogether acceptable. For one thing, she wasn't sure she wasn't acting like a paranoid, or someone whose imagination was too active. For another thing, Mr. Kim would not be particularly pleased to return to find the barn open, the door unlocked, the animals untended. He would not be pleased to find Zelda Fitzgibbon, future veterinarian, scared off by a door that snuffled closed in a wind storm.

The natural compromise was to step briskly to the door, calmly walk the right-hand portion closed, fit the key to the lock, and walk away with the satisfaction that she had done her duty, had not panicked but had, instead, used proper caution. There were, after all, some very strange things going on around campus. She didn't have to be reminded of that.

She took two steps forward. She held the pitchfork in front of her, waist-high, and looked in at Jaspar. She could no longer see his head. He had probably returned to munching hay, which was a good sign, because Jaspar would not have been comfortable with a stranger in the barn. That meant the barn was empty, no one had come in the back after all . . . of course, she couldn't *see* the mule.

The door was only three steps away now. Two steps up, and one to the right in order to grab the heel of the door and begin walking it. Really, there was nothing to it, nothing at all, because the whole thing could have been her imagination. The whole thing could just be the nerves of a nervous young woman in a nervous barn working around nervous animals on a nervous campus. Get it done, that's what she had to do.

She took the steps, grabbed the door, and began to push. The door moved without a glitch. The dark wedge between the doors closed rapidly. Finally the two doors jolted together, springing apart a few inches after the impact, and that was that, it was over, all she had to do was lock it.

She hooked the handle of the pitchfork under her arm-
pit and dug in her jean pocket for the keys. She had the
keys out, had them in her hand, the pitchfork still more or
less under control, when she heard the barnyard go quiet.
It wasn't something she could point out, wasn't something
she could define precisely, but the barnyard was inexplic-
ably silent. Maybe it was the snow, because the flakes were
coming faster. The flakes were wet and soggy, and it was
one of those dark holy moments on a November afternoon
in New Hampshire where winter was breathing, fall was
over, and every sparrow under heaven stopped for just a
second or two in order to take stock.

Silence.

The odd part was, Zelda felt the silence working on her.
It was draining something away from her, some conviction
to keep moving. The door was still open and hands could
come out of doorways. Hands could easily come out of the
doorway, and she happened to be standing near the open
slot, the barn a dark roll of film between white doors.

She leaned the pitchfork against the door. At the same
time she heard Jaspar start. He stepped quickly across his
stall, his head looking first forward, then to the rear of the
barn, and a pig grunted and the mare nickered and something moved in the barn.

Something advanced, something started up the center
aisle, moving quickly. She couldn't see it, couldn't tell what
it was, but it was approaching. It hurried through the barn,
not running, but moving under control, moving with purpose, and it was Mr. Hotchkiss, it was him after all, it was
Mr. Hotchkiss stepping out of her bedroom closet to make
the dolls rattle. To make the bell tinkle on the clown hat
of BoBo the circus doll, who always sat closest to the closet and who always smiled and smiled and smiled. BoBo,
who was Mr. Hotchkiss's pal, Mr. Hotchkiss's familiar, Mr.
Hotchkiss's buddy. BoBo, who always smiled the most late
at night, when Mr. Hotchkiss started the clothes swaying in
the closet.

She tried to move calmly. She spread her arms and
pinched the doors closed. She had to hold them for a
second to make sure they were in position, but now she

heard steps on the plank floor inside the barn. Heard boots, or shoes, clumping down the center aisle, and Jaspar sighed, she could hear that, and the doors were finally settled.

The key, the key. It was simple to think it, hard to do, but she put the key near the lock and tried to guide it in. The steps were coming, they were probably even with the mare's stall, while the key glanced off the lock. Her hand shook, her hand jingled up and down, and she felt herself begin to cry, to grow cloudy, and she had to reach her free hand to the wrist of the hand that held the key and make it still.

Go in, go in, she whispered, but it wasn't easy. It wasn't simple at all, because the steps were there, just on the other side, and it was possible the doors weren't closed properly. It was possible the doors wouldn't just click into a locked position, possible she might have to lean against the doors and hold them tight, but Mr. Hotchkiss wouldn't permit that. Mr. Hotchkiss was just on the other side of the doors, she could feel him there, and BoBo was probably riding on his shoulder, spurring him on, because BoBo enjoyed a good ride, enjoyed a night out, enjoyed smiling when the moon hit him just right.

It was astonishing that the key finally went in. Astonishing that the lock actually clicked home, because the click also stopped the steps inside. The steps halted, disappeared, and it was all silent again, completely quiet, only now the barnyard was just a barnyard, the snow just snow, the afternoon just a Currier & Ives print.

George stood next to the barn door breathing carefully. An instant had just passed, only an instant, when he had considered throwing his weight against the door. He had heard her fumbling with the lock, praying to get the doors closed, and he had simply placed his cheek against the grainy wood of the door.

He smelled her through the door.

He smelled her fear and her perfume and her shampoo. He smelled her over the odors of the horse and pigs. He kept his cheek against the wood and listened while the key finally slid in, the tumblers clicked, and the doors settled once and for all. He waited for a moment to see what she would do next. She didn't do anything. She remained silent, her breathing somewhat ragged, but her attention focused inside. He knew her attention was focused on him because he felt it. It was a sharp, intelligent curiosity. It was badly colored by fear, true, but that only made it sharper.

He placed his gloved palm flat on the door and kept it there until he heard her moving off.

He let her go. There was no sense in trying to run through the barn, circle to the front, and attempt to catch her. Besides, he had had a moment of communication and it had stirred him. He put his wrist against his penis and realized, for the first time, that he had been hard most of the morning. He had been hard following her on her round of errands, and he had been hard now, particularly hard, in scuttling up the center aisle of the barn after her. This one was proving to be delicious. She was aware of him. That was satisfying. It was enough for now.

He walked back through the barn, careful to keep to the center aisle. He did not like animals. When he went through the small office at the rear of the building, he pushed open the back door. The smell of manure increased here; there were large stacks of the stuff, probably set aside for compost. He closed the door after him, careful to lock it even though it hadn't been locked when he arrived.

The snow was falling harder. That was a mild concern. He would leave tracks at least until he reached a major road. The black officer, the one he had seen the night he had killed Toni Glennon under Potter's Bridge, had another German shepherd. He had seen it around campus, more often than not barking its fool head off at a squirrel. Although it wasn't a scent hound, it possibly had been trained to trail. It made sense to get a decent head start.

He entered the woods directly from the rear barnyard. A small stone wall divided the pasture from the encroaching soft woods. He moved quickly, hopping the wall, then continuing straight east. Ten minutes travel in that direction could bring him to the vault, though that, of course, was out of the question. Instead he headed southwest, looking to intersect the trail that led back to the campus from

Cooly's Stream. He passed through a stand of birch, then
another of sugar maples. Finally he picked up pine trees,
spruce mostly, which were rapidly surrendering their green
to the softly falling snow.

It was in the middle of the pine that he saw the boy ahead
of him. He vaguely recognized him. The boy was sometimes around Coldbridge with a father who wore military
clothes. Skin-headed, both of them, the boy with funnels
on the side of his skull. He deliberately ignored the boy.
He scooped up a little snow and touched it to his tongue.
In lapping at the snow, he let his eyes look once down the
trail, catching the briefest glimpse of the boy as he ducked
out of sight.

George used the moment to check the trail. Snow-lined
footsteps flanked his own perhaps five or six feet to the
right of the trail. The boy was clever, George gave him that.
He had consciously stayed off the trail, so that he, George,
might not have noticed he was being watched. The boy was
also wise enough to remain ahead. If he had lagged behind,
then been spotted, George would have had a clear plan.

But this was more perplexing. Really, the boy had nothing on him, even if he could identify him. They were
only, George calculated, approximately a half mile from
Dunbarton Road. If he started to jog right now, gaining
on the boy little by little, the boy could still make it to
the road and safety in time. No, it was better, he thought
now, to continue on at a steady pace. Let the boy reveal his
intentions.

He continued walking at a regular pace. It took him
twenty minutes to reach Dunbarton. The boy, now that he
understood he had been spotted, had finally left his prints in
the trail. George followed the sneaker grids. The boy's feet
made a deeper impression near the toes. Running George
thought. The boy wasn't going to stay around to see if he
was being chased.

When George finally pushed through the last pine
branches and stepped onto the sidewalk running parallel to Dunbarton, the boy was gone. At least that was
his first thought. When he had a moment to adjust to
the street noise, however, he saw the boy watching him

again. This time the boy was even farther away, well on his way into town, but he had something up to his eyes. Binoculars, George guessed, although he couldn't catch a reflection from the lens.

George checked the traffic, saw the street was momentarily empty, then turned calmly to face the boy. He squared his shoulders, bent back from the waist, then reached down to his crotch. He squeezed and flexed farther back, jiggling his hand up and down at the boy.

The boy dropped the binoculars away from his eyes.

Then he ran.

Archie did not look like a murderer, not like a psychotic, and definitely not like a guy who wanted to dress up like a woman and run through the woods.

Archie looked like an accountant. Or rather, Barney figured, a future accountant. Right now he looked, for Barney's money, like a high school kid with an exceedingly large forehead. Archie was timid, and pudgy, and about as athletic as a bowling pin.

Which made it a long shot indeed that he had killed Jam Stiefken. Made it a long shot that he crept out at night and tiptoed into the vault. Made it a long shot because the guy wore his top button closed, wore a tie as a student, and wore a lonely, frightened look that said he was more concerned about exams than about any killer stalking the campus.

But someone had called his name in to the security division. They said he was peculiar. They said he was a weirdo. That made him a candidate.

Barney sat in one desk chair, Archie in the other. Archie had crossed and recrossed his legs four or five times. He was nervous, but that was to be expected when a security officer dropped into your room. Archie had been studying on a Monday afternoon a day before Thanksgiving break started. Not exactly the profile of a serial killer.

"So, you were saying," Barney said.

"I took the summer courses to give myself a leg up," Archie said.

"How so?"

"Well, if I can graduate in January instead of June I'll be ahead of my class and ahead of other applicants too."

There was more. There was Archie's life plan, for example. There was a lifetime of accounting they could discuss, but Barney wasn't in the mood. What he wanted to do instead was to go home, crawl onto the couch, maybe watch some ESPN hoop and take a snooze. Take a long winter's nap, because it was snowing outside. Because, let's face it, he told himself, he was getting nowhere. The campus was in a panic, the F.B.I. was making definite statements about setting up a temporary office in Coldbridge, and all he could think to do at the moment was interview Archie the future accountant.

But it wasn't easy to turn off Archie, because Archie was lonely. Archie roosted in his dorm room by himself, studied, went to meals, attended a few hockey games, and kept copious statistics on professional football. He kept wall charts, in fact, although he had already assured Barney that he never wagered on the outcome of any sporting event.

Outcome was Archie's word. So was the phrase, "sporting event."

"I see," Barney said when Archie finished telling him about his "leg up" on his classmates. Barney stood. Archie stood.

"Thank you for talking to me," Barney said.

"No, I mean, I understand. You have to check things out."

Barney shook the boy's hand, opened the door, and felt like he might faint. It wasn't a big thing, wasn't a swoon, but he felt decidedly weak. The hallway in front of him felt overheated. He closed the door on Archie, then walked carefully down the hall. He kept one hand on the wall to guide him, because he hadn't eaten all day and he was no closer to anything at all except his own fatigue and sense of futility.

Outside, he sat for a few minutes in the patrol car until he was steady, then drove cross-campus toward the office. The car smelled of Goliath, but he didn't particularly care at the moment. Mostly he wanted something to eat. He considered bellying out to the highway strip on the way to New Market, where he could pick up a Big Mac with a large fries and a vanilla milkshake. But someone—he couldn't remember who at the moment—had told him recently that the milkshakes at McDonald's were only one molecule away from being plastic. Not pretend plastic, not an aesthetic differentiation, but actually a liquid frisbee. One molecule, which sounded crazy, but he couldn't get the idea out of his mind.

His mind was so squarely centered on food that he almost missed the girl who was walking parallel to him on the other side of the road. He almost let her spin away into the wide snowflakes. He would have grouped her with the other students he saw hustling through the snow, if he hadn't seen her carrying a pitchfork.

For an instant he thought it was the scalp lady, dancing through the snow, carrying her own version of a broomstick. He even put his hand to the overhead beam and started to turn it on before he saw that it was, indeed, a young woman carrying a pitchfork. Eighteen or nineteen, walking down a well-populated sidewalk, carrying a pitchfork. It could be a prop for a sorority party, or a present for a boyfriend, or an antique. It didn't have to mean anything, nothing at all, except that he sensed that the girl was just on the edge of panic. Just on the end of a full-out, lung-splitting explosion. Just ready to run through downtown Coldbridge yelling, because her legs were pumping hard and she held the pitchfork out like a WWI soldier, with fixed bayonet, ready to dive into an enemy trench.

He pulled over and got out of the car. He felt dizzy once again and had to put his hand on the trunk to steady himself.

"Miss?"

Maybe it should have been Ms. This was 1991, after all. Never mind. She stopped. She squinted, then put her pitchfork down, tines sticking in the dirt.

"In the barn," she said.

"What? Are you okay?"

He raised his hand and stopped traffic while he crossed. It was a bit of a scene, what with the snow coming down, the lights of the cars throwing his outline onto the road, the few students who stopped to watch.

"My name is Captain Barney," he said, approaching her carefully.

"I think he was in the barn," she said.

"Who was?"

"I might be imagining it, but I had to lock the door and walk away. You understand."

"Who was in the barn?"

"The man who has been killing women on campus . . ."

Just that. The girl was a rock, or at least determined to be a rock. A flat statement that she had almost lost her life.

Despite her efforts, she was on edge. Barney felt it was possible she could lift the pitchfork and have at him. Not that it would be directed at him, but that it would be directed at the man in the barn, at the scalp lady, at something.

"Could you just drop the pitchfork, Miss?"

She let it fall, her hand simply dismissing it. The wooden handle bounced on the sidewalk. The tines chipped four narrow furrows in the dirt in front of her.

"Okay," he said.

"Okay," she said, and then began to cry.

Tony felt major-league bored. He had stayed home from school with an upset stomach. It had been fun in the morning, scrunching down in bed and knowing he didn't have to go to the last day of school before Thanksgiving break, but now he found it boring. He had been through three back issues of *Sports Illustrated*, the leftover Sunday comics, an old copy of the *Great Brain* by John D. Fitzgerald, exactly thirty-seven soap operas or talk shows, and one black-and-white movie about girls falling in love in Rome.

And it was only a little before six.

He smelled dinner cooking downstairs and felt his appetite kick in. His dad, he knew, would be home in about forty-five minutes. He was watching Popeye beat up Bluto when his mom called up the stairs.

"I'm going to run to the store. Do you need anything before I go?"

"No, Mom."

"I'll just be ten minutes. I'll be right back."

As soon as she was gone he walked into his parents' room and pulled out the Victoria's Secret Catalog from the stack of magazines and catalogs on the bedside table. The Victoria's Secret Catalog was the fifth one down, placed exactly between a *McCall's* and a Tweeds Catalog. He pulled the catalog out slowly, careful not to upset anything. He left the other magazines slightly crooked so that he could slip the catalog back to its proper position in an instant.

Right now, he wanted to look at page thirty-five. Because on page thirty-five the most beautiful woman in the world was dressed in black panties, a black teddy, and white garter belt. There were other pictures he liked almost as well—one on page twenty-two came to mind—but with only ten minutes to spare, page thirty-five was the hands-down winner.

So he sat on the edge of his parents' bed, opened the catalog, and thumbed through the pages. Page thirty-five popped open almost at once because it was situated near an order form. The order form was stiff and worked like a bookmark, so that he had only to rifle the pages once in order to be gazing down at a sandy blonde woman reclining on a luxurious bed. A sandy blonde woman in silk underwear. A sandy blonde woman in picture frame *F*, seventy-five dollars for the teddy, twenty-seven for the garters, thirteen for the panties. Every woman should have an outfit like this once in her life, the ad said.

That was when he heard the back door open downstairs.

Tony's first movement was to stand and push the catalog back into position five among the magazines on the bedside table. He moved so quickly, tried to get the whole thing perfect so fast, that he managed to smear the magazines across the table like a deck of cards fanning out. At the same time he heard a step on the kitchen floor. The sound made him stop and listen, because it did not make sense that anyone was home. No car had come up the driveway. It was too early for his dad; his mom had just buzzed away. Was it the scalp lady? The stairs were groaning, and whoever was coming up had arrived.

"Hey, Tony how's it hanging?"

Ryder, the living bone-head, bopping up the stairs and going into his room as casual as a dickless dog.

"You flaming a-hole!" Tony shouted. He knew Ryder had meant to scare the shit out of him and was immensely pleased to have done so.

"What were you going to do? Crawl under the bed?" Ryder asked. "That's the first place anyone looks, man. The first place anyone looks is right under the bed."

"What are you doing here?" Tony asked.

"I saw your mom go out. I was waiting. Your dad's car isn't around. It wasn't hard to figure out, Sherlock."

"You better get out of here. She's coming right back."

"So I can't even visit you? What do you got, malaria or something?"

Tony shook his head. He took a good look at Ryder. Ryder was dressed like a marine. He wore baggy army pants, a combat jacket, and a beret his father had given him. His black sneakers were wet.

"What do you want anyway?" Tony asked, going past Ryder into his bedroom.

There was something embarrassing about having Ryder standing there in the hallway. Something a little embarrassing, too, about being caught watching Popeye cartoons.

"Ryder, what do you want?" Tony said.

"You got the flu or something?"

"I puked."

"You going to be out tomorrow?"

"I doubt it."

Ryder smelled like someone who shouldn't be closed up in a room. And maybe it was just the smell, or maybe it was the look on Ryder's face, but Tony realized Ryder had been out in the woods.

Which was nutty, because they had both been forbidden to go into the woods. It was out of bounds. Lieutenant Giamoona had visited the school and had made a speech at assembly. He told everyone to stay out of the woods. He told everyone to stick to backyards, playgrounds, the school yard. Only Ryder didn't listen.

"I saw the guy," Ryder said.

"What guy?"

"The killer guy. I saw him in the woods. I tracked him in the snow."

"You're crazy."

"I saw him, Tony. He was out by the barn. The school barn. He didn't see me. I had these," Ryder said, digging in his big loopy pockets on the side of his army pants. Ryder pulled out a pair of binoculars, only they weren't binoculars, Tony knew, because one of the eye pieces had fallen out a couple of months ago. They were cheap to begin with, but now they only had one eye. Ryder used them around the girls' dorms to get a glimpse of his own page thirty-five.

"Ryder . . ." Tony started.

Ryder held the binoculars to one eye.

"What if the guy saw you?"

"He didn't see me, but I could have outrun him. I kept a distance between us, Tony-Bony. You don't think I'm that dumb, do you?"

"How did you even know it was the guy? You're bullshitting me."

"It was the guy, all right," Ryder said.

Tony realized it didn't matter if it was the guy or not, Ryder was going to do what he was going to do. He had the bone-head look on his face. The guy represented something to him. Tony couldn't guess what it was exactly, except that it had something to do with Ryder's dad. It had something to do with being locked in a closet as a kid, then going into the vault a half-dozen years later. It hadn't so much scared Ryder as made him nuts. Tony knew that much, and Tony knew Ryder knew Tony knew. Ryder had to find the guy and had to come and tell Tony.

"You should drop it," Tony said.

"I'm pretty sure the guy was checking out a woman. There was a woman in the barn but she got away."

"You should tell the police."

Ryder smiled widely and stuck his binoculars back in his pants' pocket.

"Scared, Tony?"

"Sure."

"I'm going to get the mother. My dad said there should have been a reward. I'm going to get the mother."

Before Tony could say anything else, he heard the whine of his mom's car.

"Here she comes," Tony said.

"So?"

"So get going."

It came to Tony with a start that he and Ryder were no longer friends, not the same way, anyway. The vault . . . Ryder's behavior . . . They might pal around now and then, might even combine to fight off Wayne Steele, but they weren't going to be friends in the same way. A friend didn't come creeping into your house to scare the shit out of you. A friend didn't swing a machete over your head and smash it into a tree, did he?

Maybe Ryder felt that way too. He hung next to the bed for just a second, and Tony saw the bone-head look appear. For all these months, Tony now realized, it wasn't Ryder's look after all. It was Ryder's dad. Ryder was a miniature of his dad, an off-the-wall military guy who as soon as he was seventeen was going to get a car with a lot of engine, then a wife he could push around. It was sad.

Ryder spun away from the bed, hit the wall slightly with his shoulder, then ran down the steps. He yelled some sort of greeting to Tony's mom, then headed somewhere. Headed home, or headed back to the woods, or headed to the dorms, where he could creep around and use his binoculars to watch the girls change for dinner. He was gone, thought Tony, in more ways than one.

It was like watching a doll unwind. Zelda Fitzgibbon sat across from him, a jacket over her shoulders, her head heavy and loose on her neck. She held a cup of coffee in her hand, the cup tipped to one side, almost spilling.

"Zelda," Captain Barney said softly.

She woke. She jerked the coffee upright and it splashed a little on her jeans. She looked at him.

"Why don't you just stretch out on the couch for a second? You'll be okay here. I've got to check on some things, then I'll be back. How does that sound?"

She nodded.

Barney stood, gently took the coffee from her hand, then moved to one side so that she could switch to the couch. She crawled onto the couch, her muck boots ludicrous and too heavy for the office, then pulled the jacket around her shoulders. She was asleep an instant later.

"Okay," he said to no one.

He stepped out of the office, closed the door behind him, then dumped the coffee in the first wastebasket he found. Afterward he went to the front desk. Eddy sat next to the radio, the headset on his ears, his stomach wide enough to almost take a perch on the desk in front of him.

"Who's out at the barn?" Barney asked.

Eddy looked up.

"Lester Draabo," Eddy said.

"Tell him to wait for back-up. Tell him by no means do I want him to investigate on his own. I'm going out there myself. After you've done that, I want you to check the records for early October. I don't know the exact date, but the young lady says she called in a report and no one ever got back to her on it. Check that through, okay?"

"Yes, sir. Any specific date?"

"Second weekend in October. Somewhere around then. I want to know if she called it in and what we did about it. That's top priority."

Eddy nodded.

"The girl is asleep. Keep her here if she wakes up. Get her some dinner if she's hungry."

"Gotcha," Eddy said.

Barney went to the side wall, back behind the desk, and used his key to unlock the gun cabinet. He took down a twelve-gauge, removed a box of shells from a storage drawer, and headed for the door.

Some part of him didn't want to listen. Some part of him wanted to believe things were under control as he heard Eddy trying to raise Lester on the radio. Heard Eddy speaking to static, speaking to air and early snow and nothing at all.

● ● ●

Let the dog go.

That was the first thought Lester had when he stepped out of the squad car onto the dirt driveway in front of the barn.

Let the dog go.

He understood that letting the dog go was not an entirely new idea. He recalled thinking the same thing somewhere near Potter's Bridge on a hot night in July, out in the frucking jungle of center campus, the bugs and heat and piss smells and the small stream going under the bridge and the screams, plenty of those.

Right now, he didn't feel like letting the dog go. He didn't feel like risking another dog, this time his own money to boot, or letting a dog go up against the scalp lady. He didn't feel like letting anything or anyone slip into the barn, because the barn was one ugly place. The barn was one open-jawed, hollow-throated, hay-breathing ugly place. The barn was dark, and right outside, right by the barn doors, the pick-up belonging to Charlie Summers idled with no one in the driver's seat.

Which was not a good sign, because Lester had already called three times and no one had answered. Not even the animals in the barn. No squawks, no honks, no whinnies.

The other thing, the other blessed thing, was the *feeling* around the place. The barn felt like a place where some old time farmer had gone a little crazy with an ax. Some old guy in bib overalls who got tired of chopping kindling decided he was just a mite fatigued at listening to his wife's directions, so he slipped into the front parlor, turned on a clunky 1930s radio, adjusted the dial for a little swing music, walked down a wide-board hallway that tilted left, raised his ax, and stepped into the kitchen. Caught mother in her gingham washing up or peeling spuds, and did nothing at all to her for a second until she had time to turn around, to appreciate the situation, then stepped forward and gave her a little *pit-a-pat* with the sledge end to get her started, and finished her off with a good chuck right down to the eyebrows.

The barn felt like that.

Only this was 1991, and it was snowing, and the pick-up truck idled with no one sitting in the driver's seat. The truck ran dirty, kicking a bit over an old set of points or plugs, and the driver's side door occasionally rocked and strained against its hinges because the wind rose and tried to make the truck fly. The wind blew a snow beach up onto the upholstery of Charlie's truck. The wind made a hollow sound as it gouged out the inside of the cab, looking for Charlie.

It was a bad move to turn off the truck. Lester understood that an instant after he had done it. Turning off the truck also meant turning off the headlights, and that meant the whole area was suddenly dark. Maybe it was just a coincidence, but as soon as it was dark it was also colder and quieter.

Goliath seemed to take a new interest in his surroundings. Part of that, of course, was the fact that by turning off the truck Lester had made the environment more suited to animals. More suited to smells and sounds, to predatory instincts.

"Hey Charlie!" Lester shouted. "You in there, Charlie?"

No answer.

Goliath started barking.

Not really barking, not at first. For a second he just snarled, curling his lip back and taking two steps to the rear.

Don't go into the barn, Lester told himself. Charlie Summers might be dead in the barn for all you know, but that's no reason to go inside.

That was it in a nutshell. That was it in a gnat's ass. Let well enough alone. Keep your gun in your hand, your dog on his lead, and let the light of the Lord shine through you.

Amen, end of case.

That was exactly what Lester intended to do, only Goliath began to bark like a crazy thing at something in the barn. Goliath barked like a frucking he-wolf, cracking his jaws again and again, straining the lead hard enough to jerk against Lester's shoulder muscles. Goliath wanted to get at it, which meant that he wanted to get into it, wanted to run into the barn, because whatever was going down this quiet November evening was going down inside.

So Lester tightened his grip on the choke collar and said, "No."

When that didn't work he tried "stay" and "sit" and "down" and even "heel." Something to divert the dog's attention, since whatever the dog barked at was directly behind door number one.

The dog pulled against the lead, because, let's tell the truth here, Lester thought, Goliath was getting a nose full of something. The odd thing was, it was one of those quiet November afternoons with snow falling and ice forming and the green pine trees taking on beards of winter, the very reason he had come up to Live-Free-or-Die land to begin with. This was the kind of afternoon that counted, made more sense than anything he had known in the Boston Combat Zone, only now he was holding onto a dog who was holding onto a scent that came from right behind the door.

"Easy," Lester said to Goliath, then yelled one final time to Charlie Summers. "Hey, Charlie, come on out! What the hell you doing in there anyway?"

You should let the dog go, Lester thought. What's the point of training him if you don't let the dog go? Anyway, Lester didn't feel as if he could hold the dog. He wasn't about to let go of his revolver, which left only one hand to control the dog. The dog was heavy. The dog had already picked door number one.

"You want him, boy? You got him."

Charlie stopped, his hand jamming his shirt down the back of his trousers. Fifty-five-years-old, paunchy, a bit red from alcohol, and a face pinched under a red snow hat. He was dressed for snow-blowing in an insulated brown overall, thick fleece-lined mittens, and the fattest boots Lester had ever seen. He had a corn-cob pipe in his mouth. The pipe bowl was almost entirely black.

"You going to shoot me, Lester?" Charlie asked, fiddling with his gloves. He smiled and pushed the right hand portion of the door open wider.

Lester shook his head. He lowered his gun.

"I almost shot your stupid ass, Charlie. You been here all this time? I've been calling you . . ."

"I heard you. I was back on Mr. Kim's crapper catching up on *Field & Stream*. I yelled back but you didn't hear me. Tough to yell on the john. Give yourself a heart attack that way." Charlie pointed to the gun. "So what's with the gun, Lester?"

Just then Captain Barney pulled off Dunbarton and squealed to a stop not ten feet away, then jumped out of his car, toting a shotgun.

"The marines will be here next," Charlie said. "One of these animals hold up a bank, Captain?"

"Lester?" the captain asked.

It wasn't really a question. At least it wasn't anything Lester felt he could answer. Even after the captain seemed finally to take the situation in, Lester wasn't sure about the captain. The man was wrapped way too tight. Lester looked quickly at Charlie. Charlie looked at him, shrugged, then turned to stare out at the open fields.

"I got to get these animals put to bed before Mr. Kim gets back," Charlie said.

Lester turned and put Goliath into a down-stay.

The picture postcard was back. All was safe and serene.

George Denkin ordered a bowl of lentil soup without looking up. He was seated toward the rear of Penguin's, the only natural food restaurant in Coldbridge. He smelled the waitress's perfume disappear as she went toward the kitchen with his order.

A meal at Penguin's was a treat, one he rarely permitted himself. Tonight, however, there had been no internal debate. Tonight he had decided to take care of Mr. Maslo. Later, in a day or two, perhaps sooner, he would see to Zelda Fitzgibbon. He was not concerned that she would be on her guard, or that the police would intervene. The snow had continued for most of the late afternoon, so that any tracks he had made were covered. It would be her word—her very nervous and near-hysterical word—that someone had been in the barn. With the town suffering from a general state of nerves, the police would soon dismiss the testimony of a young woman who had become alarmed by the sound of barn animals side-stepping in their stalls. No, the best of all things had happened, he reminded himself. He had established contact without being seen. The girl knew. He knew. The waiting was already delicious. It was going to be exquisite.

Now he sat at the small table—the surface nicked by knives and forks—his hands alive with excitement. The waitress came back. She wore a hippie-length skirt, an alpaca sweater, socks, and sandals.

"Did you want anything to drink with that?"

"No thank you."

"Tea is on the house."

"Just some water, if you would."

"You know, I think I've seen you around. Do you work on campus?"

"No."

"Funny," she said, then walked away again.

He did not care to be recognized. He considered standing and leaving, then realized that would merely draw more attention. It was possible, he had found, to live in a town for several months without being recognized. If you were conscious of your habits, if you varied your patterns, you could become invisible. People did not observe things closely, faces least of all. He had been in Coldbridge for almost three months and had only been accosted by over-friendly fellow employees on the street once or twice. Even then he found he could dissuade them from overtures of friendship if he set his face a certain way, looked down at the ground, was deliberately distant and cold. Still, after all his careful work and restraint, it was now time to move. In fact, he had delayed too long. In the past he had kept his stays to a ten-month maximum. The conditions were so excellent in Coldbridge, however, that he had decided to stay on. He had the vault, decent quarters in Mrs. Cutrer's boarding house, and an adequate job. He had become comfortable, which was, he knew, a dangerous thing. Only lately had he felt himself growing more active.

And only lately, he reminded himself, had the young boy been watching him.

The waitress returned with his soup.

"You know, you really do look familiar," she said as she placed the bowl in front of him. "I mean, I guess everyone looks familiar to everyone in a way, right? Like, we're all animals at some level, aren't we?"

"Some more than others," George said.

"Wow, you've got that right."

He picked up his spoon and waited for her to leave. She stood near the table, her thighs pressed against the corner to his left.

"You a veggie?" she asked.

"If I could just get some water."

"I talk too much, don't I? Sorry, it's this whole insecurity thing I'm into right now. Water coming up."

While she was gone, George Denkin removed a cheese grater from his coat pocket. It was a small grater, shaped like the bottom of a steam iron. From the same pocket he withdrew a piece of Ms. Fizz's flesh. The flesh came from the inside of her wrists. George had cut away two rectangles of the softest, palest flesh, one from each wrist. He had rolled the flesh into a single tube about the size of a shotgun shell. He had used white thread, lashed carefully in the center, to keep it tightly rolled.

It looked, George thought, like a small flesh bedroll.

He held the skin and the grater over his soup and scraped a dusting of flesh on his lentils. The skin was not at all resistant. It shredded nicely, the curls of epidermis as consistent as Parmesan.

"Oh wow, goat?" the waitress asked suddenly from his side. "I used to be really into cheeses."

George stopped grating, both hands still suspended over the soup.

The waitress put the water down.

"Would you mind?" she asked. "Just a taste? I stayed in this place once up in Port Hood, Nova Scotia, where we raised goats. You wouldn't believe the cheeses. I really miss them."

She held out her hand. Without a word, he swiveled and grated a small dusting of skin onto her palm. She waited to make sure the cheese was centered, then lifted her palm and nibbled at the flakes.

"I was right, wasn't I? Goat? That's delicious."

"You like it?"

"Mmm," she said, her tongue dotted by flecks of Ms. Fizz.

Professor Farley Simon stepped out of Molly's Luncheonette at half past eleven in the evening with a single thought: preserve your dignity. Or maybe it went like this: preserve your dignity, old chap. He felt like an old chap, felt like a hearty fellow who had been out on a small bender, had had a few too many vodka twists, a handful or two of Molly's barside cigarettes, and had become gloriously drunk.

He amended that last immediately. Not drunk, he told himself, but glowing. As he pushed out of Molly's, lifting his hand and waving as he departed, he felt filled with good fellowship. Most of all he felt filled with vodka and the tangy pulp of five or ten lemons. VT's, Molly called them, which made the drinks sound like a dance or a disease.

Above all, preserve your dignity.

That was important because he was a professor of psychology, and it wouldn't be appropriate behavior to get drunk and fall down on the street in his own campus town. Theodore Fuzpuci, the smart-as-a-whip son-of-a-bitch in the science department, lost his tenure for drunkenness. So did Angel Samara, the demographer. Drunkenness was a morals violation, and a morals violation was an excellent way to have your tenure revoked.

At the thought of tenure being revoked, he forced himself to straighten up. Throw back the shoulders, tuck in the stomach, concentrate on walking. Nevertheless he was aware he wasn't walking with great steadiness. He passed the Bayberry Card Shop, Britches Clothing Store, Viking House, and Luce's Hardware. He stopped for a moment in front of the hardware store in order to adjust his sails and to catch a whiff of fertilizer and lime. An outdated sale sign in the window said it was the time to lime the grass again. Farley took one big breath, then walked on.

He was halfway down Power Street when he remembered the manuscript. It hadn't been out of his mind much that evening—in fact he seemed to recall talking rather too

much about it in Molly's—but it had slipped away tempo-
rarily in his anxiousness to leave Molly's gracefully. Now
that he was a good block away from Molly's he felt justi-
fied in letting the memory of it return. He thought of it now
waiting at the bottom of the tubby blue-and-white mailbox,
ready to spring up the moment the postperson opened the
latch. From there to New York City, where it would be
reviewed, chewed up, scrutinized, and, of course, finally
accepted. It would appear—he closed his eyes to consider
lag time, how long the magazine would require to edit it,
fit it into a suitable spot—probably next fall at the earliest.
Yes, definitely next fall, since it dealt with the prolonga-
tion of adolescence, and that was a proper topic for autumn
when students were going off to college and high school
seniors were preparing applications.

The thought of the manuscript carried him all the way
to Charlemont Street. He lived six houses down the block,
bringing his walk to not more than a mile and a tenth
total from his front door to his office. His house was by
no means lavish—a ranch, two-and-a-half baths, two-car
garage, a back deck—but he enjoyed the street, actually
enjoyed his neighbors, and he liked to think of himself
as doing his part to keep his corner of the world safe. At
times, when he was being sentimental, he considered himself the uncle figure on the street. Single, a bachelor, but
not a fussy old hen who needed to keep things in order.
Children could talk to him, for example. He might lend a
hand fixing a bike, or allow the local pack to run across his
yard in one of their games. No child would ever be afraid
to retrieve his baseball if he knocked it into Farley Simon's
shrubs.

That was why, when he heard the baby cry, he stopped
at once.

It wasn't a typical cry. It wasn't a hunger cry or an "I'm
wet" cry. It was something coming from further down in
the throat. It came from deep down, with pain, so that it
carried in the cold air like a reminder that all wasn't good
in the world, which, thinking vaguely of his chats with Captain Barney, he already knew.

"Yes?"

He was answered by a low growl that came directly from his right, from the large front bushes—lilac, Farley guessed—that circled the Victorian porch. The bushes circled most of the house, actually, so that Farley only had to take one step onto the lawn to be within reach of the bushes. The cry came again, this time like the mew of a newborn, whimpering and scratchy.

He took another step onto the lawn, slick with early snow. The VT's and Molly's cigarettes pushed him forward. He took another step, this time with one foot dragging behind him so he could run if need be. He suddenly felt vapor and heat explode at him, and realized with a start that he had stepped into the dryer vent leading up from the Reading's basement.

Before he could adjust himself to the vapor, the sound came again. It came almost at his feet, and he looked down to see a gray cat resting on the ground just to his right. The cat was huge and completely motionless. It rested with its legs tucked under it at the base of a patch of day-lilies, staring straight ahead at a second cat, which Farley saw a moment later.

"Oh, come on, you guys. Cut it out," Farley said, relieved.

He didn't like the looks of the cat who sat back in the vapor. There was something vaguely unearthly about the cat, sitting as it did in a hiss of white spray from the dryer. Its coat was flecked with ice and fog so that it looked silver, looked to him in his drunken state, almost ghostly.

He bent to pick up the cat nearest him, slowly slid his hands under the cat's belly, began to lift when the cat let off a scream. He tried to drop the cat at once. Only the cat was apparently confused, worried that this man was going to carry it closer to the ghost cat. It turned in Farley's hands and made a dive for his chest. It hit Farley with surprising force, so that Farley came close to falling backward, close to falling into the steam and vapor and day-lilies.

"Christ," Farley said.

The cat climbed, the cat grabbed any damn thing. Farley felt something open in his palm, felt a nick . . . more than a nick, old chap . . . on his wrist, and he tried to hug the cat, to reassure it, since that seemed the best way to be rid of it. But the cat was panicked. Farley began to run, run with a cat in his arms. The vapor was around him, the ghost cat was somewhere, but finally he broke through two branches of lilac bushes and spilled out onto the front lawn, his legs spinning out from under him. He felt himself going down, felt the cat mounting still higher on his body, and he had a brief image of himself, Farley Simon, diving over the end zone in the Fighting Mules' stadium, scoring the winning touchdown with a flailing cat in his arms.

Except it wasn't funny, because the cat came up across his neck and face. The cat used his cheeks like tree bark, used his forehead like a springboard, then was gone, one of its nine lives left behind in the vapor of a dryer's vent, its fur a ghostly white.

Tony Corposaro wasn't doing much better than Professor Farley Simon.

It was a nightmare, the night sweats.

He was aware of the closet door standing open, its door cutting off moonlight, so that the interior looked particularly dark, looked as if it had no back wall. It looked endless, which was to say it might have given way to a staircase. And on the staircase Fred Astaire and Ginger Rogers dancing. Only it wasn't the real Fred and Ginger team. It was a pair of dancing corpses, a pair of spry, spinning cadavers. They were dancing nimbly up the stairs, the Fred in a seedy smoking jacket, the Ginger in a pale yellow chiffon gown. They danced and danced, sometimes going up, sometimes, in that Astaire way, clipping down a few steps, soft-shoeing, and it was only when you looked real close, when you concentrated, that you saw every time Ginger touched Fred she left a blot of blood on his jacket. And Fred's feet weren't always feet, weren't always clothed in shoes as a matter of fact, because sometimes they were hooves, they were hooves with claws, and that was the source of the tap sound, the clicking, dancing, *ta da*, Freddy Boy.

That was what was going on deep in the closet. Tony heard them tap dancing on the dungeon steps, now and then spinning to face the top of the stairs with a vaudeville look on their faces. Faces covered in cobwebs and smelling of moth balls. Fred was doing a sort of pinwheel move, his arms out, his tails flinging around as he did quick precise circles while Ginger stood to one side still moving to the music. The way to turn the closet back into a closet was to close the door. He was too old to be having Fred and Ginger nightmares. They were a bunch of hooey, as his dad would say, a bunch of trumped-up silliness to get attention in the middle of the night. A mature man would get up, go to the closet door, shut it, and get back in bed. *Basta*.

He threw back the covers releasing an explosion of Vicks VapoRub in the air and stood beside the bed. That started Fred and Ginger dancing at a greater rate. Fred was hopping up stairs one at a time to the beat of the Copacabana Band, a drum marking each step while Fred smiled and made excellent progress up the stairs.

To cut him off Tony took two steps toward the closet door. He heard Ginger start her run toward the finale. She ran up the stairs on her high heels as Fred, still doing his one-step hop, his knees bent, his arms out to balance him, started hopping faster.

Tony took another step toward the closet, at the same time reaching his hand up to grab the door. One more step and he touched the door, *sayonara*, Fred and Ginger, except before he could close it the clothes at the back of his closet began to separate. Fred and Ginger were going to stick their heads through, smiling, grinning, mugging for the audience as if they had put the wraps on a big routine. They were going to put their heads through, wink, smile, a way to end the number, except their heads were going to be ugly, were going to be scary as hell, their faces two dingy bulbs at the back of the closet.

He began closing the door. He swung it quickly, but it wasn't fast enough to keep the clothes from rippling open. He saw his good blue suit, the one that cost $129.30 at Warsaw's Department Store in New Market, shimmy sideways on the closet pole. Next to it a western shirt from his Aunt Adele, which was a Christmas present the year before, did a sort of limbo walk to the left, opening up a gap at the rear of the closet. And now it was a race. Now it was a matter of getting the door closed soon enough, because he heard the Copacabana Club Band become brassy and loud, finale time, spotlight-memories time, and he saw the top of Ginger's head coming through, her hair covered with maggots, and Fred followed, his pate bald but moving with pulsing veins, and they were about to look up, to smile for the audience, when Tony took a step away and let the door slam.

It was over. Faintly he heard the band begin playing "Good Night, Irene," which was the send-off song. It was no problem at all to imagine Fred and Ginger going disconsolately down the stairs, Fred occasionally giving a tap for the hell of it, while Ginger pointed her toes and concentrated on proper posture.

He fought to wake up.

Near midnight George Denkin moved slowly down the hallway of Mrs. Cutrer's boarding house. Mrs. Cutrer was off visiting her sisters in Putney, Vermont. Mr. Collier, the tenant who lived downstairs, was on his way to Montreal.

George was alone in the house with Mr. Maslo.

When he was only five or so steps away from Maslo's room, George heard the old man snoring. Maslo's sinuses were clogged. Ever since he had returned from Penguin's, George had been treated to the sound of Maslo hawking. George went on his toes to be more quiet. Wind hit against the roof somewhere. A shade cord tapped once against a windowsill. In his right hand George carried a present for Mr. Maslo.

He halted at the door and listened. Nothing except the intake of Maslo's breath. He passed by the door, then stopped directly under the white smoke detector that was anchored in the ceiling. The red battery light pulsed. George removed a Bic lighter from his pocket, flicked it to get a strong flame, then held the head of the lighter against the smoke detector.

It took approximately thirty seconds to get it buzzing. Underneath the buzzing he heard Mr. Maslo scrambling out of bed. Heavy braying springs, a short hawk, then feet

shuffling toward the door. George crouched just to the left
of Maslo's door, the present in his right hand.

Maslo fumbled with his lock, then stepped into the hallway. His hair was rumpled. He wore only pajama bottoms.
He looked up and down the hallway, blinking to clear his
eyes of sleep.

George's present for Mr. Maslo was a Boy Scout hatchet.
He used the blunt end to hit the man on the right knee cap.
He heard the cap break, then listened to Mr. Maslo fall back
against the wall. George swung the hatchet again, this time
aiming for Maslo's left arm. The square head cracked down
on Maslo's fleshy bicep. The arm suddenly had a second,
unexpected elbow where the bone had snapped in two.

"Do you understand now?" George asked as the man
slumped down, his arms up to protect his head.

Maslo did not answer.

George broke the other knee cap as the smoke detector
stopped buzzing.

"Do not speak," he told Maslo. "Do not say a word, you
filthy animal."

George was not certain Maslo survived the basement steps.
The man was a boneless weight. It disgusted George to
think what the animal had consumed over the years to give
himself such a flabby, shapeless body. His skin was white
where it was not covered by coarse black hair. His nose
and cheeks were dotted with large pores.

George had dragged Maslo down from the top floor of
the apartment house. Now he stood, out of breath, at the
bottom of the basement steps. He looked around quickly
and saw everything was ready. He had cleared an ancient
laundry table near the wash basin.

"Mr. Maslo?"

Mr. Maslo did not answer. George bent and checked the
man's pulse. It beat irregularly. A few bruises had come up
on the man's neck and forehead from bumps he had sus-
tained on the way down the stairs.

George dragged Maslo to the laundry table, then let him
slump. Both of the man's kneecaps were broken; the legs

were swollen. Maslo gave a slight groan when George released him. George put his foot on Maslo's head, then hopped to let his weight crush down on the man's right ear. He heard something give, then let his weight drop to the floor again.

"Mr. Maslo?"

He waited a moment to catch his breath. The man did not respond.

George placed Maslo's hands together. He forced Maslo to sit up, then pinned the man's hands down flat on the laundry table. His feet slipped a little on the cement floor, but he balanced himself, then reached under Maslo's arms, hoisted the man up and dumped him across the table, face down. Maslo let out a deep sigh, almost as if his lungs no longer bothered to hold oxygen.

"Do you hear me, Mr. Maslo?"

The man did nothing. He appeared like a blob of white flesh bent forward over the table. George removed the man's pajama bottoms, careful to keep Maslo centered on the table. It occurred to George that Maslo could be faking. He reached forward and took Maslo's hair, then bounced the man's head twice on the table.

Convinced Maslo was unconscious, George left him for a moment and went to turn on a light over the wash tub. Mrs. Cutrer had placed an old mirror above the basin years ago, and now George checked to make sure it caught Mr. Maslo's reflection. He walked behind Maslo, looked in the mirror, then returned to the mirror and adjusted it again. He performed the adjustments twice before he was satisfied.

Maslo moaned slightly after the final adjustment.

"Coming, Mr. Maslo," George said.

He stood behind Maslo, the man's broad behind directly in front of him. He looked in the mirror. He was there, radiant, the dim light turning his skin soft. He reached to the right hand side of the laundry table and picked up a scalpel. The weight felt good in his fingers.

He made his first incision just beneath Maslo's shoulder blades. The man groaned more loudly this time. George continued with the cut, slicing skin deep across the man's back. A thin line of blood followed the blade, then in pulses the blood became thicker.

George's second incision was above the shoulder blades. He cut to the same depth, keeping the incision parallel to the first. George wiped the two cuts clean with the rolled pair of pajama bottoms but he could not keep up with the flow.

When he finished with the second incision, George reached into the first cut and pushed his hand up and through the strap created by the surgery. The skin was loose, baggy.

"Not yet," George said to Maslo. "Please don't go yet."

George returned the scalpel to the right end of the table, then closed his eyes. He did not want to see himself in the mirror. Not at first. He pressed his hips against the man's rear end, then placed his chest on Maslo's back. He raised the strap of flesh away from Maslo's backbone, the one he had just created, then slid his cheek along the man's spine.

The skin yawned. George lifted harder with his hand, his head turned sideways and sliding upward. He felt warm blood touch his forehead as it slipped under the strap.

I am inside him. I can feel his heart beating. With a slight shove, his head popped through. At the same moment Maslo put his hands out wide on the table, as though groping for something. Perhaps for the scalpel, or perhaps he merely tried to stand. Too late, George was inside him.

George lifted backward with all his strength. Maslo rose. George jerked him up and down, sensing the strap of skin stretching to accommodate his head and neck. Maslo was sliding down him, or he was crawling up through Maslo. It no longer mattered, Maslo's life was entering his own.

"Do you see? Do you *see*?" George said. Because *he* now saw. He saw his head, the top of it, protruding above Maslo's left shoulder. He saw it in the mirror, a man climbing inside another man. He shucked himself deeper into Maslo's skin, his eyes rising above the man's shoulder. He felt Maslo's weight slip, the skin-strap bag wider, while he began to walk the old man to the right, circling the laundry table.

He did not know if Maslo had died or not, but the man's body was limp. He carried the hulk closer to the mirror, because this was what he wanted to see, this was what he wanted to discover.

Balancing Maslo's weight, he reached back and picked up the scalpel. Then, standing directly in front of the mirror, he brought the razor across Maslo's throat. He felt the old man's body go rigid for a second. He wasn't dead! George threw away the scalpel and hugged the man's chest.

So now he knew. This was what they felt when they died. This was what he gave them, he thought, watching himself watch Maslo become a ghost in the mirror.

CHAPTER SEVEN

FINALE

Zelda stood in her bathrobe and watched Martha struggle to close her last suitcase. She had to prop one knee on it to shut it, and even after it was buckled it looked as if it might explode any second.

"Okay," Martha said.

"You have everything?"

"Doesn't it look like it?"

Zelda saw Martha glance at the clock. It was early, barely 7:15. The bus to Boston left at 7:59, but Martha, Zelda understood, was compulsively early. She could walk to the campus bus stop in front of Luce's Hardware in five minutes, which would give her—Zelda did a quick calculation—roughly forty minutes to stand outside.

"So," Martha said.

"I know, you have to get going," Zelda said. "Have to be early."

"I can't help myself."

"I know you can't."

Zelda watched Martha take a deep breath. Here it comes, Zelda thought.

"Come home with me," Martha said in a burst. "It's crazy for you to stay here. If you won't call your parents, at least come home with me."

"We've been all over that. I'm staying here."

"I'll cancel my trip to Richie's. He can come to my house or something. I don't want you staying here by yourself, Zelda."

"It's not by myself. There are other people on campus. It's not a big deal."

"I don't like it," Martha said. "Zelda, the guy was right in the barn when you were there."

"The security people didn't think so. There wasn't any proof. All the tracks were gone. It might have been my imagination, that's all."

Zelda held up her hand, palm out. Stop. Martha started to say something, then checked the clock again. Still thirty-five minutes to spare, but Martha was anxious to get going. Besides, they had been over this. They had talked about it continually since Captain Barney had brought her back to the dorm room. Zelda's brush with the boogey man, they had called it.

Zelda wasn't crazy about staying, hardly, but somehow she felt she had to. Sometimes, she thought, you just have to stick by what you say, even if it does scare the hell out of you. She'd made a stand with her parents about going home, and she'd meant it. Mostly, of course, it had to do with being on her own, finally. And she really had looked forward to being alone for a change. But now . . . well, this was something else. She was tempted to give in, to go with Martha, but she also told herself that she'd better see if she really had grown up enough to do what she'd said she was going to do. Better see if she could put Mr. Hotchkiss away, out of her life, not let him dominate her anymore the way he had for so many years. No, damn it, she would stay.

When Martha saw there was no point in arguing, she took a breath. Zelda took a breath. Snoopy, on the wall, still hung from his dog house.

"You have a great time," Zelda said before Martha could think of anything else to say. "Say hello to Richie for me."

"Okay, you too. You have a great time too."

Zelda hugged Martha. It felt like hugging a barrel. That wasn't a particularly kind thought, so Zelda hugged harder, hugged Martha for real, and felt Martha hug back.

"I'm out of here," Martha said.

"Can you carry all this stuff?"

"Sure."

She did. A large suitcase, a huge pocketbook and a smaller overnight bag. She picked everything up, stood for a moment in the middle of the floor, adjusted her shoulders, then nodded at the door.

"Get it, will you?"

Zelda opened it. Martha had to turn sideways to get through the doorway. She shuffled through, banging once against the door frame.

"You sure you can make it?" Zelda asked.

"Positive."

Zelda remained in the doorway and watched Martha walk down the hallway. When Martha reached the top of the stairs leading to the lobby below, she turned and looked back. She couldn't wave so she simply smiled and headed down, the noise of her bags hitting the railings, the only sound Zelda heard in the entire dorm.

Barney stretched out on the sofa with the sports page. If it had been a perfect world it would have been the Boston *Globe* sports section, the biggest and most complete in the universe, but it was not a perfect world. He had to settle for the Coldbridge *Chronicle*, which alternated stories about the Celtics and Patriots with personality sketches of regional coaches and players.

Not that he didn't care about regional athletics. He was a guy who always threw in a few bucks when he came out of the grocery store on Saturday and found some muffin-faced kid standing there with a donation can. It was just that today was a day off, a glorious day off, and he wanted the Boston *Globe* as a mini-vacation from the real world.

But the *Chronicle* was okay. He folded the paper neatly and lay on the couch, the afternoon growing dim, the street noises distant. He was just starting to fall away, just having trouble holding onto the paper, when Matty joined him on the couch. She stretched out exactly on top of him, pushing the paper aside with her shoulders and neck, then settling as comfortably as a cat on top of him.

"Where's Seth?" Barney asked.

"Napping," she said.

She wasn't in the mood to talk. That became obvious a second later when she scrunched up a little higher on him and kissed his lips for the first time. She kissed him lightly but firmly. He let the paper drop overboard. It was high-school necking, and it felt shy and tentative and right. A little later, when he slipped his hand to her breast, she clamped her elbow on his wrist. The clamp felt like a throwback of twenty years. She shook her head and kissed his cheek.

"But I really do love you," he said. "I'll take you to the prom."

"No, not now," clamping the elbow tighter.

"I really do."

"I have a reputation to think of."

"That's true."

It was a game, a time warp, and it was a warm afternoon the day before Thanksgiving. Barney kissed his wife, not thinking, for the first time in months, of the crazy man stalking his campus.

By two-thirty in the afternoon George was finished packing his car. It had taken him less time than he had anticipated. He had carried everything downstairs to his Volkswagen Golf, loaded each item carefully, then finished by hosing off the car. He had vacuumed it earlier so that now he was able to step into an immaculate car.

He had also left his room clean. Mrs. Cutrer might have complaints about what she found in the basement—and she would find Mr. Maslo's body had already started to go— but she would find no fault with his room.

He checked his room two or three times to make sure he hadn't forgotten anything. He reminded himself that, of course, he could return to shower if Zelda proved too messy. There was no reason not to if he felt so inclined. Still, he knew he would prefer to do it clean, then move on. To return to the boarding house might be bad luck.

His final move before leaving the boarding house was to spread his road atlas on the large living room table and check his route once more. He was heading south, probably to Atlanta, perhaps even to Florida. He did not want to live through another New England winter, that was certain. Once he reached his destination he would have to change identities. He had done it before; it wasn't difficult. Then, for a month, he would abstain. He would have Zelda and that would have to satisfy him for a time.

When he finished examining the atlas he folded it carefully and carried it out to the car. Zelda, he knew, would be in the dorm. He had called her roommate Martha from the registrar's office. It was so simple, really, to manipulate people. Three or four questions about their room, about their course selections for the following term, and Martha had given him a complete schedule of their Thanksgiving plans. Martha was going. Zelda was staying.

He closed the front door of Mrs. Cutrer's boarding house, leaned against it to make sure it stayed shut, then went down the front stairs. He patted the pocket of his coat to make sure he had the razor. Then he unzipped the pocket at the rear of his jacket, the game pouch, and pulled it around until he could smell it.

Blood. Old blood.

People magazine.

It was a mandatory addition to the laundry pile. Arm & Hammer liquid laundry soap, a roll of quarters, two Twinkies from Martha's stockpile, and a dime and a nickel so she could get a can of Tab.

When she had everything neatly stacked in her laundry basket she checked herself in the mirror. She was going for a . . . what look? A sharp, younger image, a Big Chill look. A young professional doing laundry look. A bandana over the hair—but not completely, there was still a curl near her forehead—sweatpants, and moccasins look.

She picked up the laundry basket, balanced it, then walked sideways through the door. She set the basket down afterward and listened to the dorm while she locked her door. Late afternoon quiet. No sound came to her except the ticking from heat vents. She was certain she wasn't the only one left in the dorm—she had checked that—but nobody seemed to be around at the moment. It was the time of day when you went downtown, maybe wandered over to the library, or did something to get you out and about. It was errand time, only her errand consisted of muscling a bunch of laundry down the stairs to the basement.

She picked up her laundry and headed downstairs. She deliberately walked with a confident stride. She pushed through the swinging fire door, then clumped down the steps. She kept the laundry basket at her side. There was hardly any light left. That was one thing Zelda couldn't ignore. The stairway was illuminated by one security light on each landing. There was also a window on every landing, but outside the day was fading. Winter solstice was only a month away, and in New Hampshire the sun went south in a hurry.

She stopped on the second landing and listened for the sound of dryers. She would have been very pleased to hear some sneakers batting around the dryer drum. The machines were always busy in a dorm the size of Sheppard, but today business was slow. She heard nothing except the heat vents and the long-shadowed hollowness of empty hallways.

Hello, she wanted to call. Hello, anybody home?

She continued down to the basement. The laundry room itself was a square of cinder blocks on the northeast corner of the building. It was hot. It was painted gray, with low dangling pipes and cement floors. It was the kind of place where a fire extinguisher provided a welcome change of color.

She put her laundry basket on a wooden table. Before she began sorting colors, she listened to the building once more. It was quiet, but that was all. It wasn't the silence she remembered from the barn. It was just empty space ticking softly during the last real hour of daylight.

Ryder was right. There was no forgetting the face.

It was the guy who had stood under the Kon-Tiki deer blind a couple of months back. The guy who had turned the forest silent, who had listened to the jay screaming, and who had made Tony one frightened cowboy. Made Tony jump on Ryder's back and tell him to shut his basket. When the Tony-Ryder friendship had begun to frazzle.

The guy who had been making deposits in the vault.

"Did I tell you?" Ryder asked.

"Yeah, just hold on."

"It's him, man, it's him."

Tony watched the guy cross the street, then took his eye away from the single lens of Ryder's binoculars. Ryder grabbed the binoculars, put them up to his eye and squinted behind the eyepieces. His cheeks worked on a Tootsie Roll. His sideburns were sweaty even though they sat in a forsythia bush beside Sheppard Dorm, where a cold wind curled around and sawed at them.

"Okay, you're right. It's the same guy," Tony said when Ryder put down the binoculars.

"I told you."

"You told me you told me. So what?"

"So that's the guy I saw out at the barn. That's the killer."

"You don't know that. Come off it," Tony said, and stood.

He was cold and tired. Besides, he felt a little strange hanging around with Ryder again. Ryder was like a leech who had hooked onto him and wouldn't let go. Tony also knew this whole Hardy Boys routine Ryder was going through was mostly an effort to resurrect their friendship, to make them pals again after Tony had seen Ryder the other day in his house.

"I'm telling you, man," Ryder said, reaching in his pocket for more Tootsie Roll. "We could get a reward."

"Geezum, Ryder, I don't want a reward. Just call the police if you're so sure you're right."

"That guy would be out of here too fast. Come on, let's go in the dorm."

"In?"

"Yeah, in. We got to follow the guy. We'll check it out, then come back down."

"Are you out of your mind? Especially if you're right about him being the killer."

Ryder did nothing for maybe a count of three, then started walking fast around the building. He walked in a miffed way, slapping the bushes as he went, heading around to the rear of Sheppard Dorm. Watching Ryder leave, most of Tony's good sense said one thing—it ain't your potatoes. That's what his dad would have said in the same situation. It ain't your potatoes, so just let it be. Ryder was going to do what Ryder was going to do, and the smart thing now was to push away from the bushes and go home. Once he got there maybe he could get his mom to make some tomato soup while he watched old episodes of "Bewitched."

But of course he followed Ryder.

Not to go in the dorm. He didn't have any intention of doing that. Yet he felt he owed it to Ryder, his once-upon-a-time best friend, to save the kid from himself. He had to try and talk sense with him, even though that was normally a waste of time.

"Ryder, wait up," Tony said.

Ryder was already around the corner of the building. The bushes still wagged where he had pushed through them, but that was it. Ryder had vanished.

"Oh Jesus, Ryder," Tony said.

Tony hustled around the corner, keeping low so he could remain hidden by the bushes. The whole idea was nuts, because you couldn't be sure it was the right guy. And if he was, it was still crazy.

By the time Tony made it around the corner of Sheppard Dorm, Ryder was already diving through a basement window. It looked ridiculous, just two legs wiggling out into the bushes and the rest of Ryder, his entire upper torso, inside the building, snaking forward.

"Ry . . . der," Tony whispered.

"Nuts to you," Ryder said, his breath choked from his awkward position. "I went after your stupid vampire . . ."

"Just hold on. I'll go with you. Just hold on, is all I'm saying. Think it through." His father liked to say that.

The legs slid forward. Tony watched Ryder scrape his shins. They went right along the windowsill until Ryder slithered in with a final squiggle. An instant later he was at the window, his bone-head looking up and smiling.

"It's easy," Ryder said.

Don't go in, Tony thought as he put his books beside the window, put his lunch box on top of the books. Don't go in you freaking peg head.

But he did. He slid on his belly through the basement window, then stopped when he saw the drop on the other side was approximately five feet. No, actually it had to be more than five feet, because Ryder stood on the floor below, holding his hands up to assist, and that added up to more than five feet. He stayed where he was a second while Ryder flexed his fingers like a guy telling the driver of a large truck how far he could back up.

"Come on, you're crazy," Ryder whispered.

"This is crazy. Why didn't we just go in the front door?"

"Because it's locked, you a-hole. Just come on."

"This is wrong—"

"Oh Geezum."

Tony slid forward on his belly, still telling himself this was not a good idea.

"Easy," Ryder said.

And it was. Tony slid into Ryder's arms. He smelled Tootsie Rolls on Ryder's breath as he dropped his feet to the cement floor. He stood for a moment afterward, checking to make sure he hadn't ripped his pants. And trying not to look as scared as he felt.

The one thing Barney didn't like about being married, a father, the whole ball of wax, was that he couldn't eat anchovies on pizza. Sausage, hamburger, pepperoni, mushrooms, even pineapple slices were okay, but not anchovies. Seth claimed he was going to be sick every time he saw an anchovy, and Matty wasn't much better. Matty insisted the fish were dehydrated, and moisture from the average human throat caused them to expand and stick, cutting off air and making seven out of ten individuals sick.

So it was one large to go, half pepperoni, half mushroom, three diet cokes, easy on the oil.

That's what Barney had ordered a few minutes earlier when he stepped into the pizza parlor. Now he sat at a computerized trivia game, punching buttons to answer questions in the general knowledge category. You could wager x-amount of points and if you won they doubled or tripled until you became a professor, a rocket scientist, or, finally, a genius.

Right now, in the student bracket, he was confronted with a tough question: What is the longest river in the world?

         (*a*) the Amazon
         (*b*) the Mississippi
         (*c*) the Nile
         (*d*) the Volga

He picked (*b*), got it wrong, lost half his points, and ended up in a category called "dunce."

But that was okay. He felt good. He had slept nearly three hours in the afternoon, waking up to find he had drooled on a small dinosaur Seth had evidently propped near his face. The dinosaur was a Stegosaurus. It possessed a spiny back with huge plates guarding its vertebra against Tyrannosaurus Rex. It was molded from blue plastic. Seth had chewed its tail.

He was thinking about dinosaurs, actually thinking about what the world must have been like then—the giant ferns, the weird swamps, the volcanic heat—when Lester Draabo showed up at the front door of the pizzeria, Goliath in tow. He came in, went straight to the counter, and ordered three slices. Lester took a soda from the machine against the side wall and was about to sit down when he saw Barney. Barney smiled. Lester walked over.

It was a tad strange to be out of uniform and see one of his officers. It made him feel smaller, which probably said something about Freudian symbolism wrapped up in the uniform, but it was true nonetheless. Barney felt like he might give an order to Lester Draabo and Lester would have every right to ignore it, because right now Barney was just a middle-aged guy out buying pizza—no anchovies—for his family, sitting in front of a trivia game that he had no appetite to play any longer.

"Hi, Chief," Lester said.

"Hello, Lester. How are you tonight?"

Before he answered, Lester gave a short wave across his waist.

Goliath sat.

Then Lester made a sign as if he wanted traffic to stop.

Goliath went down on his belly.

"Fine, chief," Lester said, taking a seat. "Just getting a little breakfast before I go on duty."

"Goliath is really coming along."

"What did I tell you? Suds says Goliath's almost done his training. This dog is sharp."

"I'm going to see if we can't reimburse you when this thing is over."

"Well, whatever," Lester said.

"No, I think you're right. I think it's a good idea to have a dog on the force. Good public relations, if nothing else."

"You got it."

Barney liked Lester Draabo. He liked him as well as any man working on staff. But he was a subordinate, and Barney was the captain, and—be honest, Barney told himself—Lester was a black guy, he himself was a white guy, and there was still some tension in that, say what you will. The tension didn't have to stick, but it probably would because Barney held the other man's job in his hand. They could pretend all that didn't matter, they were just two fellows bumping into each other in Vermichelli's pizza parlor, but that wasn't the fact of the fact.

"Hey, your pie is ready," the counter guy called.

Barney didn't like himself for feeling grateful for the interruption. I feel more comfortable in a uniform, he thought. He stood and heard something go off, a pipe, or a toilet. It took him a second to realize Goliath had growled. Head on his paws, Goliath didn't budge but sent his eyes once to his boss, Lester. Lester simply shook his head to make the dog stop.

"People move quickly around him . . . he's just checking," Lester said. "Him and me, we're in synch, you know? We're reading each other's minds all the time."

"It looks like it," Barney said.

Barney went to the counter, paid, and grabbed the pizza. It was hot and he had to put on a pair of gloves before he carried it. He put the sodas on top of the box, then turned back to Lester for a second.

"Hey, Lester, you going to check out that girl Zelda in Sheppard? The one who was out at the barn?"

"A little later tonight."

"Good. Did that dorm empty out pretty well?"

"I guess so. I haven't been over."

"Give me a call, will you? When you've checked her out? I don't like her sitting up in that dorm."

"If it was me," Lester said, bending to pet Goliath, "I'd be out of there. No way you'd catch me sitting up in a dorm like that."

"Give me a call, okay?" Barney said, backing out.

Lester nodded. Barney pushed outside, carrying not even a whiff of anchovies.

"Let's go," Ryder said.

Tony checked his pants again. The shins didn't look ripped, but the skin underneath was hot. Probably, Tony figured, a couple streams of blood heading down to his socks. A couple streams of blood that would stain his socks, stain the inside of his pants legs, and cause his mom to start barking about the price of clothes today, was she made of money, did he think his father enjoyed breaking his back for—

"Let's go," Ryder said.

"Go where?" Tony asked.

Because at that moment he didn't see anywhere to go. He didn't see anything except a couple of soda machines, a money-changing machine, and a staircase leading to the scalp lady, or to some nut case, or maybe just to a security officer on patrol who had a bone to pick with piss-ant kids breaking into college buildings.

"We got to go up," Ryder said.

"Ryder, you sure you want to do this?"

"I'm sure, Tony-Bony. What's wrong with you, anyway? You chicken?"

"I'm not chicken. But this is a crime, breaking and entering. We can get arrested."

"Frug it," Ryder said in a frog voice they sometimes used.

"Frug it," Tony answered out of habit.

"Frug it, frug it," Ryder said, heading down the hall and up the stairs.

Tony followed. But something was wrong, and it was not until Tony was on the first landing that he knew what it was.

Ryder was leading, that's what it was. And Ryder never led. Ryder was a born second banana, born second lieuy. He was the guy who always got killed in the "Star Trek" shows. The guy you never really recognized, maybe the botanist sent down to study the new planet's flora and fauna, an extra type of actor who had to be sacrificed so that Kirk and Doc McCoy could feel terrible, judge the full extent of danger, and act accordingly. Certainly not a leader.

So Tony hustled up the stairway and caught up with Ryder as they came to the first floor.

"Wait a second," Tony said, grabbing Ryder's elbow.

"Wait for what?"

"Just wait."

Ryder stopped. Tony thought, if we're going to do this we have to do it right. But he didn't know how to do it right. The dorm seemed empty, there was no one around, and the hallways beyond the large fire doors were straight and clean and shiny as hell. Someone had left a waxing machine over against the side wall.

"What are we looking for?" Tony asked.

"Come on."

It was definitely not right. The tone was wrong. Ryder hiked up the stairs, taking them two at a time, and Tony did nothing but follow. Now, walking after the talking bonehead, Tony heard his own steps going up and down the stairwell. The sound bounced way down, down to the soda machines, then up, up to whoknowswhat. He didn't like to think of the scalp lady listening. He pictured her down on the bottom landing, just turning past the newel post, her hair waving, her hand reaching out to grab the banister because she couldn't see very well. Maybe she couldn't see very well, but she could hear, and right now they were making way too much noise.

"*Shh,*" Tony said.

Ryder stopped. "What now?"

"Just be quiet. You can hear us all over the building."

"So what?" Ryder said in a deliberately loud voice.

"But you don't—"

He didn't finish because at that moment he heard a door shut somewhere on the staircase below. Someone came out of one of the hallways, or maybe headed down to do laundry, and maybe it was a security officer, and maybe it was—

"Come on, come on," Ryder whispered.

"Let's get out of here, Ryder."

"Come on, come on."

And Ryder ran up the stairs. Tony admired the way Ryder ran. He kept to the center of the stairs, placing each foot with precision while Tony himself scrambled. He couldn't tell a thing about any potential sound below. Everything was clamor, everything was fast breath and empty hallways, and for a second Tony saw a fire extinguisher and thought: there's a weapon. But then he passed it, ran up another flight of stairs, where Ryder stood with the door open, the hallway open in front of them.

"He's coming," Ryder said.

"No," Tony said.

No, because that wasn't possible. No, because he didn't want anyone to follow on the stairs. No, because Ryder couldn't know for certain, couldn't have heard any better than he had himself. It was just panic on Ryder's part, just a goofy jolt delivered to get them all wound up.

Then Tony heard steps and someone whistling, someone mounting the stairs with a song in his heart, a spring in his stride, a rose in his cheek. It was impossible the guy hadn't heard them.

But before he could move, Ryder laughed.

"We know who you are!" Ryder shouted down the stairs.

Then he laughed again. He laughed the great bone-head laugh, the pure, unadulterated Ryder laugh. When Tony looked at him he realized Ryder was gone a notch.

In that instant Tony really gave up on him. Because the steps they heard stopped—just like they did that day in the tree house—and Ryder's clock was on the wall but no one had thought to wind it.

Tony heard a little scrape. Someone turned on the steps, someone had changed his mind, and the steps listened. They listened because someone was piecing this whole thing together.

The shoes scraped again.

That was when Tony ran. He ran down the hallway, hitting doors as he went. He hoped for one of the doors to open because there was nowhere to go otherwise. He heard Ryder sucking wind beside him, Ryder giggling and running down the middle of a terribly empty hallway.

It was the type of running you did in dreams, the kind where you felt something closing on you and you sprinted as fast as you could and nearly let yourself scream, only the toothy strangeness was on top of you so the only thing you could do was dive forward and tuck yourself into a ball and let the dream beast take you.

It was sort of like that for Tony on the third floor of Sheppard Dorm as he ran down the hall and heard the sounds of someone coming up the staircase.

"Try the doors, Tony," Ryder said as he slowed in front of him and began yanking at the room doors on the left hand side of the hall.

It took Tony a second to begin on his side, because Ryder was jumping from door to door, and Tony had to concentrate, had to keep from going *tharn*—the state rabbits in *Watership Down* entered when they were suddenly caught in the headlights of a car—a state of acute consciousness, and acute paralysis. Tony felt it starting to cover him when Ryder turned again and shouted.

"Check the doors!"

Which broke tharn.

And that wasn't any better. Tony began yanking on the doorknobs, but his hands seemed like spider monkeys that leaped from doorknob to doorknob with no sense of what they attempted to do. It did no good to remind himself that he shouldn't be in the dorm in the first place, or to think of his mom waiting dinner, his mom pacing the kitchen floor, his mom getting itchy each time she looked at the phone. He was too caught up in it.

The door directly in front of him opened.

It opened so suddenly that Tony didn't believe it at first. It swung open, flapped slightly, then closed again. Tony turned to say something to Ryder. Ryder stood beside another door, staring down the hallway at the guy.

The guy from the Kon-Tiki deer blind.

"Hey, fellas, what are you doing up here?" he asked.

He raised his hands, palms out, to show he was just a curious good guy. He didn't mean any harm. In fact, he was there to help them. He took a couple steps down the hall toward them. Tony wanted to catch Ryder's eye because he suspected Ryder was going tharn.

"What is it? What are you guys doing up here?" the man asked. "You can get yourself into some real trouble."

Then it came down to timing.

A math problem. How close does the guy have to get, and how fast does he have to run, in order to trap two shaking and nervous kids who have to squeeze through a door and then lock it?

To Tony's mind it was broken down into stages and seconds:

One: The guy took two more steps forward, his hands still out at his sides, his smile full and warm. Tony had a glimmer that it was a con job, but the guy really did seem sincere in his attempt to straighten them out.

Two: Tony glanced at Ryder. Ryder was tharn.

Three: The Kon-Tiki man saw Tony look at Ryder and tried to speed up just a fraction. Tony saw it out of the corner of his eye. It reminded him of a game they played as kids called "Mother, May I?" You had to creep forward to the person who was "It." Net gain, one more step for the guy.

Four: Tony turned to face the guy dead-on and realized Mr. Kon-Tiki was leaning forward, ready to sprint. At the same time Tony noticed the guy's face had changed. While before he looked open, now his smile was gone and his eyes had become serious. A change of look, a cloud going over, just like, say, the way a child's face might crumple right after he falls on the sidewalk and an instant before he cries.

Five: Tony pushed on the door beside him and felt it open. It flapped, actually, because it was a swinging door, a saloon-door type of thing, and the thought entered Tony's mind that it might not lock.

Six: Tony said to Ryder, "Hey."

Seven: Which started the Kon-Tiki man moving. It was this movement, coupled with Tony's small shout, that finally shook Ryder out of tharn. Ryder looked at Tony.

Eight: Who had the door open and was twisting through it. The floor underneath was tile, just tile, and it took an instant for Tony to understand that this was the bathroom door. Tony tried to yell, "Hurry," but something locked his voice, or gave way to the sound of footsteps out in the hall, and he turned in time to see Ryder look once down the hallway . . .

Nine: . . . in slow motion, because it was too late, the math had worked against them. Kon-Tiki man had a better solution to the equation. As Tony turned to start closing the door he saw a hand come past the door frame and hook onto Ryder's throat. It was a neck tackle, a lunge, and a grab. Ryder ducked at the last instant so that Kon-Tiki man's forearm whapped off Ryder's head.

Ten: Ryder fell one step back. Which meant he also fell away from the door. Then Kon-Tiki man was in the door frame, grabbing Ryder. Which was when Tony saw the razor flick open in the man's hand.

Eleven: A moment when everyone knew everything. Tony knew the guy was the guy and he had the razor straight up, ready to bring it down. The guy knew that he could do what he wanted to Ryder, and he knew Tony was watching, and he knew Tony was next, and he started to lower the razor across Ryder's chest. Ryder, held tightly by the guy's arm hooked around his throat, had his eyes go wild, go utter bone-head, because he saw Tony standing an impossible distance away in the doorway, saw the razor start to descend, and he knew he was about to receive a razor smile.

Twelve: Tony started to shut the door. It was abandoning his friend, but he saw the razor smile start on the left hand side of Ryder's throat. Just a knick, a shaving cut, but then it went deeper, the razor explored. It wasn't Ryder's neck Tony watched anymore but the look on Kon-Tiki man's face. The guy's eyes closed, like a cellist hugging his instrument to his crotch and sawing the bow softly across the strings.

Thirteen: The door was nearly shut. Tony's hand swept down the inside for the lock. Found it. Through the crease left by the closing door he saw the razor halfway across Ryder's throat, right to left, the skin opening like a slit in a plastic shower curtain.

Fourteen: He felt the Kon-Tiki man's foot slam against the door, trying to keep it open. Tony shoved his whole weight against the door, bucking upward with his shoulder. The door shut. It continued to tap nervously, because the guy still tried to keep it open.

Fifteen: Tony turned the lock on the door. It clicked.

Tony couldn't catch his breath. He squatted in a crouch against the wall breathing murderously fast, because Ryder was gone.

Ryder's throat was a shower curtain. For a moment Tony tried to pretend it was a *Friday the 13th* kind of make-believe but it didn't work. It didn't work because he wasn't a kid up on a phony-baloney movie screen waiting for Jason to come and chop him into chum.

Ryder really was dead.

The guy who killed him was outside the door, which left Tony trapped in the bathroom. Tony squatted against the door, his head averted from the bottom of the door because he did not want to see any more blood.

He did not even want to look down at his shirt, certain as he was that Ryder's last act had been to send blood in a red scatter across his clothes. He stayed against the wall, thinking he should think, but all his mind came up with was the message that the guy was right outside.

Don't go tharn.

That thought pushed his back up the wall, his breath slowing somewhat. He stood for a moment, calculating what he should do next. He made a quick inventory. Toilets on the left, showers on the right. Directly in front of him was a row of sinks. He forced himself to walk the width of the bathroom in order to look for anything like a weapon. He listened for sounds from the door, but the scalp lady seemed deliberately silent.

Think, Tony told himself

In almost the same instant he came up with a plan.

He walked to the showers and turned on the hot water. There were seven stalls in all. By the time he flicked on the last nozzle the steam from the other six showers already hovered at his knees. He hurried back to the row of sinks and turned a stream of hot water on in each. The mirror above the sinks turned foggy before he finished.

He stopped when he had them all going and listened to the door.

Nothing.

Okay okay okay, Tony muttered under his breath.

The bathroom was clouding up. The showers had already disappeared in haze. The larger area near the sink would take longer, but it was working.

Okay okay okay.

Tony stood in the center of the bathroom, trying to think of something else to do. He didn't hear anything coming from the doorway, but that didn't mean zip.

Then he had it. He walked to the light switch, took a deep breath, then started tapping out S-O-S. He knew how to send it because he had once read a story about a guy trapped alive in a coffin who had come awake down in the ground and had rescued himself by tapping on the lid of the casket with his college ring.

Three short. Three long. Three short.

The light made little lightning bolts in the foggy air. Tony kept the S-O-S regular, his hand mere inches from the edge of the door.

In her room Zelda stopped in the middle of folding a towel and listened.

It was nothing, she told herself.

Only it didn't sound like nothing. It sounded like a scream. But that was surely her imagination. She went over to Martha's CD player and turned down the volume. She had been listening to the radio, NPR's "Fresh Air" out of Philadelphia, when the sound had started.

She turned the volume down further. Whatever had made the sound was gone. Whoever had made the sound was gone, although for a moment the sound seemed to echo in the walls. She heard it pass down from above her, lock into the steel beams, then go chiddering down the walls until it hit the street.

She hugged the towel to her chest.

In the next breath she came up with an explanation. Some girls on the floor above were horsing around and one of them had become a bit carried away and had let out a yelp and that was the sound and there was no problem.

But Lisa, her R.A., had said the floor above her was going to be empty.

Which was impossible.

She heard footsteps. The footsteps went fast, too fast to be just some girls frolicking. She also heard a door slam shut and something else that sounded like . . .

She turned up NPR again.

The volume covered everything and she cranked it even higher because what she had heard was a scream. No mistaking it this time. The sound carried and took a lot of time to fade away. She turned the volume on the radio louder, as though what she couldn't hear couldn't hurt her.

Thuds, then something smacking on the floor.

Her bedside lamp shook.

Get going, get *going*, she told herself, because if Mr. Hotchkiss somehow came upstairs, then she had time to get out. She pushed her face into the towel and closed her eyes. The radio blared behind her. Time to make a decision, maybe the whole thing was just her imagination running wild after all the scares earlier . . . but she didn't think so.

Phone, get to the phone.

She threw down the towel and opened the door. The dorm was quiet now. She stuck out her head, looked left, right, stepped into the hallway.

Suddenly she was sprinting, the doors passing her, their surfaces like black bone. She kept her eyes fixed on the fire door leading out to the lounge, because the phone was out there, the steps were out there, the exit was out there. She ran as fast as she could. For a moment it was like some slow-motion movie. The floor was slippery under her and the ceiling felt much lower than normal. Everything was movement, misshapen images. The fire door appeared to break free of its frame and rush at her.

She hit the handle of the fire door at full speed. It slapped backward and banged against the wall. In the exact same instant the lights in the entire dorm went out.

George closed the fuse box. It was better in the dark. He had always been good in the dark, and, besides, other people became more frightened while he remained calm. That was an advantage.

He went back up the stairs, taking them two at a time. He didn't worry about the boy locked in the bathroom. The boy would stay there. The second boy, the one who had seen him out by the barn that day, was not going to be a problem again.

George was only halfway to the second floor landing when he heard someone walking in the second floor commonroom. Someone was either going for the phone or trying to take the stairs down. He dropped to one knee and waited. The exit landings still had a single light each—doubtless hooked to an emergency generator—that illuminated the stairs enough to see. By going down on one knee he was able to bend to his right and see above him to the next landing. At the same time he was confident he remained in deep shadow.

He saw her, Zelda, standing there, her breathing quick, her hands up in her hair. Obviously she wasn't sure what to do. He considered waiting for her to begin down the stairs. Stand in the stairwell, deep in shadow, then step out at the proper moment. He imagined what her face would look like, what she would understand in that instant.

But he did not have time to wait. Besides, there had been enough waiting. He would have to hurry. Turning out the lights might bring the campus security guards. Somewhere on campus there was probably a master fuse board. If the lights stayed out in Sheppard for any length of time, the reaction would be automatic.

He could not wait for Zelda to come to him.

He started up the stairs toward her.

It sounded like a Biblical passage: Barney saw the light.

But it was like that. The light blinked up above, and Barney, pizza beside him, saw the light.

The light spelled out S-O-S.

Three short and fast, three long and slow, three short and fast.

Not that he believed it at first. He had simply been on his way home with his pizza, a good-natured, dutiful dad, when he had looked up and seen the light blinking on the third floor of Sheppard Dorm. His attention had been focused on Sheppard Dorm anyway because of the girl, Zelda, who was still in residence. That was the official phrase, still in residence. He had cruised by because she was a good kid, a nice girl, and she was now inside apparently blinking the lights.

Playing S-O-S, Mayday, 911. He hadn't seen anyone try an S-O-S since the Boy Scouts when kids would go out into the woods, pretend to get lost, then beat two sticks together near a lake so the sound would carry to any potential searchers.

Knock, knock, knock. Knock (long pause) Knock (long pause) Knock (long pause). Knock, knock, knock. S-O-S and the other Boy Scouts came running. It seemed pretty nifty near Lake Wachapanoogun, seemed like you never needed to worry about getting lost in the woods as long as you could find two dry sticks and remembered your Morse Code.

Hey, it's a fuse going, that's all, old scout, Barney told himself. Just a fuse blowing out, because most of the dorm lights are off anyway, so maybe there's been some sort of power surge or brown out, and the light is blinking randomly and it only looks like S-O-S and besides it's not your problem tonight because whoever is on rounds will check it out.

Except the light continued in its steady pattern.

Barney sat behind the steering wheel of his car, leaning forward to catch the light again. He couldn't be certain, but it looked to him like a bathroom light. The window looked frosted.

His own regulations stipulated that you didn't investigate anything suspicious without some back-up. To do anything less, to plunge in was just plain stupid. It was the way to end up like Jam.

But the light kept blinking.

He did not have a radio, did not have a gun, did not have anything but a passkey hooked onto his regular key ring. The thing to do was to drive to a pay phone and get Lester or somebody over here and check it out in tandem. Check it out with a gun pulled and maybe the K-9 squad. Check it out and follow procedure.

Which was exactly what he did not do. Because, looking up, he saw the light blink faster, and it was too easy to imagine somebody, the girl, getting closer to being dead.

So he pushed open his car, left the pizza smell, and hurried to the dorm door. His key went in, the lock turned, and the heavy door swung open. When he reached around the wall and tried to flick on the lights, they didn't respond. He flicked twice more, checking. It was dark, the electricity was gone, and he felt a solid tingle take a walk up his backbone.

The lights went out in one surge. Zelda heard things go quiet throughout the building. Refrigerators, washers, Pepsi machines. The entire building went silent and that meant she was trapped near the commonroom in complete darkness.

She felt herself getting ready to scream. If she screamed, however, she knew it was going to go on and on and on. She saw herself running downstairs screaming as she went. It was only with effort that she forced herself to stay in control.

Then she heard the footsteps.

They came upstairs lightly but not surreptitiously, so that it was possible, for an instant, to believe it might be a maintenance man. She knew that was probably wishful thinking, but the steps were steady.

"Hello?" she asked the darkness, trying her voice.

She thought, run, run, you idiot, you know who it is.

Then she saw him.

She saw him through the fire door, his body becoming gradually visible as he ascended the stairs. He was illuminated by the landing lights, which must have been powered by an emergency generator. He wore jeans and a flannel shirt. The shirt was soaked with blood.

He stopped on the next to last step.

He held up a razor blade. He turned it back and forth, appearing to examine it. Then, in pantomime, he pretended the razor blade had come to life. He put his free hand on the wrist of the hand with the razor blade and began to struggle. The razor blade came closer and closer to his face. He bent over the stair railing, pretending the blade was about to cut him. He made a choking sound, then the razor slashed and disappeared behind his head. Next he stood and threw something at the fire door. It collided with the glass portion of the door, spreading and sticking. Like some desperate creature pleading to be let in, because it spread on the glass and slid in small squeaks down to the wooden frame of the door.

It took Zelda a moment to see it was a scalp. See but not believe.

The man on the steps held up the razor and gestured with his finger to her.

Come here.

She began moving away from him. She stayed against the wall because it was dark. He came through the fire door and let it settle behind him.

"Please no," she said.

He raised the razor again.

"Let's see your room," he said.

It was a kid feeling to be climbing steps in the dark. Barney sensed he wasn't alone, and the thing to do, the professional decision in this case, he told himself again, was to back out, close the door behind you, then head to the nearest pay phone.

Actually he was pissed off with himself, because what he did by walking the dark hallways by himself was stupid. Or worse, it was some sort of macho thing, the Mounties always get their man kind of stuff. Barney knew he took this whole thing way too personally. That had been the problem all along. It bothered him to know a killer could wander around his campus, chop up a security officer along with a couple of women, and not even worry about being caught. It made him feel like Barney Fife, the Andy of Mayberry geek deputy who always made a mess of things and was so incompetent Andy had to rig things so occasionally his deputy could have at least a taste of success.

Of course this Barney knew some of the guys in the office called him that Barney behind his back. It hurt, not because they were disrespectful, but because there was some truth in it. He was, after all, a small-time peace officer in a sleepy town where ordinarily nothing much ever happened. Well, it was happening now.

He hustled up the last landing toward the third floor, figuring it was doubtful anybody was going to jump out at him on the stairs. He came to the door and began to push through it. At the same time he had an odd thought, extremely odd coming as it did right at the moment . . . it was about pizza, and how the pizza would be cold for Seth and Matty, and for a moment he thought this was an omen and he'd better pay attention. But it was too late, he was going through the door. Which was when he felt something coming, something speeding at him. He ducked, ducked almost to the floor, and saw nothing.

So it was a phony omen, an empty reaction, and as he straightened—it was dark, ladies and gentlemen—he saw just a long black hallway with nothing odd about it. But his hand remained on the door. It started to swing shut, and it was then that he felt something swinging shut with it. Something knocking softly against the door, and it reminded him, just in that instant, of being a kid and hanging his pants and shirts on a hook his mom had screwed into the rear of the door. Whenever he had closed the door as a kid there had always been a little counterweight action so that the pants and shirts ticked and rocked. It was the same feeling now, the same sensation, which meant there was something on the back of the door.

He turned with a jolt, his hands up. Somehow he knew what he was going to see, because it was just like the vault, the same feeling. He wasn't prepared for a body to hang there, though, wasn't prepared for it to be the body of a twelve-year-old boy. Most of all he wasn't prepared to see the young boy's forehead peeled back, the top of the scalp gone, the skull as gray as an overcooked hardboiled egg.

Dark. Dark and hot and wet and filled with steam. Tony flicked the lights a few more times just to make sure they no longer worked.

They didn't.

He walked to the showers, tested the water with his fingers, then pulled his hand away quickly. Hot. The water still ran hot. The steam was so thick by the showers that breathing was difficult.

Tony moved to the toilets. He did a short calculation. Heat rises, which means steam rises, which means the foggiest place in the bathroom is going to be the ceiling. With that in mind he stepped onto the first toilet in the row and climbed onto the surrounding stalls. He had to climb like a mountain climber spanning a chasm, or maybe a little kid making a tunnel for other little kids to pass underneath. Feet on one side, hands on another, he stayed arched there, looking around to find a place for a more comfortable position. Eventually he worked his way to one side of the stall and perched there. A squirrel sitting on a limb. It wasn't easy, it required balance, but he held onto a sprinkler head above him.

Then he waited.

George Denkin bent close to Zelda and cut a snip of hair from her head. He used the razor.

"My my," he said.

He straightened. Zelda was tied by strips of pantyhose to a desk chair. Her hands were tied behind her.

George touched his tongue to the small shank of hair. It tasted clean.

"Lovely hair," he commented.

The young lady refused to speak. He considered that a temporary setback. Soon she would be willing to tell him anything he cared to know.

He went to her dresser and felt on the surface for her make-up. It was difficult to see in the darkness. His hands registered a mascara wand, an eyeliner. He bent close to the mirror but had difficulty seeing his reflection clearly.

"Do you have a candle?"

When she did not answer he knelt before her and removed her shoe. It was a Treetorn, size 7. He held the sneaker to his mouth and nose for a moment, then tossed it aside. He looked up at the young lady. She had her eyes closed. That, too, was merely a temporary setback. He snatched up her foot by the heel and placed it against his thigh. She didn't struggle.

"You won't feel this but that doesn't mean it isn't happening," he said. "If you won't cooperate I'll feed your own toes to you one by one. What will it be?"

"In my roommate's dresser, the dresser on the right top drawer." Said in one breath.

"A candle?"

She nodded.

He dropped her foot, stood, went to the dresser. In a minute he had the candle going. He set it by the mirror to double the light.

"Ah," he said, checking through the make-up once more. He stopped his examination and turned to Zelda.

"I'll still feed you your toes. You understand that?"

The young woman said nothing.

He turned back to the mirror. His hands moved automatically through the make-up. He applied eyeliner, mascara, a dot of rouge to each cheek. He bent close to the mirror, straining to see.

"There," he said when he finished.

He turned around to let her see him. At the same time a faint noise came to him. It came from upstairs. It sounded like keys jingling on a ring.

"I'll be back," he said.

He picked up the razor and went out the door.

Here he comes.

Tony checked his balance on the stall, checked to make sure he could jump free when the time came, then listened intently. It was hot, incredibly hot up by the ceiling, but he also felt pretty well covered. It was possible he could make a jump, hit the floor running, and get out before the scalp lady got him.

Here he comes, he thought again as he heard a key go into the lock. He told himself to remain as calm as possible, because if he wobbled on the stall door, then it was all over, the scalp lady would be on him, and his throat would be cut like a shower curtain.

Like Ryder, who was now a dead bone-head, a dead knuckle-head, a dead friend. Now, he knew it. Somehow Tony couldn't help thinking about Ryder's dad, the sarge, who would probably go on a tear when he heard about Ryder, probably drink himself crazy, beat up his wife, go over to the army base, and get sad with a bunch of his friends. He felt a little faint, felt lightheaded, and the door finally pushed open, air whooshed in, and the guy called out.

"Anyone in here?"

Which wasn't a bad trick. Tony almost fell for it. He felt a reply rise in his throat. The guy left the door open, which was another break, because if the guy went to the showers first, he could take a jump and beat it out of there.

Except the steps came his way.

Tony closed his eyes. As a little kid he always believed that if he couldn't see someone the person couldn't see him, and that was kid stuff but he closed his eyes anyway, because the steps kept coming in his direction. He tensed his legs, ready to jump, when suddenly through the fog he could make out the security officer.

The guy who had been in his house that night. The guy who had been sitting with his mom the night he came in after finding the vault. Captain Barney, a good egg. Tony could just make him out through the fog, but it was definitely the guy. Tony started to say something, started to hiss that he was here, up here, when he saw the scalp lady appear through the fog.

It was other-worldly, it was strange, because the scalp lady was suddenly there, just beside Captain Barney. Her face appeared in the fog right behind the captain. And the face was melted. The face was wax. Only Tony saw it wasn't wax. It was make-up and the fog had made the gunk run so that the scalp lady's eyes were black and about five inches long. Her lips looked like they belonged to a bloodsucker, there was something endless about the mouth, something hungry, and Tony saw the lips spread as the scalp lady lifted the razor and brought it down—

"Look *out*," Tony yelled.

Brought it down on the captain's shoulder, raising in its wake a geyser of blood. The blood was red against the white steam. A second chuck of the razor brought a sideways slick of blood from the captain's neck. The captain spun, but it was too late, the captain's eyes understood that. Tony tried to kick at the scalp lady. He tried to give the captain a chance, but the scalp lady was quick. She looked up at him, her face melting, her tongue coming out for just an instant in a sort of tart's wiggle, and then down came the razor again.

The captain took this one on the forearm. More blood, and it was over. The captain waved his arm around, and that was when the scalp lady grabbed for Tony. He grabbed up, the captain was gone, so now it was time for a small fry— only Tony kicked and caught the wax face with a heel right in the face. He kicked again, and felt a slit open on his thigh. It didn't hurt, it was just a seam of red, and he tried to kick once more but the blood made the stall slick and he had to hold onto the sprinkler head above.

That was when he heard it.

It started far away, but it came fast, came with increasing momentum. The scalp lady was intent on the razor, so she failed to hear the clicking, the tattoo of bone on tiles. But it grew louder, the sound increased, and then Tony heard a jingle of chain, a clink of a tag hitting a collar, and he remembered—the door was open.

Before he could think much more Tony saw something appear at knee level, something brown and moving fast. The steam swirled with it, broke around it, and then a short growl came up, filled the room.

That was when the dog bit the scalp lady in the throat.

Which was an illusion. It wasn't real. But Tony saw something jump up, high, and the dog was on the wax head.

It was on the scalp lady's throat from the side, and the scalp lady hacked at the dog with the razor, but the dog was too heavy. The dog growled and thrashed and the scalp lady fell back. Tony heard skin ripping, the scalp lady's throat giving, and then they faded under him into fog.

"HOLD IT EVERYBODY JUST HOLD IT DON'T ANYBODY MOVE YOU GET AWAY FROM MY DOG I DON'T CARE WHO YOU ARE . . ."

It was a black guy with a gun out in a stance like he was just getting ready to sit down. The guy looked almost as crazy as the scalp lady. Down on the floor, just through the fog, he saw the dog chewing at the scalp lady. The scalp lady screamed, and Tony wished she could scream for the next eternity, scream her guts out down in Hell.

"Off, Goliath," the officer yelled.

The dog let go. The dog skulked away, its muzzle covered with blood, its skin criss-crossed with razor smiles. Then the black officer almost lost it, almost walked over and shot the scalp lady. As it was, he put his hands on the dog's coat, tried to use pressure to stop the bleeding.

"Aw shit," the officer said.

That was the last thing Tony heard. He felt himself sliding off the stall, only the floor came too fast, came in a rush, and he banged his head on the wall, banged it on the bottom of the stall.

And in his last glimmer of consciousness he found himself almost face to face with the scalp lady.

Who wasn't dead.

Who was waiting.

As soon as he left, Zelda managed to scooch the chair over to her work desk and fish a pair of scissors from the top. It was difficult to twist her wrists around until she could line up the cutting blades, but again, she managed.

As soon as she was free she closed and locked the door, began piling furniture in front of it. She slid Martha's bed against the door, then her own bed, and finally both desk chairs. It wouldn't brace the door particularly, wouldn't keep him out for very long, but at least he couldn't just climb in. While she moved the furniture, she kept the scissors in her hand.

She would have stayed in her room forever if she hadn't seen the scalp. It was resting on Martha's desk, one tentacle of hair dripping over the edge. The top of her desk was bloody. She saw part of the person's ear still attached to the flesh cap underneath the hair.

She still might have remained in the room if she hadn't happened to hear a police radio squawk. It came from upstairs, from where she had heard the keys jingle. The police were here. She heard a dog bark, then some shouting. When the dog continued to bark she began pulling the

furniture away from the door, careful to keep her eyes away
from the scalp.

Lester first tried to cover Goliath's cuts with his free hand.
When the blood kept coming, he tried to mash the cuts
closed with the heel of his gun hand—sort of pinch things
shut and staunch the flow, but it wasn't working, the blood
oozed and Goliath whimpered and put his head at Lester's
feet and waited for his master to make him better.

It was a damn soul-wringer, but Lester wasn't anybody's
fool, so it took a good two or three minutes before he put
the gun down just to the side. He put it no more than a hand-
grab away, then looked at the Voodoo man, looked back at
Goliath. Too much fog in here, too damn hot, too stuffy.
What he needed to do right away was pull out his walkie-
talkie and reach out and touch someone, because the good
captain was bleeding something ugly back near the johns.
Bleeding from his neck and shoulders, pumping out little
artery vapors now and then, and here was the dog under his
hands, the kid frucking crash-landing on the floor.

He squeezed a cut closed on Goliath's skin, reached
behind him for his walkie-talkie—which was when the
Voodoo man jumped to his feet. The frucking Voodoo man
was on his feet in nothing but a flicker, and he had the razor.
He had the razor and it was going to be one of those time
things, one of those tussles where two go for the gun in the
same instant. Lester saw it coming. He reached for the gun
as fast as he could and managed to hit it and make it skid
along the tile floor just as the Voodoo man gave one big
swing of his razor. The weird thing was, all Lester heard in
his mind was the noise Houston control center used in those
early space flights, all that squawking and tweeting each
time the space capsule spoke, then more tweeting and static as Houston responded, and the whole thing had occurred
in some imaginary world out in the stratosphere and that's
what it was like to feel that *psst* of the razor flicking across
his shoulder. As it caught him again, this time across the
back, there was no pain, just some robotic Voodoo man
crouching beside him and going after the gun that kept
skidding along the floor. It was fog and blood and dead

dogs while the razor continued tic-tac-toe on his back.

The Voodoo man stopped. He stopped and looked up. Lester looked up too, looked through the fog. The person standing above them was a woman.

Or rather a girl. A girl he vaguely recognized. A girl who right this blessed moment had the gun in her hand.

"Stop it," the girl said.

The Voodoo man stopped. When the Voodoo man stopped, the girl standing above him took careful aim and blew his right knee to shreds. Then, while he writhed on the floor, she walked over to him, put the muzzle of the gun on the Voodoo man's left knee and spoon fed him a little Smith & Wesson.

CHAPTER EIGHT

THAW

Tony Corposaro returned to school on the Monday before spring break. He didn't take the bus, which was unusual in itself, but he was accustomed to things being out of whack so it hardly bothered him. What did bother him, however, was the look on his mom's face when she pulled the Vega to the curb in front of Coldbridge Junior High. She had a doubtful look, had had it all morning, and he understood he was the cause.

He ducked when her hand came over and touched his hair.

"Mom . . ." he said.

"I'm not saying you don't belong in school, Anthony. I just want you to be careful."

"I will be. We've been all over this."

"And you understand that Mr. Almroth is on your side? I don't want you to think of him as a principal. He understands everything that's happened. You go to him if you have any problems. Do you promise?"

"I promise."

237

He had promised seventeen times already. He had promised every day since they first realized he couldn't spend the rest of his life inside the house. His dad had contributed a couple of nuggets about getting back on a horse when it bucks you, take a fresh start, putting the past behind him, but that, even Tony realized, wasn't the point. Mrs. Tocqueville, the school psychologist, didn't think much of getting back on bucking horses. Tony's mom, on the other hand, thought a great deal of fresh starts. He had listened to her talk about the virtues of a parochial education, a change of schools, a change of student body, until he had finally piped up and put an end to it.

Because he had to go back.

He wasn't sure why, but he was certain he did. He was even aware that his parents pulled for him to return. Not because they wanted to save money, not because they thought Coldbridge Junior High was the best school in the state, but because his return signaled he was cured, or at least well on the way. That he was Tony Corposaro, typical seventh grader once again.

"You'll come home right after school. I'll be here to pick you up."

"Yes, Mom."

"We can get McDonald's if you like. The place out on Loudon Road has the new McRib sandwich, the one you wanted to try."

"Okay."

"You sure you'll be all right?"

"I'm sure."

But of course he wasn't sure. He felt his stomach knot and turn as he pushed open the car door. Several kids stopped playing hackey-sack when he stepped outside. He ignored them, but they didn't ignore him. They weren't going to ignore old "sufferin' succotash" because they knew, just as he did, that he was the kid who had survived.

"Okay," he said.

He closed the door. Get going, he wanted to tell her. Please. But she sat in the driver's seat watching him.

"I'm okay," he whispered, bending back to the car window. "You can go."

She didn't leave, although she pretended to get ready. He shrugged his book bag higher on his shoulder, then headed for the door. He saw Mrs. Tocqueville step out on the doorstep. She wore a cardigan sweater over her shoulders. It was obvious she had waited to watch him make his progress across the playground. To watch his adjustment. He wasn't sure how he was supposed to be adjusted, but he figured it meant he should be steady. Walk straight, nod, and say hello.

He tried to keep his feet from scuffing. He tried, also, to keep from heading toward Mrs. Tocqueville. He had to go past her, that was obvious, but he didn't want to appear like a heat-seeking missile looking for a haven.

He was halfway across the playground, kids clearing for him as he went, when he saw his ancient enemy, Wayne Steele. Wayne stood on the corner of his vision, hanging back with his boys. Tony didn't look at him. He wanted to be adjusted, which meant he had to keep calm, look straight ahead. But he knew Wayne was trying to catch his eye, trying to tell him something.

At the same time Tony was aware of Mrs. Tocqueville scoping out the situation. She was one point of a triangle. Wayne and he made the other two points, and he felt a current pass among them all. It was a moment they had been waiting for, a moment they had discussed, and he knew if he turned around he would see his mom rising in her seat, trying to see what occurred.

Someone ran close, chasing a superball in its crazy bounces. Someone else let a book drop flat on the asphalt. It made a bang and Tony turned. Then he let his head turn back toward Wayne on the other side. He saw building bricks, saw Mrs. Tocqueville take a step off the stoop, and then saw Wayne Steele purse his lips and blow a kiss at him.

Before Tony could respond he heard Mrs. Tocqueville.

"Wayynnee?" she said, her voice rising into a question.

"Hello," Tony said to her when he passed.

"Hi, Tony," she said.

It was warm, it was welcoming. And it would have meant even more if he hadn't seen her give a small wave to his mom. A little wave, just rippling the shoulders of her sweater.

I have your son now, the wave said. I'll return him to you later. He'll be okay. Really . . .

It was a week later when Captain Len Barney returned to duty. He drove slowly up Capitol Street, cut south on Beaumont, and finally pulled into the security office parking lot. He carried a cup of coffee into the building.

And he was pleased to find a wave of bunting hanging from the doorway saying: "WELCOME BACK, CAP."

Mrs. Shell and Mrs. Cawdor stood directly under the bunting, hurrying to light candles on the cake. Eddy was there, and so was Lester.

The sight of Lester nearly touched him off, so he tried to take deep breaths because he had been emotional lately. At the same time he saw them checking him out, which was understandable since he had two scars running down his cheeks. One scar, the biggest and reddest at the time, actually went up to the bridge of his nose. That's what they tried to see without giving anything away.

"Surprise!" they yelled.

And welcome back. And Mrs. Shell gave him a kiss with a slice of cake, and Mrs. Cawdor, not to be outdone, kissed him and told him he really did look . . . terrific. But when he mentioned he might think about growing a beard, or maybe having plastic surgery, no one tried to say *pshaw*.

He ate some of the cake. While he ate, as he talked to Eddy, he heard a strange sound. He knew the sound an instant later. It was the big surprise, no one had told him, and he looked around for Lester, didn't find him, then looked down the hallway at the odd clicking.

As soon as he saw Goliath he started crying. Not loud, but it had been stored up too long. Now here came Goliath walking stiffly, walking like a dog fifty times his age, but walking nonetheless. The dog creeped to where Lester stood, his front left leg shot, his right rear leg half-amputated, his fur criss-crossed and pulled together. The sight of him made Barney hand his cake to Eddy, then go down on a knee.

"Come here, fellow," Barney said.

Barney gathered the dog lightly in his arms, and he put his face in the dog's fur.

It was strange to be outside.

It was extremely strange, but Zelda forced herself to continue walking. She dug in her pocket and checked for the shopping list her mom had written out. Pears, apples, Mr. Clean, microwave popcorn, shoe polish, heavy cream, and brown sugar.

She was so involved checking on the list—she didn't have a good mind for details these days—that she almost forgot she had deliberately taken a different path to Hampton Market. She had taken, in fact, an entirely different path, the other way around the block, as it were, because she had wanted to check her progress. She wanted to check whether she was ready to get back to living. It was spring, April 12, to be exact, and she had to find her way back to college soon or she felt she was in danger of becoming . . . what?

A recluse? A narrow, frightened young woman? A woman for whom other people could safely feel sorry?

So she was out. It was a gorgeous street, actually, with forsythia, dogwood, and even some lilac in bloom. It was so beautiful that she almost failed to notice she had arrived at the branch, the exact spot where Mr. Hotchkiss had once appeared on a Halloween night.

There. On a branch.

She stopped and looked up, and for an instant she felt terror. Because it wasn't over, he was still out there somewhere, still waiting in that hot bathroom forever, his face runny with makeup, his hair cut from a scalp, his—

Stop it, she told herself.

Miraculously, she did. Not that it was all over. She understood that it was never going to be all over. But at least the branch above the sidewalk, Mr. Hotchkiss's swing, was now merely a limb of oak.

A year and a half passed before George Denkin killed again. This time he killed in prison. An additional life sentence was added to four others he had attached to him. Punishment, however, the presiding judge noted, was not going to be a strong inducement for good behavior.

George killed his attorney during a conference.

It was, for its kind of a killing, a text-book study. George laid the groundwork for months. It showed, several doctors claimed afterward, an enormous amount of cunning. It also revealed George's understanding of psychology. George had played the young lawyer perfectly.

For months, whenever George met with his attorney—which he did often—he was bound and chained, sometimes in a straight-jacket, sometimes in simple handcuffs. The lawyer did not object. By allowing his client to be restrained, they were able to sit and talk in privacy. If, on the other hand, the client insisted on being unrestrained, then they would only be able to consult between the bars of his cell.

George understood, he never complained. In fact, he was docile. He agreed that it was necessary to have himself restrained. He could not control himself, he said.

This honesty, naturally, was all the young lawyer needed to hear. The lawyer was—it must also be pointed out—a bodybuilder. His suits were full-cut, expanding to considerable proportions to accommodate his shoulders. George, who understood vanity, had been, after all, exposed to it early on in his mother's shop, knew how to appeal to the lawyer.

One day the conversation went like this:

"I'm sorry to complain. I can't concentrate right now. These restraints are digging into my flesh. They make my hands go numb."

"Are they too tight?"

"A little maybe."

"Well, we'll see what we can do."

The restraints were not removed the next time. Nor were they removed during the next five or six visits. But on a spring day in late April, a year and a half after George had murdered the young boy named Jimmy Ryder, he met his lawyer for the first time without restraints.

"How did you get them to let me meet you without cuffs?"

"It wasn't easy," the attorney said. "They figured we've established a relationship. And how much can go wrong in this room? There aren't any weapons. Besides, I can handle myself pretty well."

"The bodybuilding?"

"Right."

For the last statement, George planned to take the man's tongue out.

There were contradictory reports about how the murder took place. Everyone agreed, however, that it was done with amazing speed. A guard was posted outside the conference room. He heard the act but couldn't get inside in time to do anything about it.

The way it occurred was simple. In addition to being a bodybuilder the attorney was also making a great deal of money for the first time in his life. As a result he was spending most of what he made. His suits were custom-fitted not only to accommodate his large shoulders but also to accommodate his dandyism. He was a good dresser. He wore expensive cologne. His first major purchase, however, was a replacement digit for the index finger on his right hand. He had worn one since he was ten-years-old—the finger had been cut off in an accident with a lawnmower—but it had always been a rather cheap prosthesis. His parents had paid to replace it the last time, in the middle of high school, with a newer, more natural looking finger manufactured by the Disinksi Prosthesis Co. out of Weymouth, Massachusetts. He didn't think a great deal about his missing finger at the time. If anything, he saw it as a social asset. To draw attention to himself—he wasn't particularly distinguished in high school and had to settle for this means of notoriety— he developed a number of small routines he liked to spring on newcomers who weren't aware one of his fingers was false. For example, whenever it was cold, which was much of the time outside of Boston, he liked to turn to the wind, stick his artificial digit in his mouth to wet it, then lift up his hand to test the breeze while the finger remained in his mouth. Or, he would pretend to close his hand in a heavy door, catch it under a sled runner, or perhaps hold it out to a dog, let the dog nip, then raise his hand minus a finger.

Most of the guys thought it was pretty funny. The girls he dated tended to shiver and look away.

In any case, with the first flush of money he was earning as an attorney, and with the demand to spend time with a better and more observant clientele, he felt obliged to buy a new finger. After doing some research he finally settled on a Silver-Ray prosthesis, one fitted precisely to the dimensions of his hand. The finger was constructed of plastic, although a new material, Doylar-6, made the skin surface remarkably lifelike. It was possible, sometimes for days at a time, for the lawyer himself to forget he was even wearing an artificial finger.

The finger cost him $1,750, which he charged to his credit card. Because it was made of hard plastic, the finger did not trigger the metal detector when he entered the prison that day.

The young attorney probably never considered the possibility that the finger could somehow be turned against him. He was new, after all, and did not have a veteran's caution about being around extreme cases such as George Denkin. It was also possible, some said, that he had forgotten to declare the finger, even though it was standard procedure for guards to inquire of visitors if they wore any type of prosthesis.

George knew about the finger. He had seen the lawyer touch it repeatedly during visits. George had imagined endless uses for the finger. It did not, for example, escape him that the finger was, among other things, phallic in nature.

When the conference was stalled—they were going over some appeal material—George squared himself at the table. He knew enough about body-communication that often, although not always, people sitting across a table from one another will occasionally adopt the same body posture. To encourage this, George sat square, his palms flat on the table before him. It took the attorney some five minutes to arrive at the same position. When he did, George made his move.

The first thing he did was to reach out his right hand and squeeze the right hand of the lawyer. George looked down, pretending to be sad. When he felt the lawyer's hand respond and grip his, George jumped clear of his chair, leaned his weight on the lawyer's wrist, then reached and cracked the artificial finger straight up. It did not leave the attorney's hand without dislodging some underlying bone. It happened so quickly that the first thing the lawyer did was try to pull back, forgetting his hand was pinned by George's. He yanked in two reflexive jerks to get it free, but he was sufficiently startled to have lost any purpose to his movement.

In one motion George turned the finger in his hand so that the jagged edge stuck out from beneath the part of his palm used in a karate chop. In the next motion he plunked the thorny tip precisely in the lawyer's left eye.

The lawyer screamed. The guard looked in the window.

Meanwhile the lawyer had fallen back, both hands to his eyes. He got tangled in the chairs and went down on the floor. George did not circle the table. He went over it, then jumped so that both feet landed on the lawyer's chest. He heard ribs crack. The lawyer cried out again.

George allowed the lawyer to grab his legs. He even said *oww* so the lawyer would think he was doing some good by holding the legs.

George then bent at the waist and popped the second eyeball with the tip of the Silver-Ray Doylar-6 index digit prosthesis.

The attorney's hands went to his face again. The door of the cell was opening at the same time. George waited as the lawyer's mouth opened wide in pain and confusion, then rammed the finger down the man's throat until it lodged in the soft wet tissue.

He did not cut the tongue out. There wasn't time.

But he did stab the finger hard enough so that it emerged out the back of the lawyer's throat.

Afterward, when they finally shot George with a stun gun and locked him up again, they found—since the plastic finger was harder than the soft linoleum floor tiles—that the finger had left its mark underneath the lawyer's head. As he squirmed and chugged, trying to get a breath that would never come, his head continued to go back and forth, back and forth, sketching ghostly drawings on the floor.

The cops said the sketches didn't look like anything.

Except one fellow who was more imaginative than the others said he thought the scribbling looked like a child's drawing of a cyclone.

Avon Books presents
your worst nightmares—

...gut-wrenching terror

BY BIZARRE HANDS
71205-9/$3.99 US/$4.99 Can
Joe R. Lansdale

THE ARCHITECTURE OF FEAR
70553-2/$3.95 US/$4.95 Can
edited by Kathryn Cramer & Peter D. Pautz

...unspeakable evil

COLD SHOCKS   76160-2/$4.50 US/$5.50 Can
edited by Tim Sullivan

EYES OF NIGHT   76011-8/$3.95 US/$4.95 Can
David C. Smith

...blood lust

THE HUNGER   70441-2/$4.99 US/$5.99 Can
THE WOLFEN   70440-4/$4.50 US/$5.95 Can
Whitley Strieber

Compelling True Crime Thrillers
From Avon Books

BADGE OF BETRAYAL
by Joe Cantlupe and Lisa Petrillo

76009-6/$4.99 US/$5.99 Can

GUN FOR HIRE:
THE SOLDIER OF FORTUNE KILLINGS
by Clifford L. Linedecker

76204-8/$4.99 US/$5.99 Can

LOSS OF INNOCENCE:
A TRUE STORY OF JUVENILE MURDER
by Eric J. Adams   75987-X/$4.95 US/$5.95 Can

RUBOUTS: MOB MURDERS IN AMERICA
by Richard Monaco and Lionel Bascom

75938-1/$4.50 US/$5.50 Can

GOOMBATA:
THE IMPROBABLE RISE AND FALL OF
JOHN GOTTI AND HIS GANG
by John Cummings and Ernest Volkman

71487-6/$4.99 US/$5.99 Can